TREASURE AT BATTERY POINT

An artist's sketch of the Brother Jonathan, which went down off California in 1865.

TREASURE AT BATTERY POINT

by
Helen Corbin

To: Connie with warm regards Helen Corbin June, 1998

Wolfe Publishing Company

6471 Airpark Drive
Prescott, Arizona 86301

This is a work of fiction; however, the unique Battery Point Lighthouse and the information regarding the wreck of the *Brother Jonathan* and the tidal wave were the inspiration for this novel. All the characters and events contained within are purely fictional. Any resemblance to real persons and real events is entirely coincidental.

ISBN: 1-879356-50-3

03 02 01 00 99   5 4 3 2 1

Published April 1998
Printed in the United States of America

DEDICATION

To those who go down to the sea in ships,
may they find treasure
if only in the search.

Other Books by Helen Corbin

Heroin Is My Shepherd

The Curse of the Dutchman's Gold

King of the Ice

Senner's Gold

CONTENTS

Foreword

*B*rother Jonathan left port on July 28, 1865, on her regular run from San Francisco to Portland and Victoria. Commanded by Capt. Samuel J. DeWolf, she carried 244 passengers and crew and a large amount of freight which allegedly overloaded the steamer. Included in the cargo was a very large ore crusher, two camels, an army payroll and gold.

On Sunday about four miles above Point St. George, Quartermaster Jacob Yates, taking his turn at the wheel was ordered by Captain DeWolf to return to Crescent City as a storm with mountainous waves made it impossible to continue on course. Within an hour of changing course the ship struck a sunken rock. The force knocked the passengers from their feet, and the steamer started to break up. Lifeboats were launched, but with the exception of one, all capsized, their occupants suffering the same fate as the passengers and crew who remained aboard. Only 19 persons survived the greatest maritime disaster in California history.

After an initial search and the recovery of those bodies that washed ashore, the *Brother Jonathan* lay quietly in her watery grave for 130 years until her rediscovery in 1993. The lure of treasure – gold – provided the incentive to seek and find her resting place. Now, however, a new struggle was to take place. The finders, Deep Sea Research, Inc., wanted to recover the gold. The State of California, in whose territorial waters the *Brother Jonathan* rests, wanted to preserve the historic integrity of the vessel. The resulting litigation in the federal courts has consumed thousands of hours of effort by attorneys for both parties. During the six years of litigation, in recognition of her historic significance, the *Brother Jonathan* has been declared eligible for the National Register of Historic Places. Despite that status, a federal judge, over California's objections, has permitted the salvors to recover what is reputed to be "a large number of gold coins."

The final chapter to the litigation, unlike that of this book, has not yet been written. The United States Supreme Court has the matter under consideration. Regardless of its outcome the court's decision will have a profound effect on the ability of states to preserve and protect historic shipwrecks.

Author Helen Corbin wrote this book without knowledge of the on-going legal battle. It is a fictional mystery that happens to involve the California Attorney General's Office and its efforts to obtain the contents of the famous paddle wheeler. Is the conclusion of the book an omen for the outcome of the case?

Peter Pelkofer, Esq.

Mr. Pelkofer is Senior Counsel for the California State Lands Commission where he specializes in shipwrecks and maritime matters. He has been an attorney for the California Lands Commission in *Deep Sea Research, Inc. v. the Brother Jonathan* since 1991.

ACKNOWLEDGMENTS

Peter Pelkofer, Esq.
Senior Counsel for the California State Lands Commission

Vern and Virginia Fergeson
Historians

Gerry and Nadine Fugel
Caretakers, Battery Point Lighthouse

Loretta Robertson
Artist, Medford, Oregon

Roberta Montgomery
Editor

Del Norte County Triplicate Newspaper
Crescent City, California

Times Standard Newspaper
Eureka, California

Humboldt County Historical Society
Photographs

Del Norte, California, Historical Society

**Battery Point Lighthouse, Crescent City, California.
Erected in 1856, automated in 1953, decommissioned in
1965 and re-activated for private aid to navigation in
1982. Open to visitors during low tide.**

Lighthouses of Del Norte County

Two lighthouses stand sentinel along the beautiful Del Norte coast. At the northern tip of the Crescent City Harbor is Battery Point Lighthouse.

Lit in December 1856, only two years after Crescent City was incorporated, Battery Point Lighthouse is one of the oldest inhabited lighthouses in California. Built in a traditional Cape Cod style, the quaint structure is only accessible at low tide.

The lighthouse is now a museum run by the Del Norte County Historical Society and is home to historical society curators who maintain the building for visitors and give tours during the summer.

The logs of the lighthouse keepers are kept here and visitors can read about the day-to-day struggle to keep the beacon lit against the fury of the sea and of harrowing rescues performed off these shores. The original lighthouse lens, memorabilia, and original furnishings are also all on display within this architecturally exquisite building.

Several miles offshore stands the St. George Reef Lighthouse, the tallest and most expensive American lighthouse ever constructed. Built in the wake of California's worst maritime disaster - the sinking of the side-wheel paddle ship *Brother Jonathan* - it took nine years and $704,000 before the 140-foot tall lighthouse was completed and operational.

For the next 92 years, until it was decommissioned in 1974, the lighthouse's bright beacon protected ships at sea from the numerous perils of the reef. The lighthouse, a national landmark, was recently turned over to the St. George Reef Lighthouse Preservation Society, which is raising money to restore the structure.

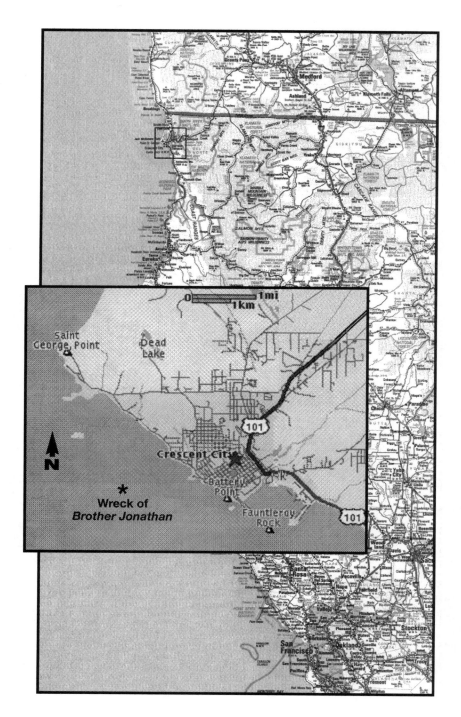

Chapter 1

Death at Dawn

Northern California's historic Battery Point Lighthouse, perched on a rocky, fog-shrouded promontory in the sea, appeared ghostly just before dawn on June 6, 1996. The weather had been foul. Rain soaked it and the nearby town of Crescent City eliciting loud curses from fishermen whose livelihood depended on their catch during, what had become, a carefully controlled short season. The bay, dotted with their trollers came alive as they readied to leave the huge harbor under a blanket of dark, swollen clouds. Jetty bells clanged regularly coupled with the foghorn's distinct moan giving warning of impending danger.

At the parking lot just north of the bay, a young woman moved away from her Jeep and followed her big German shepherd while trying to balance herself under the weight of voluminous gear. The pair crossed the macadam road above a cement ramp that led down to a rocky spit some 300 yards across to the base of the island where the lighthouse was barely visible. In front of them irregular, ocean-darkened boulders lay strewn here and there down the beach. Terry Hamilton hurried down the ramp toward them.

The artist was almost a fixture on that beach at low tide, which was the only time the lighthouse could be reached. Soon the tourists would be invading Crescent City to see the famous structure, but for now, at least, she had the place to herself. Fortunately, the rain stopped but damp air seeped into her bones as Terry huddled low into the big collar of her all-weather coat, exhaling steam from plump lips. Her long, red hair had been tucked neatly into the collar for warmth. She sighed. Her eyes drifted up to the tower where the lamp glowed, sending an eerie shaft into the fog. The Pacific, barely visible, slapped against the jetty accentuating the familiar horn near the entrance to Crescent City's harbor. There was no wind, just gloom.

Her dog darted toward the sea gulls busily picking at small fish left in the rocks by the receding tide. He barked loudly. A hundred wings fluttered simultaneously as they took flight, their raucous, screech proof he was depriving them of their morning feed. Watching, Terry laughed lightly. He was her protector. It would have been foolish to have come to so lonely a spot without him. *Besides*, she thought, *I love Baron, and I couldn't have a better friend especially now that he weighs almost 100 pounds.*

Shortly she opened the Thermos and poured herself a steaming cup of coffee. Taking a quick sip, she reached for a bakery bag and took out an apple Danish purchased that morning. A nearby rock acted as a table. Sitting down the girl munched contentedly before taking a second pastry out to give to the dog; then, she withdrew a tin bowl from her knapsack and filled it with water for the panting animal who anticipated the act and raced to her side. The pastry and coffee were rewarding. Waiting for the fog to lift usually took awhile, *a good time to reflect*, she thought. A blue gaze lifted toward the lighthouse; she always wondered if the lighthouse keeper were scanning with his telescope as he had so often, although they'd never met. Refilling the cup, she shivered and zipped the down coat up close around her slender neck before pulling her woolen stocking cap tight around her face. Last night's storm hadn't made life more bearable, but this ritual

2

would become impossible once summer came. Terry shrugged and began to set up the portable easel.

After awhile she became completely engrossed sketching the unique red-roofed lighthouse framed by several wind-bent California Cypress trees. It was now, just past dawn, when the surrounding light and the thinning fog actually enhanced it. This particular structure fascinated the artist – she painted it exclusively. The studio was filled with sketches and watercolors from every conceivable angle. In fact, she was almost to the point of being satisfied for a change. The look grew on the comely, young face; so intense was the act, Terry didn't notice the dog had wandered away.

Baron's repeated barking startled her, causing a glance in the direction of the sound. Not wanting to stop work, she frowned at the distraction. "What's wrong?" she yelled. Suddenly, replacing the paintbrush on the pallet, she set it upon a nearby rock and hurried down the beach toward a rock outcropping where the dog was hidden from view. As she approached he ran to her. "Something's got you all stirred up, boy. Okay! I'm here now. What is . . . Oh! dear God." The body, face down in the ebbing tide, appeared to be a man in a down jacket and jeans. His hair was dark with congealed blood and water. His outstretched hands reached for her, but his floating form was tethered behind the rocks. A scream rent the air.

Running as fast as possible, Terry headed for the path up to the lighthouse, following the dog who had already anticipated her desire and raced ahead. It was barely daylight. The climb up the rock strewn, twisted path was difficult, but her adrenaline was up. Puffing noticeably, she neared the door to the museum, which she knew was locked. The hours were 8:00 A.M. to 5:00 P.M. if changing tides allowed. She hoped the old man was awake and willing to open the door to strangers at such an early hour.

Everyone in town knew Captain Tillman. He limped, smoked a deliciously aromatic pipe and wore a peaked, woolen seaman's cap winter and summer. Terry saw him occasionally.

3

She also knew he watched them from the lens room. It hadn't occurred to the girl that he might be friendly. The keeper usually walked slowly, head down – totally oblivious to anyone around. He'd taken the job some seven years ago, and it was apparent that the townspeople thought he belonged there. Terry was a newcomer; no one would discuss him with her. People were usually clannish, or so her grandmother had told her. And since Letty Baldwin had spent thirty summers in Crescent City, Terry believed her word to be gospel.

The dog barked incessantly as they neared the lighthouse entrance. It was futile to try to quiet him; he knew there was trouble, and they needed help. Her small hand grasped the brass door knocker and banged it. Shortly, the door opened; they were face to face.

In a gravely, stern voice he said, "What do you want?"

"Look! I'm sorry to intrude, but there's a dead man down below in the surf. I think you'd better call the sheriff."

Surprise registered – it was probably the last thing he thought she'd say. Suddenly, he turned and invited them both in. They followed down a narrow passage into a parlor that opened into the captain's almost round kitchen. It was well equipped but antiquated, and off to one side was an alcove that contained the all-important ship-to-shore radio and a telephone.

Terry tried not to be rude, but her curiosity was peaked. Quieting the dog with a command, her eyes roamed the room quickly, covertly. The walls were painted white. There were red checkered curtains that had been shirred with eyelet; they were tiebacks. The equipment, although very old, had been polished – everything looked immaculate. On top of the refrigerator was an incongruous cactus plant. The old man didn't look like he cared for plants. Terry snickered. One of the ladies from the historical society probably brought it out to him. The table was an old, porcelain-topped one with two small chairs tucked into either end. On the top was a napkin

4

holder, salt and pepper shakers, a sugar bowl, a tray and a book that sat open as though he had been reading when they knocked. Everything in the room was well used, clean and somehow very appealing. Even the dish towels that hung on a rack over the sink matched the curtains and were folded neatly, hanging as though they were matched before they were folded. This was a precise man.

"He minds good," the old man said, limping toward the stove where he poured two mugs of coffee and motioned to the girl to come and get one. A jar of non-dairy creamer and a bowl of sugar were next to the stove. "Help yourself. I'll make the calls."

After he went to the alcove, the radio began to crackle and static broke the silence as a choppy voice came through. The captain explained and closed the transmission before he picked up the phone to call the sheriff's office in Crescent City.

Terry, comforted by the warm liquid, relaxed while glancing out at the view. The windows opened a vista of ocean and huge rock formations whose very existence caused shipwrecks on days just like this one. A low moan from the fog horn nearby raised the hair on the back of her neck as she stared out into the cloying air where only the ghost of the rocks could be seen. The sea seemed too close for comfort. Occasionally, a wave broke over the huge boulders just below the building. Watching spray ravage the salt-stained windows was mesmerizing; Terry almost forgot why she was there.

"They're on their way, miss. Be here shortly," the captain said.

Terry nodded thoughtfully. "I appreciate the coffee, Captain Tillman. Baron and I will go on back now."

"Wait a minute! I don't even know your name."

"Sorry . . . Terry Hamilton. In the excitement I forgot my manners."

"I seen you on the beach. You work there a lot, don't you?"

His thin mouth creased into what might have been the suggestion of a smile. The weathered skin, reminiscent of days spent on the bridge of the ship, neatly contrasted with his cobalt blue eyes that were crisp and honest. Beyond them just a faint view of steel gray hair sprang out in kinky clumps from under the dark, woolen cap. He was sturdy – not a big man but strong in appearance, enough that Terry thought him reliable.

"I'm an artist, and I love this lighthouse. If I paint it a couple hundred times, I just might get it right," she grinned, and the entire look was enticing.

"Modest – I like that in a woman. I like your dog too. He's very protective but good mannered; that's pretty special in so tough a dog. I often thought of having a dog here to keep me company of a night." Having said that, the seaman bent to scratch Baron's head. They heard sirens. "I must have left the door open," the captain said absently. "You can't hear nothin' through these walls. That'd be the ambulance and the law. We might just as well go together to the beach. They'll have questions," he said walking toward the passageway.

Once they were outside, the sound was deafening as many vehicles converged on the mainland parking lot above the beach. Loudspeakers barked commands while the ambulance people assembled and started down the cement ramp carrying a stretcher. Several officers, the sheriff and some additional personnel followed.

From their vantage point above the spit, Terry and the captain watched the rocks below come alive. After coming down to the cove, the young woman and the dog led the way to the place where the body was floating. Baron started to bark. Terry pulled the lead taut, cautioning him and retreating a safe distance. The dog obeyed. They watched as men in rubber hip boots pulled the dead man out of the surf. Terry glanced away, shuddering as they flipped him over into the rubber body bag and closed the zipper.

6

"Are you the woman who found the body?" a sharp voice asked.

The woman's red curls moved in tandem as her head jerked around. "Yes, I came up to the lighthouse to ask the captain if he would call you."

"What were you doing here?"

The question seemed impertinent. The questioner was about 35 years old, very good looking, smug beyond words and tall enough to make Terry strain to look up into his face. He appeared serious. Two dark brown eyes pierced her soul, and his mouth seemed almost cruel. She disliked him instantly.

"You don't think I had anything to do with his death?" she asked in an incredulous voice.

"I don't know what to think, but you were apparently the only one here. Isn't that so?"

The artist's look widened. "WHO ARE YOU?" she asked with such indignation that it actually took her by surprise.

"Assistant District Attorney Martin Delaney, and I will be trying someone for this murder. Well, if it turns out that it is a murder."

"So, you believe I murdered this man, put him into the ocean, then ran up to the lighthouse to call the sheriff?" Terry's blood boiled – deepening her skin color around blue eyes the color of glacial ice. "You can't be serious?"

Captain Tillman's crusty voice rose in the cove. "Mis' Hamilton din't kill nobody. She and her dog come everyday to paint on this beach. I can vouch for that. I get up at 5:00 A.M. and am up on the catwalk with my first cup o' coffee. There weren't nobody else out here then; besides, young fella', the tide was in."

Terry felt a smirk rising. She looked away.

"Well, it is possible he was murdered somewhere else and dumped here."

Captain Tillman's look soured. "Or, out there. It's jest possible he floated in here with the tide. Wouldn't you agree?" The cobalt blue eyes leveled on the prosecutor who nodded silently in the face of the old man's mounting anger.

Sheriff Cameron Ripley approached. His considerable size left deep footprints in the sand; he sounded breathless. "They've finished with the body and are removing it to the morgue. Did you interview the witnesses, Martin?"

"Yes, sheriff. Miss Hamilton was painting on the beach this morning. Her dog was with her. Other than that, no one. The captain can vouch for that."

Terry eyed the captain curiously. A black Mercedes was in the parking lot when she drove in. She remembered it because it was strange for anyone else to be around at that time of day. The restrooms were on the edge of the parking lot, and she decided to go in before her trip down to the beach. She didn't see anyone, but the car was gone when she came out. Of course, that didn't mean they were on the beach or had gone up to the lighthouse – still it was mighty unusual.

Ripley, who had lived in Crescent City all his life, knew everyone and made it his business to check on newcomers. He was polite but suspicious because he was paid to be. He was also a political animal, re-elected so many times there was no opposition. "I believe you are Letty Baldwin's grand-daughter, aren't you?" he asked.

Terry nodded. "Did you know my grandmother?"

"Yes. She was a fine lady. We were all sorry to hear of her death."

"Thank you."

Terry's answer was directed at the lawyer. He shifted feet and looked down, causing his dark brown curly hair to fly about in the wind. Watching it ruffle, she wanted to laugh. He poked his hands into the all-weather coat pockets and leaned over, ignoring her gaze.

"I suppose you are staying in her house up the beach, aren't you?"

"It is my house, sheriff; I inherited it."

Ripley nodded knowingly. He loved picking up information and processing it. "Oh, will you be living here permanently, then?"

Terry appeared annoyed. "I haven't decided. May I go?"

The sheriff scratched his head unconsciously. He received the message loud and clear. "Yes, of course. Now, there will have to be a coroner's inquest. We'd like you to be available. You, too, Captain Tillman. That okay with both of you?"

His attempt at charm was lost on Terry. She nodded thoughtfully and turned away.

"Mis' Hamilton," the lighthouse keeper called after her. He limped toward her and waited until they were alone. "I was wonderin' if you might like to come to dinner one night? I don't get many visitors, and I'd like to have you both, and ifn it would be okay, I'd like to see some of those paintings."

The invitation was certainly unexpected but pleasing. Terry looked appreciative. "On one condition, Captain."

"What's that?"

"That I can bring dinner. I'm pretty good in the kitchen."

"Is my cookin' that well known?" He broke into a salty grin. "Okay, Tuesday next. The tide will be out at 5:00 P.M. for an hour an' a half if we're lucky."

"It's a date."

The wind was rising and the tide was beginning to seep onto the spit as Terry hurried to pick up her equipment before the incoming sea swallowed it. Without looking back, she knew he was watching them both leave.

Chapter 2

The Prosecutor

Martin Delaney, new to prosecution, had recently been accepted at the California Bar, the most exotic moment of his life so far. He wanted it too much to blow it, and now he realized he had been completely overbearing with the girl on the beach. *Perhaps*, he thought, while parking his Volvo in the courthouse parking lot, *I'd better learn some people skills. I just made an ass of myself. That won't sit very well with the district attorney or the sheriff.*

The young prosecutor had been offered the job to work in Crescent City by District Attorney Frank Starbuck after he submitted a resume and while he awaited the bar results. Reasoning that starting in a small town would have definite advantages, Martin opted for a two- or three-man office. He knew he would pass the bar; that fact alone was strange. No one else thought they would pass it, but Martin's dedication became abject passion.

He hadn't spent a lot of time with women while he was in law school, deciding rather to wait until after he acquired his dream to find a mate. Naturally, there had been women along the trail. Summers, while he worked on the yachts in the southern California basin, he admired and enjoyed the suntanned beauties he encountered.

He loved boats. His father was successful, and the family

had always owned one. Martin could sail before he could play tennis; his father classified him a natural. When his father died, he willed the sailboat to Martin, but there had been little time for it these past few years. Instead, the sleek motor sloop he named *Sea Dreamer* languished in its berth in the San Diego Yacht Basin. He often imagined himself impressing some beautiful young thing and taking her out for a sail now that he was making good money. However, in his mind's eye he saw himself eventually running for district attorney and then, maybe, attorney general, which required careful plotting. After all what was there to prevent any of that from happening? "Nothing, stupid," he said aloud, "except more of what you pulled this morning on the beach." He resolved to call the sheriff and invite the man to lunch after first questioning the dispatcher regarding Cameron's favorite spot.

Martin arrived first at the weathered, old Seafood House on the dock and selected a booth overlooking huge rusting hulls being prepared for scraping and repainting. Some of them were on hoists being moved into dry dock while others were still floating in their berths. Since he loved ships of all kinds, this place held a special charm for him. Inside was cozy. Out beyond the boat yard was the gray-blue Pacific stretching to the horizon. Martin grinned listening to the constant screech of the sea gulls hanging around the docks and restaurant. That sound created nostalgia, reminding him of all of the pleasant times he'd had with his father on the *Sea Dreamer*.

The sheriff pushed open the door and removed his ten-gallon hat before looking around for the lawyer. Martin stood and offered an extended hand as the lawman approached.

"Glad you could join me, sheriff. I understand the food here is quite good."

Ripley waved to the chef and waitress before sitting down. "Yep, this is one of my favorites."

Martin picked up the menu and appeared to be studying it. "What do you suggest?"

12

"Crab sandwich with cheddar. I can't get my fill of that one."

After the waitress took the order, Martin used the moment to apologize for his indiscretion on the beach.

Ripley's plump face broadened. He laughed out loud before saying, "Oh, I know you were just showing off for that good looking artist. Kind of don't blame you. Her grandmother was pretty well off, and it sounded as though she left it all to Miss Hamilton. You are single, aren't you?"

Martin colored. "Yes, I am." If that were his motive, he hadn't been aware of it. But, at least, it seemed he hadn't upset the lawman.

The sandwiches were deposited, and the conversation turned serious. "Look, I think we ought to talk about the salvage of that wreck," Martin said.

Ripley's eyes sobered. They were gray becoming ocean deep as he spoke. "What is it you want to know?"

Martin knew this was serious business in Crescent City, but there was so much he didn't understand. "Sheriff, I'd really appreciate you filling me in on this matter. I hate not being able to make informed decisions. After all, I am new here."

Ripley responded very positively. "It is very involved, but first you need some background. Well . . . in 1865 there was a big paddle wheeler that sailed out of San Francisco on its way to Portland, Oregon. The storms on this coast are legendary. The captain of the *Brother Jonathan* refused to sail, telling the owners in no uncertain terms that she was carrying too much tonnage and it was dangerous. Those greedy bastards forced him to sail or else. She was carrying over 250 innocent souls and a reputed fortune in gold. In fact, Abraham Lincoln's aide was on board, bringing pay to the troops stationed up in the Northwest."

Martin whistled. "That's really interesting."

"Well, she hit a raging squall just off Crescent City right after sunrise. Her captain, DeWolfe, ordered the crew to turn back and put into Crescent City's harbor. It was about 16 miles.

After turning they struck a ledge. The crew tried vainly to back her off. She wallowed for five minutes helplessly and then, there was a deep thump; a section of her keel floated to the surface. Her foremast tore loose, dropped, punched a hole through her bottom and crashed to rest with her foreyard across the promenade deck. They actually lowered three life boats. One of them made it to Crescent City three hours after the sinking. Eleven men, five women and three children were rescued and taken in by the people of this town. One of them, a quartermaster named Yates, told what actually happened. If he hadn't been such a great seaman, we probably would never have known the whole story. She just sank like a rock. Now, she's resting on the bottom somewhere out there," he pointed toward the ocean. "She is a veritable bank vault of gold and artifacts, which a lot of folks would give an arm and a leg for. So, what we have here is a big fight between California, Crescent City and the National Ship Salvage Corporation."

Martin was savoring the gourmet sandwich. He swiped at his mouth with a napkin and tried to swallow hastily before speaking. "Have these people actually located the wreck?"

Ripley's look widened, his white mane nodded. "That's a good question. Nobody knows, but everybody is concerned. The historical society doesn't want them to get their hands on the artifacts. And, there are plenty of folks here about who think it is a graveyard and shouldn't be disturbed. Then, of course, there is the matter of 50 million in gold bullion, which is not to be snickered at. California wants it bad. You're a lawyer; you can see what a can of worms this might be."

Martin had to admit he was fascinated. "Can't they arrive at a compromise?"

Ripley's raspy laughter echoed across the room. "Lawyers always say that. Listen, son, did you ever know a state willing to compromise about anything? They pay a battery of lawyers who work around the clock. It is big bad government against everybody, and don't quote me. By the time they are finished nobody wins. It's stupidity personified. These salvage compa-

14

nies spend upwards of a half million dollars trying to locate. Then they have to spend that much defending their position in court. Now, remember, if they locate and they get too much hassle, what is to stop them from just opening up the wreck and taking the loot. Who would ever know? Better yet who could prove it?"

For the young lawyer the problem seemed challenging. If a person wanted to make a name for himself he might never get a better opportunity. He shook his dark mane and appeared to be completely engrossed in his companion's conversation, but his brain was reeling. He knew this was a small place, and the people who controlled it were on each other's boards and committees. He would have to be very careful to find out who the players were before he misspoke. At that moment he decided he would get interested in the historical society.

After lunch Martin headed for his office to handle his mail and calls. It was half past three by the time he finished. It suddenly occurred to him that he'd better call Ms. Hamilton and do some fence mending. He dialed the number on the DR report.

Terry was napping. She shook her head and glanced at the porcelain clock on the nightstand in her grandmother's front bedroom. *Umm, I was tired. Who could that be?* "Hello," she whispered.

"Miss Hamilton, this is a very embarrassed public servant. I believe I owe you an apology for my inexcusable behavior on the beach this morning."

Terry held the phone out staring in disbelief. "That is very nice of you, Mr. Delaney, but really it is forgotten."

"I'm not sure what got into me, but I would certainly like to make it up to you."

"I assure you, Mr. Delaney, that is not necessary."

Martin wasn't on solid ground. He could hear the uncertainty in her voice. "Please, could I take you to lunch sometime soon?"

"What a lovely offer, but it just isn't possible. I'm very busy right now and besides, Mr. Delaney, I'm not the least bit upset. Don't give it another thought. Thank you for calling. Goodbye."

Terry giggled as she replaced the receiver. She looked at the dog who sat up and glanced over. "Ha, Baron, that lawyer thought he could snooker us. Hmph, men are all alike." For an instant she saw her recent boyfriend from art school in her mind's eye. Clark became much more interested after she invited a few of her classmates to the estate for the weekend after graduation. It never had occurred to Terry to discuss her family or their affluent circumstances. That fact had always been taken for granted. Terry remembered now, sitting in the comfort of her Crescent City home, how little the money mattered, especially after she lost her grandmother. But, in her earlier youth, her grandfather, the more pragmatic of the two, had lectured her on the future as it pertained to her fortune. He had said many times that she had to be extremely careful because people would do a lot to get their hands on that kind of wealth.

Climbing out of the canopied, king-sized bed, Terry pulled on her pale blue woolen robe. She snuggled into it and smiled softly. Her long hair was in disarray, and she moved to the Pinewood dressing table and sat down. The face in the mirror was quite beautiful. Her blue eyes, which matched the robe, sparkled as she rethought the recent telephone conversation. Putting a brush to her long hair caused her to frown, and her full lips pouted slightly as she worked the tangles. Then, she reached for a clip to tie back the hair. "There," she remarked to the dog, "I'm presentable, Baron. I suppose I should get dressed and go to town. I'm about out of everything." The dog barked. There was nothing he liked better than to get into the Jeep and take a ride.

Later, they drove into the parking lot behind the grocery. Terry cautioned the dog to sit and behave himself. "No tricks, boy. You hear me?"

16

The dog yipped twice. Terry grabbed his face and hugged him saying, "Where would I be without you, old friend?" Baron's huge brown eyes stared into her soul, and Terry knew he was heaven sent.

The aisles in the grocery were quite crowded, but then, it was Friday afternoon. The artist spent a lot of time selecting raw things – her favorites. She filled the cart with fruit and crisp, fresh vegetables from the Imperial Valley of California. It was such a treat after having lived in Boston for so long where everything came out of cold storage. She was bagging some tomatoes when a voice called her name. Turning, she saw the handsome face of Martin Delaney under a neutral colored suede hat. He had on a tan turtleneck sweater and blue jeans. The effect was definitely pleasant. He didn't look so formidable somehow, but she still didn't trust him.

"It is Terry, isn't it?" He was really attractive when he smiled.

"Yes."

"Do you mind my calling you that?" Boy, this guy was pulling out all the stops. "No." She snickered, "That is my name."

Martin looked nonplussed. This lady was really mad at him. He decided to keep his losses at a minimum. "Well, it was nice to see you. Have a nice day." He tipped the suede just ever so slightly and moved to a new aisle, leaving the lady quite surprised.

Shut your mouth, Terry, you are gaping, she chided herself. *I don't think you expected him to give up quite so easily.*

Chapter 3

Inside the Lighthouse

Tuesday arrived quickly. Terry prepared some wonderful delicacies for the dinner in the lighthouse, but fixing a meal for someone she barely knew required extra thought. She made an apple pie for dessert, pretty confident that no man alive would refuse homemade apple pie; the salad was for her – she hoped he would approve; fresh Washington State shrimp, plump, pink and delicious, had been precooked and would be served cold at the site with horseradish and ketchup. There was hard crusted French bread to go with her specialty, a spicy rice dish that could be warmed at the lighthouse. Everything was prepared and wrapped by noon, then placed together in her grandmother's big refrigerator. The artist realized how excited she was to finally be able to see the inside of this building her hand had painted hundreds of times.

Terry hummed as she moved into her studio to take a good look at the recent works and put a few of them into her art case for the captain's perusal. The watercolors were all hanging on a large cork board near the big window facing the sea in her favorite part of the house. The light was definitely better there. Up high overlooking the ocean, a small deck, just outside large French doors, was an extremely welcome spot on sunny summer days. The studio evoked pleasure – bright and airy with colorful wallpaper of carnations, daisies and violets. The paper hung from the ceiling to just above the middle of the wall under which was an off-white wainscoting with a ledge. Red and white linen covers on a couch and armchair complimented the big pine coffee table where her grandmother had put together an artificial flower arrangement of poppies and greens and carnations in deep blues, white and red. There were cupboards, a sink and a counter to spread work on against the corner wall. The room just begged to be used, and it coaxed her talent. All the hours spent there brought back happy memories of the woman who had decorated it with loving hands.

Remembering her grandmother's joy when Terry had seen the room for the first time, she knew it had given the elder woman great satisfaction to have decorated it. It was a present to Terry for her graduation from the Boston Institute of Art where she had gone after college. She was certain her grandmother hoped it would encourage her to settle in Crescent City. They had been happy here for a year until her grandmother's death. That thought evoked sudden loneliness.

She carried a cup of tea to the big windows overlooking the beach and sat down. It was strange to have lost everyone. Her parents were killed in an accident when she was just six. After that, grandmother Letty raised her; grandfather Baldwin was rarely home. His business of buying and selling commercial real estate took him everywhere, and Letty, tired of traveling, welcomed raising the child. The pair grew very close. After grandfather Baldwin died five years ago, Letty moved to the beach house permanently. Terry visited summers. The house in Boston had been closed now for several years, and Terry was having a hard time thinking about selling it. Recently, an estate agent had been pressing for an answer; he had a willing buyer. Letty's estate was sufficient, but there were so many memories in that beautiful house. The thought of selling Letty's priceless art work and collections raised a shudder. The caretakers were enjoying the place. Terry knew they were trustworthy; they had been with the family for years.

For a moment she thought about the request for the lighthouse painting from a San Francisco art gallery. Someone in Crescent City, an unknown benefactor who had seen her work at a local show, must have contacted the gallery on her behalf. It was quite a plumb to have them ask. Naturally, she was nervous about showing her work. Those people were very particular. If they accepted her, she would probably have it made, at least, on the West Coast. Pondering that thought took Terry some time. It wasn't the end of the world. If they didn't like it, so what? After all, she reasoned, there were plenty of other markets, but it would be nice to get an opinion from a true critic.

At four o'clock she packed the Jeep and headed for the A Street parking lot. Captain Tillman surprised Terry by waiting on the far bank of the island just as the last of the tide disappeared from the rocky bottom. He waved and started toward her, stopping momentarily to pet Baron.

"Thought you might need some help, young lady," he mumbled through clenched lips where he held his pipe tightly.

"Thanks, Captain, I'm grateful; this stuff was getting heavy."

The aroma from the pipe floated around them. "You brought a lot. It's just the two of us."

"Well, it won't go to waste. You can nibble on it for a few days," she said, looking winsome. "Oh, Captain, that pipe smells wonderful."

The wind was up. The captain cautioned her about its force before they reached the upper path that faced the sea, where it was always the strongest. The seaman hurried toward the door and opened it, led them into the hallway and walked quickly into the kitchen where they put down the packages and began to unwrap things.

Static from the ship-to-shore radio crackled into the room.

The captain went to it and opened the key. "Coast guard, this is Battery Point, do you read me?"

"Yeah, come in, Battery Point."

"You boys got any more on that earthquake?"

"Only what we gave you earlier. We've got a cutter headed up that way, Captain. Leave the radio on and we'll keep you posted."

Terry stared at him. "Is there a problem?" It felt ominous, as if it were a warning.

"Look! I almost called you to ask you not to come. There was a bad earthquake in Alaska yesterday. Did you hear about it?"

"No, I rarely listen to the radio or television, just my stereo, a music-only station." A wink surfaced. "Alaska is a long way off, Captain, maybe, two thousand miles."

"You don't understand. See, that quake was 8.5 on the scale. That's the largest ever recorded in this hemisphere. They had a helluva tidal wave after it happened. This is a big ocean, and it's got a mind of its own. You followin' me?"

"A tidal wave? Is that what you mean? HERE?" Her eyes widened as she asked.

"Well, let's eat, honey. I don't want to scare you, but I don't want you to stay too long. If that water is on the move, no tellin' what it'll do."

Terry wasn't even hungry anymore. This man knew the sea. If he had trepidations, maybe she should take Baron and get out.

Captain Tillman saw her fear. "Look! Let's enjoy our dinner. I din't mean to scare you. We're safe here cause this place has walls 24 inches thick. See, look here." He pointed to the break between the sitting room and the kitchen. "If you was to be anywhere and wanted to be protected from that ocean, it would be right here." His look softened and so did Terry's.

Once the oven was lit, they placed the rice dish inside to warm. Everything else was ready.

"Come on, Terry, I'll show you around."

The girl's face lit appreciatively. "I thought you'd never ask."

She followed him into a round hallway adjacent to the sitting room and started up the twisted staircase. The walls were trim painted navy gray, and the rope railing clinging to the wall was really useful for the dizzying climb. On the second floor he showed her three small rooms. Two were bedrooms and a third was a bath that faced the now-darkening horizon. The bedrooms were simply furnished in antique oak pieces. There was a chair in each room, a dresser, bed, a wooden clothes rack and foot locker. The windows overlooked the giant Pacific and looking down, one felt as if he were actually in it as breaking waves collided with the rocky base. Terry followed him out. They returned to the stairwell that wound up to the tower where the fresnel lens was shining brightly. The climb took her breath away, as did the view from the glass tower. She walked around the catwalk extolling its virtues.

"You like it, huh?" It was apparent he wanted to share it.

"You bet. No wonder you spend so much time up here."

He gave her a funny look. "We'd better get down to supper."

Dinner was very pleasant. The captain definitely appreciated her choice of foods and the preparation. He gave her a compliment. She imagined that was rare and thanked him sincerely.

They had coffee with the pie at five o'clock. The captain looked at an antique banjo clock in the sitting room and shook his head. "I don't want to make you mad, Terry, but you'd better go. I don't like the looks of that water. It seems to be swellin', and that don't make no sense. The tide's supposed to be out."

She jumped up and started to clean up.

"No time, girl. Come on, put on your slicker and let's git."

Terry realized the urgency. She obeyed and followed him to the path leading to the sea. The wind was howling by now. She clutched the dog's lead. At the turn in the path, the captain grabbed her arm; he pointed ahead. The spit was already covered with water and the bay filling for a real flood tide raising angry swells. The captain couldn't yell over the wind; he pointed toward the lighthouse entrance before turning her around.

Once they were back inside he chuckled. "Well, it looks as if I'm gonna have two overnight guests."

Terry's mouth gaped. "You're sure there is no other way?"

"It's no problem. I've got a guest room upstairs, and it's all prepared. Sometimes people get caught out here and stay over." He grunted. "You ain't got much choice now, have you?" His look seemed almost mischievous, as though he was secretly pleased to have some company.

Baron was very nervous. He was pacing, and once in awhile he'd bark. Terry comforted him, but it didn't do too much good. By 8:00 P.M. it was pitch black outside. She reassured herself by saying, "Well, Captain, there is no use being upset about anything I can't control – is there?"

"I told you, girl. You are safer here than any place else on the coast. Now, let's have a piece of that great pie and hit the bunks."

Upstairs Terry readied for bed. The captain gave her an extra blanket, but it was really comfortable in the building. Outside the wind was howling, but inside it was silent. She refrained from looking out into the void and tried not to think about the coast guard radio messages. There was going to be a tidal wave, but as yet no one knew where it would be.

She must have fallen asleep, and what was happening had to be a dream. A figure, dressed in a strange costume, stood by the bed. He was good looking, maybe 45 years old, and his long, dark, curly hair hung loose against what appeared to be a blousy silk shirt. His trim waist was encased in a leather belt closed by a wide brass buckle. In his hand he held a viewing scope that he manipulated as if it were used frequently. The man's deep voice accosted her. "Get up, lass. Don't you hear me, get up." Baron started to bark loudly. Terry knew the bark; it was fear. The figure spoke again. "Get that old fool up now. DO YOU HEAR ME?" he demanded.

Terry sat straight up. The figure was gone, and the dog's incessant barking grew louder. She got up and pulled on her clothes. As she did she glanced out the window. It was moonlight, and the ocean was gone. Terry screamed. Running into the hall, she yelled, "Captain, my God, get up quick!"

The captain barely had his clothes on when he ran out. "What's wrong, Terry?"

"LOOK!" she pointed outside. "The ocean has disappeared." She started to cry. "My God! What is happening? I'm terrified!"

Captain Tillman never did know what to do with women who cried. "Don't do that!" he shouted.

Terry stopped and stared at him wide-eyed, the tears still fresh on her cheeks.

He could see terror in her eyes, and he knew what it had to be. "Look! It's comin', and it's gonna be bad, but I think we're safer than those people in town. Do you believe me?"

She wanted to believe him, but where the hell was the ocean? "WHERE IS IT?" She clutched his shoulders roughly. TELL ME, WHERE IS IT?"

"It's sucking out to sea and building. Let's go up to the tower. This will be Mother Nature's big show. You won't want to miss a moment of it. Now, I gotta go to the radio and warn the town. Go up to the tower. I'm telling you, girl, you ain't never gonna see anything like it again. I'll be up as soon as I radio the coast guard."

"I'm going with you," she said, shaking and afraid to be left alone.

25

Terry followed below and tried to comfort the dog. He knew there was trouble; animals always do. Finally, she made him lie down. He obeyed but not for long.

"Mayday! Mayday! Coast guard, this is Battery Point. Do you read me?"

"We copy – go ahead, Battery Point."

"The tide is out – it's out so damn far I can't see any ocean. It's coming, and you'd better warn the town and the ships in the area."

"This is coast guard, Battery Point, we have already warned the entire coast. We have notified the state police, sheriff's office and local authorities. We know it will hit Crescent City, but it's anybody's guess what else will sustain damage. We've been calling you, but you probably were in bed. Keep us posted and that light going – we've got ships out there."

"Okay, girl, let's get up to the tower. I'll call the local sheriff to make certain they're in touch."

Terry started up the steps. She was shaking from head to foot. "Wait, Terry. Let's go outside to see if we can see anything."

They put on their slickers, and Terry forced the dog to stay inside triggering his ceaseless barking.

The night was still. Now there was a moon and she could make out strange, black rock formations dotting the ocean floor. There was no water in the harbor – the boats had sunk into the mud and rolled over onto their sides except for those tethered on four lines, which were suspended in midair. It was eerie and exciting and evoked a strange curiosity until suddenly they heard a thunderous roar, growing louder with each second. Fear encompassed them.

"Get inside quick," he ordered, pushing Terry toward the door.

Captain Tillman bolted the door behind them. He ran for the staircase and went up so fast Terry couldn't keep up. She was huffing noticeably when she finally arrived on the catwalk.

Chapter 4

A Watery Terror

At midnight in Crescent City, the bars on Front Street were still going strong. Several drunks sitting by the door of Duffy's yelled out that the law was coming as two deputies entered and demanded quiet. The din stopped. Someone turned down the radio, blaring out a western tune, so they could listen.

"There's a tidal wave coming, folks, and you've got a very short time to save your hides. Get out now, and don't stop until you are way back on the mainland. Turn on your radios and follow the instructions about returning."

People started to scream and run, almost knocking the deputies over. The bar emptied immediately. No one bothered to look at the bay except one old man staggering outside who could barely walk. He stopped and stared at the harbor. Scratching his head, he said to no one in particular, "Well, I'll be damned, somebody stole the bay." A deputy came close and ordered him to move up into the mainland. A truck stopped, and two young fishermen yelled, "Carl, git your sorry butt over here before you gits drowned."

Cars were racing out into the night with horns blaring as people tried to send a warning to others who might be left behind. Within minutes Front Street was completely silent. The bartender was the last to go, and he only wanted to grab the strongbox and empty the register of the night's receipts for which the owner would be eternally grateful.

It seemed unreal to be so quiet. The deputy remarked, "It feels like waiting for death, Joe. Let's get the hell out of here before that thing drowns us."

The pair climbed into a patrol car and headed for the docks. There wasn't much time; in fact, they didn't know how much. They were in constant radio contact with their own dispatcher, but he would have to leave shortly. Everyone concerned knew if they only had a siren or an air-raid horn of some sort, they could have warned the townspeople. The docks seemed nearly deserted except for a few guys playing cards in a service shack. The deputies yelled into the shed. "Get out now – tidal wave coming fast." Some of them ran to their boats not realizing the water was gone. The deputies did not want to be caught either and were happy they had nearly completed their mission. They searched for the night watchman and then moved on toward the fish packing sheds. The sheriff would say later that they did a bang-up job considering the short notice. They had emptied the bars while other deputies warned people in the motels and houses on Front Street and just beyond. The deputies had been ordered to turn on their sirens as they moved to create a disturbance that could be heard by anyone curious enough to check. There wasn't time to move patients from the hospital. Sheriff Ripley contacted the head nurse and ordered her to move everyone up to the second level; he also told them to pray. The hospital was a fairly new brick building and, owing to some dedication by a few knowledgeable board members, had been built sturdily and on high ground. The sheriff believed it to be quite safe.

A coast guard plane roared overhead. It must have been on alert since they finally located the wave. The dispatcher received a call shortly from the state police then relayed it to the patrol cars. "It's building high maybe twenty or thirty feet, and they said when it comes it'll be moving at speeds of 500 miles per hour. You will hear it before you see it. We've notified everyone we can, now – get out, fellows, you don't want to be trapped either."

The deputies put the car in gear and raced away. They were curious and didn't want to go too far hoping they could see it. One of them suggested the radio tower four blocks into town and up on a rise. They turned the squad car toward it.

Crescent City's bay was quite wide at its mouth and deep as it came toward the docks. A marina and boat yard occupied at least a half mile of the left side of the harbor as it faced the sea. Boulders, weighing upwards of twenty tons, were guarding the entrance on the right side. The jetty extended for a half mile as it faced the ocean. Battery Point Lighthouse sat up high just beyond the sea wall. The building overlooked the bay on the left and was just adjacent to the entrance to it. The lighthouse had a clear view of the cove on its opposite side, the bay itself, the town and the upper and lower coastal areas.

By now Captain Tillman was operating his telescope from the tower and feeling a strange exhilaration. He knew the sea. It had been his life and although he loved it, he had a true respect for its power and wrath. This wasn't his first tidal wave, and he knew what was about to happen could be so devastating as not to be believed. His only concern now was the visibly shaken young woman who stood beside him looking out at the abyss. He turned for a moment and touched her hands. "It would be better if you tried to calm yourself. Consider what nature does, Terry. There is no way to argue. If you can understand what I'm gonna say it might make a difference. What you're about to see will be like nothing else ever in your whole life. Think, girl, you're privileged and you're safe, ifn you know it or not."

He turned the glass slightly and yelled, "Here she comes, don't miss it." Terry stared out into the moonlight and could see a giant wave all frothy on top, boiling up in great mounds, racing toward them at unprecedented speed. The moonlight gave her a good view of the width. Although she wasn't knowledgeable enough to gauge distance, she guessed it was at least several miles wide, maybe more. She was too frightened to yell. Her eyes bulged as the enormous wall of boiling water hit the island and split, racing around them, but not before allowing a sluicing wave to splash up and hit the tower. They both ducked simultaneously – then, ran to the other side of the tower facing town.

Captain Tillman opened the door to the outside catwalk just as the torrent passed by, surging toward Front Street. The sound was so incredible Terry could not take it in. Breaking glass, crashing buildings, boats rising into the air and floating onto Front Street seemed surreal. The lights went out all over the docks and street lights were diminished as they toppled over into the onrushing sea. The captain hurried back inside, fully aware of the renewed destruction yet to come as the water, after having wreaked its havoc, would suck all the rubble back out into the ocean. The buildings were floating, banging against cars and wood from the docks, which had exploded like splinters. A large troller lifted from its mooring, rose up into the wave and disappeared up into one of the creeks now flooded with sea water. The usually well-lit area was dark, and a feeling of doom prevailed. At this point the street lights on the highway were still lit, getting their power from a big transformer farther away.

"Here she comes, Terry. Watch this!" The captain yelled, pulling his binocular tighter toward his eyes.

The ocean had sunk deep into the town, breaking everything in its path and now, like some giant squid, was reeling all of the houses, cars, boats and loose rubble back out into its womb. It could not be believed. It was happening so fast that her mind could barely absorb it. Terry was unaware of it then, but her dog, who could not mount the circular staircase, was howling so loudly the radio's repeated transmissions were blocked out.

It seemed an eternity when, in fact, it was only minutes before the captain yelled, "It's almost time for a return."

Terry stared at the destruction in front of her. It seemed to be over, but it was building its power for the backwater.

The captain bolted the heavy steel door that opened onto the outside catwalk. Terry felt weak in the knees. There was one realization – life was very tenuous. *A blessing for the captain's wisdom and experience,* was her only thought. She was safe in this unusual place. Gathering her strength, the girl moved closer to the salt-stained windows, not wanting to miss the show nature was providing. The captain had been right; it was unequaled in memory.

Suddenly the water began to recede. They could not hear it, but buildings, cars, boats, planking and debris seemed to be on some giant water slide tunneling out into the harbor and disappearing out past the breakwater. Terry ran to face the sea. "It's over and I'm still in one piece. Oh! Thank you, Lord, thank you." Captain Tillman was working on some charts secured to the inner wall near the staircase. Terry brushed past him headed down below to the bathroom where she vomited. In an instant she flushed water over her face, cleaned up and rushed back to the tower.

"Here she comes again." The captain was excited.

Terry gasped. "I thought it was all over. Don't tell me there's more!" The color drained from her face.

"There might be as many as four or five, but they won't all be as bad." He shook his head, "Here it comes."

Terry ran to the glass. This wave wasn't as large as the first. It passed them swiftly, raced into Front Street, engulfed the boat yard and sucked back out within what seemed like seconds. The sky glowed with light. They could see clearly. Immediately the bay drained, sinking a giant lumber barge into the mud. The captain seemed preoccupied with the telescope and his charts, anxiously marking things on nautical maps. Terry imagined it was part of his job and didn't try to disturb him – he seemed oblivious to her presence. Moving to the tower glass, Terry picked up his unused binocular and searched the horizon. Her mouth dropped open.

"Oh, Captain, THIS ISN'T HAPPENING!" she screamed.

Several miles out a giant wave was building on top of which was the coast guard cutter and two fishing boats. They must have been monitoring the ship-to-shore communications. They had tried to outrun the water, were circling about three miles out and now had been forced on top of the wave's crest racing toward the coast.

"It's coming, Terry, and it's bad. We are seventy-five feet in the air right now, and this wave is higher than this tower. Brace yourself, girl. If we make it through this baby we'll be lucky."

Terry ran downstairs to the dog. If she were going to die, she wanted to be with him. Kneeling, she clutched his warm neck and put her face close to his, talking softly to him about what he meant to her. Baron's howl rose in the kitchen, mournful and disconsolate. A watery giant passed over them with such force and speed that Terry thought the island had moved. As she glanced out, it appeared as if they were looking into an aquarium tank. As quickly as she thought that, it passed, rushing onto the unprotected town. Terry kissed the dog and leaped up the circular staircase. Once in the tower, she pressed herself against the glass.

Lights became apparent off to the right. The captain and Terry ran to the other side of the tower. On the dock the wave had hit the gasoline drums, which flew into the air before crashing and spilling. There were hot wires everywhere, igniting the gasoline that raced across the dock, eventually moving toward the Texaco storage tanks that had ruptured. They exploded instantly. The material on a huge lumber barge was flying into the air sending planks sailing around like kites. Explosion after explosion lit up the night sky just as the backwater sucked out bringing burning debris with it. Terry started to cry; she couldn't help it, and she couldn't stop. The captain put his arm around her shoulders. He never spoke but he certainly understood. That hideous wall of watery destruction defied explanation, and now he was sadly aware of how many townspeople were dead. He picked up the scope and turned back toward the sea. He could see the coast guard cutter, which appeared to be unharmed.

"What a ride that must have been, boys," he shouted to no one in particular.

There were two more fishing boats out there, but he couldn't be certain if they were manned. The water was building again. He told Terry they could relax now; he was certain the worst was over, at least, in his experience he believed that.

They went down to the kitchen where the captain radioed the coast guard cutter. The voice was breaking up badly, but it sounded as if they said it was subsiding. They thanked the captain for the flashing beacon that gave them a point of reference and protected them every time it became rough off the coast. They asked for information, and he gave it. He also learned that the other boats out there were unmanned or had lost their skippers.

"We've tried to raise them but can't get an answer," the radio operator said. They told him choppers were coming in from a Seattle military base, but it would take some time for the help to arrive.

At 12:30 A.M. some of the gang who were in Duffy's, believing the wave had passed, grouped together in two trucks and headed back into town deliberately skirting the state police road blocks. They were all shocked. It seemed as if nothing could actually do that much damage in so short a time. Duffy's was miraculously still standing – well, at least the front. The windows and doors were missing and everything inside had been rearranged, but two walls still stood. They went inside and decided to have a drink to celebrate the "Great Crescent City Wave." They were what one man termed "gin courageous." They were also about to be killed. Within twenty minutes of their arrival, the third and most destructive wave crashed in on them. They had been laughing and dancing around the empty bar when the eighty-foot wave crushed the building around them. The entire street went out to sea, and for a long time no one knew what had become of them or their vehicles.

Four blocks up the street on the highest point of the radio tower, the deputies shouted to each other, back and forth, as they were exposed to more unbelievable happenings. They were desperately clinging to a metal infrastructure that they climbed after getting onto a nearby roof. They were speechless seeing the big wave. Their place on the tower turned hot as the power fields running into it shorted out, and the water flooded into its base. They were both electrocuted. Their bodies were found the next day burned almost beyond recognition.

There were very few people uninformed of the tragedy, but one man said he actually slept through it. He lived close to Terry Hamilton's house, which was untouched. Most of the damage was in town or on the southern end of Crescent City. Naturally, much of the lower coast had been damaged also. The waves originally funneled into Crescent City Bay, sucking out and widening past the jetty, causing some unusual oceanic action on the lower coast for the rest of the night.

Martin Delaney, up late preparing a brief, usually listened to the news before bed. After turning on the radio he went to his kitchen to fix a cup of tea. He glanced at the clock and was surprised that it was after midnight. "Oh, it's too late for the news," he said aloud. Suddenly the announcer said tsunami and Crescent City. He gaped. Shutting down the stove, he hurried to turn up the sound. This broadcast was a special announcement, and the station would be on for the rest of the night. The young prosecutor's jaw dropped as he heard the information being given out.

Martin's rental, out behind the home of a local judge, was a guest house. Fortunately, it was in the country probably five

miles from Crescent City. The first wave had apparently dev-
astated the town. Martin grabbed his leather jacket and ran
toward the judge's back door.

The family was asleep. Martin banged heavily on the door
until the sleepy, bewildered judge answered. Martin explained
and then ran toward his car. Within minutes he made it to the
roadblock set up by the state police. They recognized him as
he climbed out of his car.

"What can we do?" Martin asked. "There have to be a lot of
injured people in there."

"We can't really do anything, Mr. Delaney," the officer
replied. "This thing is going to continue all night according to
the coast guard. They've got a plane up and a ship outside the
bay. Apparently there are recurring tidal waves until the
ocean decides to stop. It doesn't serve any purpose to go in
there and join the dead."

Martin turned the car around to head for home. He remembered a logging road through the woods that came out near
the north end of town. It didn't take long to reach the road.
About fifteen minutes later he came out onto a rise overlooking Crescent City. Parking, he climbed out. "Son of a bitch,"
he screamed, "I don't believe it!" Down below everything he
recognized was gone. The water seemed to be drained completely out of the bay. Dregs of boats, cars, barges, lumber,
trees, tanks and houses were all plopped down like toys all
over the mud flats. It was impossible to comprehend. There
was fire everywhere illuminating what had to be the worst
destruction he had ever witnessed. Suddenly, he realized
there was another wave coming in. It looked like a funnel rising up so high it passed around the lighthouse, headed for the
hospital, diverted and hit what was left of the town. From his
vantage point he couldn't see anymore. Mouth agape, the
lawyer prayed silently. *There must be horrible situations all
over the place of people in need, but no one can go into that
place until the water stops its assault.* He felt the frustration
but knew the police were right. Before the water retreated, he

heard a child crying just below him; he followed the sound. If the child hadn't been screaming, he wouldn't have heard her. Down the hill he found a little girl sitting in the woods clutching her knees. He stooped before gathering her into his arms.

"Go ahead and cry, little one. It's pretty bad. Are you hurt?"

The small voice sniveled in between cries, "No. Mommy's hurt. She won't talk to me, and I don't know where to go."

Martin clutched the cold body to him. He took off his jacket and wrapped her in it. "Look, can you tell me where you live? Are you far from home?" She stopped crying, shook her head and pointed across the woods. It looked as though there was a small bungalow sitting sideways off in a clearing. Martin could see the hospital; it wasn't damaged. He assumed if it weren't hit by now it probably wasn't going to be. Taking the child back to his car, he wrapped her in a blanket from the back seat. Then he drove onto the path leading down toward the hospital. Within minutes he gave her to a nurse and headed back out, hoping the little girl had given him good directions.

He drove as far as he could, then left on foot. He could see a small frame house that had been knocked off its foundation. It looked as if the roof were caving in. He saw the last wave hit and recede and decided he might have a short span before another one flooded in. The building was still upright but slanted as if it wanted to fall down. Martin guessed it was taking a real chance going inside, but he called out and listened. "Anyone – are you inside? I will help – answer me." The moaning was low, almost inaudible, but there was a sound. The door stuck because the jam was uneven. Picking up a loose board, Martin bashed in a window and climbed inside. The woman, crumpled like a rag doll, was lying on the floor against an inner wall. He moved closer and knelt.

"You're hurt bad and I'd rather not move you, but there's no telling what that water is up to. Can you help me get you out of here?" Her lips moved, but no sound came out. Martin lifted her, and she just went limp and silent. He was glad of that; at least he wasn't hurting her. Within minutes he made it to his car and laid her in the back seat. He ran back and tried to search the rest of the house for anymore people. He found a baby drowned in a crib and removed her lifeless form to the front seat of his car. Back at the hospital he told the nurse about the little girl. He imagined they were all from the same family. Another wave hit just after he left the hospital. Martin watched it destroy and suck back out. The house he found the woman and child in had been swept away. For a moment he stared in awe as the bungalow slipped silently into the receding bay, bobbing like a toy in a bathtub, before breaking up and sinking slowly out of sight.

Chapter 5

The New Hero

Terry fell asleep with her head leaning heavily on crossed arms on the kitchen table. Earlier, she had fed all three of them. The captain was still busy in the tower, and the dog was asleep at her feet when she awoke and stretched. "Oh, I'm so stiff and sore. What a terrible night – if I live to be 100, I hope I'm spared from another experience like that one." She had to admit being alive was a big plus. They had already learned from the coast guard radioman that the death toll was at eleven and the townspeople weren't finished searching.

At 6:00 A.M. Terry climbed up to the bedroom and stood staring at the ocean below. It looked deep from that vantage point but normal. On the other side of the room there was a small window that overlooked the harbor. It was difficult to look at Crescent City. She could see how much activity there was, and they had been radioing the lighthouse all morning. The tide was still up. It was anybody's guess when it would subside. The jetty, which was clearly visible, was strewn with debris and even off the cove she could see remnants of houses and boats lying all over the coastline. They had learned from the coast guard that the two other boats floating free last night were not manned but had broken their moorings and floated out to sea. The captain on the cutter put two seamen on board and directed them to try to bring the boats into the harbor where they would be tied up to buoys. The docks were absolutely unusable. Crescent City's boat works and fish packing sheds had been demolished. The pilings for the docks speared out of the bay as lone sentinels, but the loose planking was still floating like so many toothpicks.

Military helicopters arrived sometime before dawn and were able to evacuate wounded from their homes with hoist baskets. They flew the badly injured people to a hospital in Medford, Oregon, an hour away, where a triage unit had been set up. State police units from all over California flew in medivac planes equipped with supplies and extra medical personnel. Doctors were in short supply, and the additional help was badly needed.

The stories that came out of the previous night's disaster were incredible. One woman told of seeing a car with two people in it float by her window. Another man said he watched sea water rise seventeen feet on the outside of the hotel before it washed away. Someone saw a huge troller riding the water up the street, and when the water withdrew the boat was sitting in the city swimming pool. People were interviewed in the hospital and on the streets where many dazed and bewildered injured just sat looking out to sea. Shock obviously controlled them, and doctors warned citizens to come in to be checked.

Terry turned the television on to listen to the news reports. There had been a great deal of destruction further down the coast. The fire department notified the town council that twenty-nine blocks of the city had been destroyed. The entire town was out helping. Residents were housing displaced people in their homes. The needy were advised to gather at the hospital parking lot where food and clothing would be made available. Many had lost their homes. Cars, boats and businesses were missing or destroyed. Listening, Terry wondered if her house had been damaged. Of course, she reasoned, it was pretty far north, and the waves didn't seem to come into that area. Shortly, a nurse was being interviewed at the hospital. She told the story of a brave young man who had saved an entire family during the time the waves were still attacking the harbor. As the story unfolded, Terry became more interested. The nurse said he hadn't identified himself, but when she described the man, the sheriff knew it was Assistant District Attorney Martin Delaney. The nurse explained how he went back to get the body of a baby from a house that was sucked out to sea immediately after he abandoned it. "Then," she continued, "he spent the rest of the night bringing in people he found wandering in the rubble. He saved six lives because we were able to treat them plus the little girl and her mother. The mother is in serious condition but is expected to live." She answered the next question sadly. "No, she does not know the baby drowned in her crib."

The captain came in just as the story was unfolding. "Well, I'll be," he said with a wink. "You never know about anybody, do ya'?" The old man was busy filling his pipe. He lit it shortly and puffed anxiously until it caught, emitting an aromatic scent.

Terry sniffed deeply and commented on its delicious aroma while pouring a cup of coffee for the lighthouse keeper. He sat down facing her and asked if she was all right.

"I'm okay, thank you. I'm tired, and I'm certain you must be."

The woolen cap nodded in the affirmative. "I wanted to tell you about some other waves. See, I lived through some real doosies. After that I started to study them. You know, Terry, they kind of interested me. In 1755 there was a big quake in the ocean off Lisbon, Portugal. The tsunami after that one caused the deaths of 60,000 people. Then in 1883 a volcano erupted on an island in Indonesia, and the tsunami destroyed 300 towns on the shores of nearby islands and killed 36,000 people." Captain Tillman swilled some coffee before continuing, his eyes sparkling at the excitement he felt. "The worst one, though, was in Alaska. It happened in 1958. An earthquake caused 90 million tons of rock and ice to fall from a glacier 1,000 feet into the water. That collapse sent out a wave that swept the trees and soil from a mountain on the opposite shores up to a height of 1,720 feet. Can you imagine that, Terry? What we saw here was a puny wave compared to those, but I'm not trying to make light of last night. It was bad, and when the tides hit low we'll go to town and see what's what."

At four o'clock the tide went out. Terry asked the captain if he thought it was safe for them to leave.

"Yep, I think ol' Mother Nature has done all the damage she's gonna do for this year." He stared at her for a moment, and his look seemed hesitant.

"What is it, Captain?"

"I been wantin' to ask you somethin'. Well, I guess, I'll never know ifn I don't. What woke you last night?" His eyes were piercing. It seemed very important.

"I had a dream. I saw this man standing over me in very strange clothes."

The captain raised a hand to stop her. "Did he have a folding scope in his hand, and did it seem he used it regularly?"

Terry nodded.

"Did he have long, dark, curly hair and wear a wide leather belt with a wide brass buckle?" His voice evidenced impatience as if he were eager to hear her response.

"Yes. How did you know that?" she demanded.

"Can I trust you?"

"I think you already know the answer to that, Captain Tillman. You and I went through a surreal trauma last night. I feel closer to you now than I could ever have believed possible."

"That's what I thought, Terry. So, listen carefully; I got to tell you somethin'." The captain stared directly into her eyes, wanting his sincerity to be apparent.

"This place is haunted."

"WHAT?"

42

"What you seen was the ghost of Captain DeWolfe, the sea captain who commanded the *Brother Jonathan* that went down off this coast in 1865 in a terrible storm. He was apparently sailing against his will. The owners wouldn't heed his warnings that she was overloaded with tonnage. There were over 250 people on board and 16 of them survived."

The girl's gasp hissed into the quiet room. Terry gazed out at the sea. It was so beautiful, but it had caused so much havoc.

"I know there ain't many people I could talk to about this, but I was wonderin' just what happened?"

"He told me to get up NOW! . . . He was quite emphatic about it, and his exact words were "And, get that old fool up, too.""

Captain Tillman laughed hard; bending over, he slapped at his knee.

"Is that really funny?"

"Terry, he always calls me that."

"Why do you think he did that. I mean, especially last night?"

"Because I had to keep the light burning for the ships out there. It's real important, honey. Many a ship wound up on these rocks. That's why it's essential, and any seafaring man would know that. The light is visible for fourteen and a half miles on a good night. Last night was moonlit, remember?"

"Wow! I'm flabbergasted. I know you wouldn't lie to me, besides I saw him." Her voice trailed off before she said softly, "I thought I was dreaming."

"He wanted you to see him."

"But why?"

"That's a puzzle. He don't seem to do nothin' without a reason."

"Do you see him often?"

"I hear him more than I see him. That's why your dog was howling so. Animals know about storms and earthquakes and ghosts."

"This is fascinating. Has anyone else seen him?"

"Yeah. Other lighthouse keepers. Not all of them mind you. There was a guy here who hated this place, and his wife loved it. Captain DeWolfe woke him up one night and said, "Get up and get the hell off my island.""

Terry laughed. "He's forceful, huh?"

"Look, I'm glad I told you. We can talk about it another time, 'cause you need to get across to the mainland while it's safe. Get your slicker; I'll walk you out. I've got to take care of the radio, and then I'll go too."

Terry waved from the other side. The captain waited until she was up on the parking lot before he returned to the lighthouse. He had to hurry because he wanted to go to town to see the damage.

The Jeep was piled with debris. Terry spent quite a long time cleaning it off. It wasn't damaged, and for that she was grateful. She started to take her normal route through town and realized it wasn't possible. The view from the hill, near the hospital where the parking lot was, defied anyone's imagination. Terry felt tears welling up. "We were spared, old friend," she said to the dog. "Imagine how many desolate people are left here today without loved ones."

After she arrived home, she called the sheriff's office to ask if anyone needed accommodations. They thanked her and said they would call if they did. The phone rang shortly.

"Hello."

"TERRY! This is Adam. ARE YOU ALL RIGHT?"

The sound of her lawyer's voice pleased her. "How nice of you to be concerned, Adam. I'm fine, and you would not believe where I've been all night."

"Dammit," he said. "I've been nearly crazy. I've called your house every hour since I heard about the tidal wave. I thought the very worst. Terry, hold the line, I need a drink. I thought you were lying in a heap somewhere, dead or worse."

44

Terry giggled to herself. He was really upset, but it was nice to have someone care that much. Her grandmother would have been pleased. She always wanted Terry and Adam Lindquist to get together, but so far nothing had happened. They were always on different time tables.

The lawyer swigged a big gulp of Scotch whisky before resuming their conversation. "There, I feel a little better. I'm not kidding, Terry, I've been frantic. Where the hell were you for two days?"

Terry explained most of it, being careful to leave out her experience with the ghost. She wouldn't forget that conversation about Captain DeWolfe, however, and was determined to learn more. Adam and Terry talked for almost an hour before she yawned out loud.

"Sorry, old friend, but I'm bushed. I didn't sleep at all last night, and the stress of it exhausted me. Give me a ring tomorrow when I'm more coherent, will you please?"

After they hung up Terry headed for a nice hot shower in the beautiful big bathroom next to her bedroom. The ceramic tiled shower room was wide and sunken. Terry stepped down and turned on the hot water, tempering it until she oohed and ahhed contentedly as the steam billowed inside the door, frosting the glass. The hot water, pelting her tired body, seemed seductive in the aftermath of such trauma. She stayed there for a long time relaxing, absorbing the medicating heat and wondering if the past thirty hours had actually happened.

In the morning the television newscasters did their normal rehash of the entire matter. If things went as they usually did that would go on for weeks until everyone was sick of it. At breakfast Terry saw the interview the San Francisco station did with Martin Delaney. One could readily see how embarrassed he was. The news crew cornered him on the steps of the courthouse, which hadn't been destroyed by the storm.

"Mr. Delaney, we understand that you are emerging the big hero in this entire tidal wave story." The interviewer, waving a

45

microphone into the unsuspecting lawyer's face, came off overly sarcastic and pushy as he started to question him. "How do you account for that?"

Martin flushed, instantly becoming angry. "LOOK! This town has been through hell. Everybody in it is a hero. Go over to the hospital and see the women and children who were hurt." With that statement he pushed past the film crew and hurried inside the building.

Terry applauded. "Hey, good for you, Martin. I might have read you all wrong."

Shortly, while pulling on a heavy sweat suit and talking to the dog the whole time, she planned her day. "Want to go down onto the beach for a walk?"

The shepherd barked loudly and wagged his tail.

"Okay. Let's go make some coffee, and I'll take you. I really need my caffeine fix before I get going."

Down in the kitchen, Terry hummed along with the music from the radio while she made the coffee and poured a glass of juice.

Baron gave a yip, and she pulled out his bowl to fill it. While the dog ate, Terry drank her coffee. Glancing through the newspaper, which was filled with the disaster, she saw something quite strange. On the third page was a large photograph of the men who represented the National Ship Salvage Corporation. It wouldn't have meant very much except the car they were standing by, a black Mercedes, was just like the one on the parking lot the day Baron found the body in the bay. The caption read: National Ship Salvage Corporation Buys Rights to Sunken Cargo. An accompanying story explained that the corporation had purchased the rights to the *Brother Jonathan*'s cargo from the insurance companies that owned them. Their costs were $50,000. Naturally, the National Ship Salvage Corporation was now claiming ownership of the wreck. The State of California, disputing that fact, had filed a

46

lawsuit and was asking for a restraining order to prohibit the salvage corporation from doing anything until the court ruled.

After reading the story, Terry refilled her cup and scanned the photo to look at the people. The three men were identified as William LeBaron, president; Alfred Jablonski, chairman of the board; and Raymond Donovan, treasurer of the company. The story explained their visit to Crescent City to try to negotiate with locals regarding the spoils from the shipwreck. Terry thought one or all of them must have been at the lighthouse and wondered why the captain had kept it from her. That was certainly puzzling.

Picking up the coffee, Terry moved into the living room and approached the wide glass windows. *Hmm, I almost think I could see the lighthouse from here if I had a good scope. Better yet, I'll get a telescope and mount it on the deck outside my studio.* It occurred to the artist that those men might have been at the lighthouse just prior to her finding the body. It seemed hard to believe that they visited the captain; at least he didn't mention it. The entire matter was puzzling and required some pondering. It didn't make sense. Taking the steps two at a time, Terry rushed up to the studio and opened the French doors. The view of the lighthouse from this vantage point was excellent and could be greatly enhanced with the aid of a telescope. "Yes," she said aloud. "That should do it."

Later, a phone call to Adam in Boston allowed her to ask for a favor. The secretary put him right on the line. He was really pleased she called him. They traded polite banter for a short time while Terry answered most of his questions. By now the entire country knew all the information, including Martin Delaney's brave deeds. Finally, Terry asked Adam if he would do her a favor and buy her a really good telescope for the balcony. She explained how much fun it was looking for ships and watching the whales come up the coast. Adam, anxious to please her, agreed, saying he'd buy it and ship it that week. After she hung up, Terry dialed the district attorney's office

47

and asked for Martin. Determining that she wasn't a reporter, the secretary put her through to a very surprised assistant district attorney.

"Hello, Terry, how nice to hear from you."

"Martin, I called to congratulate you on your very heroic acts the night of the tidal wave. I know you're modest; I saw that on television and don't want to further embarrass you, but everyone is proud of what you accomplished. It would follow that there must be great personal satisfaction in knowing that the little girl and her mother are reunited because you cared enough to risk your life and return to that house."

The lawyer's face reddened, but he was also secretly pleased about the call. "Thank you. That is very nice of you, and I appreciate your kind words. I honestly didn't think about it, and I'm certain anyone in that situation would have done the same thing."

She wanted to spare him any further discomfort and immediately changed the subject. "By the way, what happened to the body I found? Did you ever identify it?"

"Well, he's in the morgue. No, we didn't get a positive I.D., but we sent his prints to Washington to the FBI laboratory. If he had a criminal record, we'll be able to find out more, but if not it's pretty doubtful."

"I know you wanted me for a coroner's inquest. I mean, I agreed to be there."

"Is that a problem?" he said curiously.

"Oh, I've been invited to show a painting at a very exclusive gallery in San Francisco. I'm really excited about it and I'd like to go, but I can't make any plans with this thing hanging fire."

"That's very nice. I wish you good luck, Terry."

"Thank you, Martin." It was quite sincere, and his eager ear picked it right up.

"Normally the inquest would be in a few days, but as you can

48

imagine with this destruction and the town in such turmoil – well, it will probably be weeks." He paused and then said, "I'm going down to the capitol on a legal matter day after tomorrow. Would you care to come along? I'd like the company. We can get a hotel, and I'll drop you at the gallery. Then I'll go over to Sacramento to the capitol. We can meet later for dinner."

It was sudden and unexpected, but a really nice offer. The silence was deafening until she acquiesced. They decided on a time. Martin whistled for the rest of the day in between phone calls and clients.

The artist hadn't relished driving alone down the twisted coast to San Francisco, so Martin's offer was really welcomed. *It will be a good chance to get better acquainted,* she mused while driving into town toward the veterinarian's office. After parking the Jeep, Terry went inside and called into the doctor's work room. She hated leaving her dog under any circumstance, but if she had to leave him, Dr. Benton's animal shelter was a good place. He liked Baron. The vet usually allowed him complete freedom during the day, and at night took him home to his farm outside of town. It was, she decided, the best of both worlds. Baron went inside while she talked to the vet and yipped pleasantly knowing where he was going. After the business was taken care of, she went to an art store toward the mainland for supplies, had some lunch in the only cafe left standing and started toward home. A truck behind her kept honking. Terry pulled over and rolled down the window.

"Oh! It's you, Captain Tillman. I didn't recognize the truck."

A wry grin rose before he spoke. "Listen, I need a favor."

"Okay, what is it?" she answered.

"I came over to survey the damage and see to a couple of things, and now I'm stuck. The tide came in so fast I can't get back to the island."

Terry frowned.

"I hate to ask, but could you put me up for the night? The hotel washed away, and the only motel left is full. We got all them foreigners in town because of the tidal wave. Honestly, Terry, I din' think about it when I come over today. The tide is in good now."

"Sure, no problem. Just follow me. In fact, it's kind of nice I can return your hospitality, Captain Tillman." She saw his face light up and imagined he might be happy to have a friend. The town was in a shambles. He was right; there wasn't anywhere to stay. *Besides,* she reasoned, *this would be a great chance to find out more about the ghost.*

Captain Tillman was surprised when he saw the house. He glanced up at the English Tudor's three-story facade just above him. He realized this woman had substance and liked her all the more for her subtle attitudes. Being genuine suited her and definitely suited the old sailor. Usually he avoided people; they made him uncomfortable. He knew, however, that he and Terry were becoming friends and the feeling was damned nice.

Amos Tillman was almost seventy. He had hardly any kin left, except a cousin in Maine he hadn't seen for forty years. In fact, he wasn't sure his one living relative was still around. Last time he heard, the cousin's son was visiting California and came out to the lighthouse. They hardly recognized each other, and both of them were glad when the visit ended. That was four summers ago. Living alone all the time became addictive. He didn't realize how nice it was to be in a home until he entered the house and felt how welcoming Terry was.

She moved around the kitchen preparing their dinner. The captain fussed over Baron and questioned Terry about her life.

She explained her situation briefly. The captain nodded his acceptance saying, "I guess you miss her, huh?"

"Yes, but I'm used to it now. Time does heal you, and it's better. She was a wonderful lady, but she wouldn't want me to mourn her forever. I feel as if she is here with me, because this house is so reflective of Letty in every way. Enough about me, what about you, Captain?" Terry put down the knife she was using to cut the salad greens and looked over at him.

"Not much to tell. I came from a big, poor family in Boston. I ran away when I was sixteen and signed on a freighter going to Asia – stayed on the sea my whole life. Of course, eventually I got my papers and had my own ships, freighters mostly. I was happy enough, I guess. It was a great way to see the world."

Terry put the chicken in the oven and walked toward him carrying two mugs. "Come on in the living room and we'll continue." He followed along with the dog, and they sat by the big windows overlooking the ocean.

"I've had a few friends along the trail, but they're all gone now." He said it matter of factly; there was no remorse. Then, looking down at his right leg he said, "I got my bum leg when we went aground off Japan in a terrible storm. The ship sunk. I got hurt bad, and my two buddies drowned."

"No family?" she asked politely, knowing reliving that memory had to be painful for him.

"No. I knew no woman would want the lonely life of being married to a ship's captain. It wouldn't have been fair, and I sure weren't goin' to give up the sea. NO SIR – I WOULD NEVER DO THAT." He gave her a slanted grin and winked.

"Look! I know this is off the subject, but could we talk some more about Captain DeWolfe?" Their eyes met, and she saw that he didn't mind.

"Sure. Let's face it, there ain't nobody else to talk to. It's a touchy subject for most folks. I don't think it's so strange. After all, I figure he wasn't supposed to die. I mean, it wasn't his time. Those owners forced him to sail, and I imagine he hates being dead and still stuck here."

Terry rubbed her chin thoughtfully. Paranormal activities interested the artist. From all that she'd read, it was perfectly

51

possible, but the ghosts rarely spoke. "This is fascinating, Captain. You said you hear him more than you see him. What does that mean exactly?"

"Well, he walks in the tower a lot. I hear his footsteps. He has two others with him."

"REALLY?" She was surprised, but then he imagined that would be the reaction.

"Yep, a woman and a child. I hear them laughing and talking. I seen her a time or two; she's real pretty in an old-fashioned way. Her hair is up in a knot, and she wears a long skirt and a long-sleeved white lace blouse. I ain't never seen the child, but I hear him. They laugh and talk, and he plays with the child. We even had two cats living in the lighthouse once a long time ago. They used to let him play with them. When them cats died, it was real quiet for two months, and I thought maybe they was gone. Eventually, I heard them again, and the cats is still with them." He gave her that slanted smile. "Funny, huh? I can't make heads nor tails out of it."

"Do you ever ask?"

"What do you mean?"

"I mean can you talk to him face to face?"

Rubbing his weathered chin, the captain thought about the question. "It's real strange, Terry. I don't understand the rules, but I figure it's got something to do with that ship. I mean, maybe the woman was his friend or a relative. Who knows? I don't know why, but I figure he is waiting for something."

"What?"

"I can't quite fathom it. He ain't gonna tell me, but I sense very strongly that he has a job to do here. Who knows, Terry, maybe I'm part of that somehow."

"I'm still curious. Can you actually talk to him?"

"It's like I say. He does what he wants. I mean, I can't set the rules. He talks if there is no other way – like waking you to make sure I was at the light at a time when those coast guard men were in the path of the tidal wave. He knew that light was their lifeline. They couldn't outrun that thing, but they could tell where the rocks were and steer away from them."

"I didn't realize the light would actually go out." she seemed surprised.

"Well, usually it don't. But, who knows, maybe he knew something we din't. That's what I'm tellin' ya'. See, I don't know the rules, and he ain't gonna tell me."

The bell rang on the oven. The pair moved to the kitchen to eat, after which the captain went off to bed. The tide would be out really early the next morning, forcing the old man to rise before daylight.

On the following morning, Terry received a special delivery from Boston. It was the telescope. Leaving the box lying in the hallway, Terry went to call her handyman. The call took just a few moments. Fortunately, old Charlie had worked for Letty for so long he had his own key. Terry could leave knowing the job would be completed sometime that day.

After that she had to think about packing. San Francisco was another matter entirely. She grinned, thinking about wearing something sophisticated for the cosmopolitan "City by the Bay."

Chapter 6

A Special Trip

The trip to San Francisco down the rugged, torturous coastline was especially pleasant. Terry couldn't remember having had such a fun day. It started at 5:00 A.M. Martin explained that it was at least 300 miles on the coast road. This route would take more time, but it was especially beautiful in the morning. If they wanted to accomplish anything in San Francisco, they needed to go early. Terry concurred. At nine o'clock they stopped at a charming, rustic place perched on a cliff overlooking the ocean for fruit, coffee and sweet rolls. Their conversation was comfortable, as if they were old friends. Martin was surprisingly easy to be with. He had been careful to avoid any pitfalls; he was nothing if not pragmatic.

Terry appeared elegant in a pale pink woolen pant suit with a soft green silk blouse. It was obvious the woman had exquisite taste. She was wearing her hair in a top knot, long, curly wisps hanging loosely around her face, and on her ears were drop pearls set in wire gold. In fact, Martin thought about his mother who had always been so carefully groomed. She had worn pearls also. The difference, besides their coloring, was in their manner. The artist seemed totally at ease. He wondered if she ever lost that cool demeanor, and then he remembered the episode on the beach. It was pleasant to be with her, and that surprised him. It also occurred to him that she wasn't angry anymore. Knowing Terry didn't hold a grudge was very acceptable, and he began methodically to list her qualities. It seemed appropriate to look for a wife who could fit into the political spectrum easily. It appeared evident this woman had been well educated. Martin knew she must have come into money, otherwise the sheriff wouldn't have made so much of it.

Terry relaxed with her second cup of coffee. The view mesmerized, as the early fog clung to the cliffs, fading far beneath them where only a slice of ocean was visible. She smiled at him. "I'm having a lovely day, Martin. Thank you."

The lawyer responded by picking up the check and saying, "Well, we'd better get back on the highway or it will have been for naught."

Once in the car, Terry repaired her lipstick, and they began to talk about a hotel.

"I usually stay at the St. Francis on the Square because it's close to the shops I enjoy, but sometimes I just stay in one of the hotels near the wharf," she said agreeably, giving him the option of not spending a lot of money. "I like to walk down to the dock and get a walk away crab cocktail or go to one of those great seafood houses near the water. Anytime you can take the time to overlook that beautiful bay is terrific."

Martin wasn't all that familiar with the town. He decided to take her word for it. "Great! I'd like that. I love seafood and the water." He glanced over at Terry to see the effect and decided her reaction was positive. Talking about his sailboat brought about the sudden realization of how much he missed it. It added a lot to the conversation as he relived his youth on board the *Sea Dreamer*, not wanting to brag but, perhaps, share some of those memories. He thought she seemed interested; she certainly asked all the right questions. Later, he told her why he was going to the city. He was surprised that she didn't know more about the wreck of the *Brother Jonathan*. It suited him to fill her in on the actual sinking and the ongoing legal battle over the spoils.

Terry knew more about it than she let on, but she thought keeping the captain's confidence was essential. It also seemed expedient to allow the lawyer to impress her with his knowledge of the matter.

Shortly, the great spans of the Golden Gate Bridge came into view. It was still fog shrouded in places. The ocean and bay's magnitude from this vantage point was totally captivating to the naked eye, and it was impossible to view it without being impressed.

Terry became effusive. "That is the most wonderful sight. I never get tired of looking at it. Imagine the ingenuity it took to build it. I think people with that kind of foresight are so rare and precious." Her beautiful face seemed to brighten, and the vivid blue of her stare provided such a contrast that Martin almost lost his lane.

"Wow! I'd better keep my eyes on the road," he said with a grin. "You are really very beautiful. I'll bet that art dealer has no idea who's coming to see him."

Terry's laughter evidenced a nervousness. "I can tell you've never met any of the art dealers. And, one can only imagine the disdain they might exhibit in a posh city like San Francisco. Martin, these people make a fetish out of snobbery. They condescend to allow you to show your paltry efforts and, if one is especially fortunate, they may even ask to see another piece. I can't imagine what I would do if they accepted my work."

Martin paid the toll and turned toward the bay. They rode along the water past a colorful parade of four-storied, wooden houses towering over a nearby park. There were people everywhere. The day had turned glorious and sunny. It was a short distance to the wharf area. Shortly, they pulled into a parking garage by a Hilton just up the hill from the world famous Fisherman's Wharf. They checked in. Terry asked to have a room with a view. The desk clerk obliged and called a bellman who took her directly to the room.

The room overlooked the bay. Immediately, in front and below, was a huge four-masted schooner, now a museum, floating in her berth. There were noisy gulls everywhere, particularly near the fish market off to the left, where crowds of tourists flocked to buy the famous seafood cocktails. A troller moved just beyond the dock leaving a foamy wake, and off in the distance the bay was dotted with sailboats tilting into the wind. The view compelled Terry to spend a little time enjoying it. Kicking off her pumps, she pulled a chair closer to the wide windows.

Minutes later, the lawyer rapped lightly on her door. "I've got to get to my appointment in Sacramento. I hope you won't mind?" he offered after she opened the door.

"No, please, go ahead. The gallery isn't far from here. I'll take a cab. We can meet here about 7:30 this evening, if that's okay?" She saw that he was relieved and realized he was running late for his appointment at the capitol. They agreed and he left.

The art gallery was on a side street in a posh part of the city. She knew it wasn't far from the hotel. Terry had time to repair the ravages of the trip. She carefully opened the portfolio and looked at her newly matted work. For a few seconds, studying the results, she became critical and uncertain. That evoked a fear until she suddenly straightened, looked into the mirror and said aloud, "Oh, the hell with it."

By four o'clock a taxi dropped her in front of the Gallery Henry. After entering and taking a quick glance around, she admired the collection of oils and watercolors framed in wonderful woods with contrasting mats. Here and there fan palms in ornate cement tubs decorated the space, and off in the corners were bronze sculptures on antique tables. The subtle presentation of such provocative works lent spice to the approaching meeting. It wasn't hard to imagine one of her pieces hanging in such sophisticated surroundings. A tall middle-aged woman was sitting at an antique cherry wood desk near the back of the gallery. Terry approached and assumed a businesslike attitude before asking for Mr. Henry.

The woman glanced up, quickly appraised her clothing and asked in a rather condescending manner if she could help.

"I'm Terry Hamilton; I have an appointment," she said in a tight voice.

"Oh, I wasn't expecting someone so young."

"Does that matter?" Terry answered whimsically.

A wrinkled brow appeared and the woman took off her glasses to stare more directly. "What have you brought us?" She ran a hand over her silver, coiffed hair for effect. When she stood the girl could see her dress was silk and the neckline was draped with gold chains. Age had taken her beauty, but the remnants of classic features were still there. She exuded ice.

The girl opened the portfolio and took out the two matted watercolors. They were placed against a wall where the light was best. Terry walked away to allow the woman time to study the pieces. Leaning against the desk, the artist watched the gallery owner who had yet to identify herself.

"These are the best examples you have?" she said raising an eyebrow before walking back to her desk.

Terry felt her face color. "I'm sorry, but I don't know your name."

"Mrs. Henry. I am Mrs. Henry," she answered in a brusque tone implying the name was so important she couldn't imagine having to identify herself.

"Well, Mrs. Henry, I am Terry Hamilton and my appointment was with a Mr. Henry. I really would appreciate seeing him."

Mrs. Henry was quite taken aback. Her sallow face tightened dramatically around the mouth as her dark eyes grew smaller. "I beg your pardon."

The effort to intimidate was very effective, but the girl decided to stand her ground.

"Look! Is Mr. Henry in or not?"

"He certainly is," a deep voice called from the back room. "I'll be out in a minute. Mother, please, get our guest some tea while I finish my call."

It was an uncomfortable few minutes before he entered and strode toward her. Terry couldn't believe this handsome man was this woman's son. He was tall, blond and bore a striking resemblance to Adonis – certainly not her type but pretty to look at. His manner wasn't officious but rather accommodating. He extended a manicured hand and directed her to the office but not before he picked up the watercolors to bring along. Once they were inside the very elegant room, Terry noticed he immediately pulled out a chair for her and went to get her tea from a beautiful silver tea service on an antique cart. "Do you take sugar or lemon?"

"Lemon, no sugar, thank you." Terry hoped her mouth wasn't hanging open.

"Now, let's take a look at your work." It was matter of fact. "Hmm." He raised a hand to his mouth and appeared to be in deep thought. The custom tailored suit fit perfectly and didn't have a wrinkle. Terry watched him. A deafening silence developed around them before he said, "These are fair. You have a decent perspective, and the color is vibrant enough to be eye catching."

A sweat formed under the silk blouse. Terry wanted to bolt. She felt sick, hating the moment.

Mr. Henry asked if she had other examples of her work at her studio.

After assuring him that she did, he stood as if to dismiss her. "Well, it was wonderful of you to bring these in for our judgment, Miss Hamilton." His smile was forced. "I'll be going up to see some other art work on the North Coast sometime next month. Perhaps I could call on you and see your studio."

60

Terry wanted to smack him, but to do so would surely end her career before it ever started. Under the dyed blond hair he was every bit his mother's son.

"I'm really sorry, Mr. Henry, but next month I'll be traveling. I do appreciate your kindness; perhaps another time." Terry would have given anything to have had a photo of his face. He was absolutely stunned. Collecting the art, she placed it inside the open portfolio and tied the closings. Her hands were shaking. It was so still in the room, she felt nauseous.

Recovering, Mr. Henry said, "I hope I didn't offend you."

Terry gave him her most alluring smile. "No, not at all. I have appointments with three other galleries this afternoon. There has been enough interest to warrant my trip. Thank you for your time. Goodbye." She stood as straight as possible and headed for the door. The gallery owner ran ahead of her stammering.

"Oh, you misunderstood, madam. I do like them. We would be most honored to view your other pieces and, perhaps, find something acceptable for some upcoming show."

Terry swallowed hard. "You know, Mr. Henry, I believe it would be good business to try the other galleries first. I'll be in touch. Thank you." Once she was out onto the street, she hailed a cab and gave the driver the name of her hotel. Sitting back in the seat, she felt bile rise into her throat. In her heart she knew she wouldn't be accepted, but she had never been treated so abominably in her life. "Well, Miss Hamilton, welcome to the art world," she mumbled as the famous scenery flew by. Suddenly Terry remembered her grandfather's advice. "Terry, darling," he offered, "if you go out to do business always act like a winner and don't ever let the bastards know they got to you."

Since it was still early, Terry decided to see some of the other galleries. There were quite a few of them on that street. The driver pulled over at her instruction, and after paying him, she set out on foot. Within the hour she had approached three different art dealers who had been polite, if not indifferent. The last one, Mark Luce, was actually encouraging. He said she showed great promise and would welcome seeing any future pieces but wasn't interested in lighthouses. He recommended seascapes, which he really felt would lend themselves to her style. Terry handed him a card and left. Shortly, she entered a small restaurant that had a charming outdoor garden in the back. A waiter approached. Motioning her, he directed her to a spot near some blooming potted geraniums. "This will do nicely," she said before sitting down.

It was cool and pleasant on the brick and wrought iron terrace. In fact, it was the first nice thing she'd experienced all afternoon. While she drank the tea and ate a salad, Terry replayed the encounters with the art world. *Maybe I'm not cut out for this*, she mused. *Of course, I had to get my feet wet sometime. I'd better toughen up – this is not going to be easy.* Deciding that gave her some satisfaction. She sat back, took a deep breath and admired the myriad of colorful flowers and trailing ivy cleverly placed around the patio. The waiter returned and made some comment regarding her art case. She asked if he were an artist also?

He nodded. "It's a tough business, especially here. That's why I'm waiting tables." He finished picking up her plates and paused before asking if she lived in the city.

Terry explained her situation. It felt good to expound on the bruising treatment given in the gallery.

"Look! I know a guy who is an agent. I could call him. He's real decent and will tell you right now if you've got a chance. You want me to call him?"

It was at least a hope; Terry agreed. While paying the bill, she thanked the young waiter profusely. He grinned knowingly. Later, after a short cab ride, she got out in front of an old clapboard four-storied house. Climbing the steps felt right, and she grinned when ringing the bell. The man who opened the door was probably in his late fifties and very ordinary looking. He had a friendly manner which she liked imme-diately. She entered the entry hall and followed his consider-able girth into a parlor office. He was wearing a cardigan over tailored gaberdine trousers, and around his neck was a silk scarf. The room they entered was as comfortable as the agent looked but neat and tastefully furnished. He pointed to a divan nodding for Terry to sit down.

"Come in, Miss Hamilton. I was just having my afternoon drink. Would you like one?" Alex Waxman asked. He paused to look at her and reacted with a wry smile. "I imagine if you have been shopping galleries, you need one."

Terry laughed. "No, thank you. I'd just like you to take a look at my work."

"Okay. Let's see these watercolors." He opened the portfolio and put the two pieces side by side against a wall where the afternoon light was exposed.

The artist felt completely undressed; she shivered. Exposing your gut so completely was unnerving. This matter was hard. The agent appeared to study the work for a long time. He made some notes on a white pad and put them on his desk. Minutes later he said in a matter of fact voice, "I like them." There was a long look again at the work. "You are not quite ready for San Francisco, young lady." He held up a palm. "If you will follow my directives, I will get you ready, and then I'd be happy to represent you." His look widened into a broad smile. He knew those words were music to her ears.

There was complete silence while the words were absorbed. Suddenly an ebullient smile rose. Terry's voice cracked slightly, "I'm delighted – I really appreciate your confidence. I was beginning to doubt myself."

Waxman's white mane nodded; he pursed plump lips. "I can just imagine what you've been through today. They are a bunch of vultures, aren't they?" The laughter that followed had an experienced ring to it. "I've seen many people in your shoes during my long career. It isn't fun, but you see, Terry, it is the only way. When you make it, you will appreciate it."

They exchanged credentials before she left. It was nearing dusk. The cab ride to the hotel accentuated the difference in her mood. *God*, she thought. *What a day.*

By seven o'clock Terry had luxuriated in a long, hot bath and changed into a fitted black wool designer suit. Putting on her best diamond earrings, she hummed. The matching pin, a small elegant cluster of diamonds and emeralds, had belonged to Letty. Admiring the final effect in the mirror, Terry prepared for a spectacular evening. There weren't many occasions to wear such jewelry, but a night out in San Francisco definitely qualified. Martin's message said he would be bringing an assistant attorney general to have drinks with them. The girl tugged at her suit jacket, swung a shoulder to the right while looking into the mirror, and said, "Okay, lady, I think you're ready."

They met in the lobby. The lawyer, whose name was Dan Levine, turned out to be charming. Besides being very accommodating, he was dressed in an expensively tailored but very subtle pin-striped suit and a red silk tie. Terry eyed him approvingly as he hailed a cab. Instructing the driver to go to the Mark Hopkins Hotel, they climbed in for the steep drive up Nob Hill. Having drinks at the Top of the Mark was a treat. She couldn't help but compare the two men. Once they were seated and ordered, Dan told some really funny legal stories. Everyone laughed regularly, especially as he explained how green he was initially. After that they had a lengthy conversation about the tidal wave. Dan seemed really intrigued when Martin told him Terry had spent the night in the lighthouse over which the wave had passed. Of course, Martin was flattered by the woman's description of his heroic deeds. Eventually, Terry left the men to their legal conversation and walked around the glass walled Mark's cocktail lounge. She had been gone about ten minutes when a voice behind her said, "It is spectacular, isn't it?"

"Oh! You startled me." She reeled to face Dan. Being this close allowed her a good look at his wide set brown eyes. His brows were quite bushy and black to match his hair. He wasn't photo pretty, instead he had rugged good looks that were very appealing, and when he smiled that was all one noticed. "Imagine being able to view this spectacular place from the highest point. I'm an artist, Dan, and I'm thrilled. Thanks! This has been quite a treat."

His look was hesitant as if he weren't accustomed to such honesty. Terry was used to that reaction. The style, her very own, showed maturity. She decided a long time ago that no one would change the fact that she was her own person.

"Martin had to make some calls," he said. "I'll be leaving you two to your dinner engagement shortly. I imagine you're getting hungry by now?"

Terry admitted she was. It was sad that he was leaving. His swarthy good looks and his winning personality really attracted her. She realized what a hermit she'd become. Getting out more would be healthy; right then and there, she decided to do it.

"Listen, I don't want to be out of line, but are you two an item?" It was quite direct. The lawyer looked hopeful.

"No," she laughed.

"Is that funny?" He seemed a trifle uneasy.

Terry sobered saying, "We've only just met. I found a dead man on the beach where I paint. Martin came to the scene to interview me. Weird, huh?"

Dan's smile widened. "I certainly didn't expect an answer like that, but I must admit I'm pleased to learn that you're unattached. I'll be up that way soon. Would you care to have dinner with me?"

Although she wasn't given to snap decisions, Terry didn't hesitate.

Within minutes he was gone. Martin returned, led her to the

elevator, then, out onto the terrace driveway where the door-man whistled for a taxi. The cab raced them down the steep hills toward the wharf. The drive actually unnerved her, but she could see in the rear view mirror that the driver was enjoying the imposed fear.

"Your friend Dan is very nice," Terry said, matter of factly, trying to pretend she wasn't apprehensive of the reckless driving.

"Yes, I knew him at Berkeley. Of course, he was ahead of me in law school. I think he's been in the AG's office about three years. He's handling this salvage case for California."

"He must be pretty good at lawyering to be given such a big case."

Martin admitted he was but didn't elaborate.

They drove to Fisherman's Wharf to have dinner at Tarrintino's. After they arrived at the restaurant, Martin went to see about the reservations while Terry enjoyed the fresh lobsters swimming in the big tanks inside the lobby. It was crowded. Within a few minutes they were seated. Martin seriously examined the wine list and ordered something white and dry according to her preference. For dinner Terry ordered sauteed scallops and a salad with coffee after dinner. Martin had a lobster and all the trimmings. Seafood was obviously something he relished. He even tried to talk her into selecting a lobster. Up until now their conversation had been fairly mundane. He was polite in discussing the business of the day. She told him he really didn't want to hear about her experiences with the galleries. He convinced her otherwise. After she told him the story, he reacted with indifference, which really put her off.

"Well, what did you do?" she asked defensively.

Martin was excited she could tell. He explained that the National Ship Salvage Corporation had been to court recently and the judge ruled in their favor.

Terry said softly, "You seem happy. Is that what you wanted?"

"No, I didn't, but at least he didn't rule on who owned the cargo. All he said was they had the right to locate and do the search." The lawyer seemed totally captivated by the entire matter. It seemed she had found just the right button to push. He talked on about the case for a long time, completely oblivious to her needs.

Later in the room, Terry reviewed the day and the evening. It was her considered opinion that Mr. Delaney was a self-centered, legal clod. Then, as she lay down to sleep, she remembered Dan Levine and grinned broadly.

Chapter 7

Goodbye Sweet Friend

Picking up the dog was eagerly anticipated, and he responded in kind. Terry hugged him for a long time saying how sorry she was for being away. He ran around and barked excitedly until a signal silenced him. The more time she spent with people, the more she realized just how wonderful Baron was. They had only been apart for a few days, but there was no doubt about it, she missed him.

On the way home Terry thought about her position. *I'm lucky, I guess. It isn't as if I need anything – Letty saw to that. I realize most people have a family; that would be great, but it didn't happen for me.* She wanted children someday – three or four. Enough, she decided, so if something happened to one of them the others wouldn't be alone. It hadn't hurt to lose her parents – Terry was too young. When her grandfather died she mourned for a long time. Of course, telling herself there was still Letty, who loved her unconditionally, helped. Then, when Letty became terminally ill, Terry began to suffer. There was no way to prepare for being totally alone. The pain of leaving the hospital that awful night surged into her mind and she gasped. Suddenly, she remembered how desolate she'd felt. "I'm stronger now." Her voice rose in the Jeep. Baron yipped. Terry laughed. "Right, boy, you bet."

Grinning broadly, her hand rubbed his head. "We're going to be okay."

Going to San Francisco with Martin Delaney was a test. It had been a long time since she dated anyone and for good reason. The art school romance left a scar. There were others, but they were not serious. Her grandfather's admonition had almost been forgotten, but remembering it now raised a caution. Money never entered her mind. Grandfather Baldwin's insistence that men would do a lot to marry into it came to mind. Finding a mate or companion would not be easy, but if she wanted to have children, she would have to think about it. Terry was twenty-five, and her biological clock was ticking. It seemed expedient to stop mourning and start to seriously consider the future.

Soon, after opening the front door, she dropped her bags in the entry and went to the kitchen to put on the kettle. The phone rang. It was Captain Tillman.

"Hi, Captain." The lilting voice evidenced her happiness.

"Terry, the tide's out around six tonight. Is it all right if I come by? I left somethin' in your house that I need." It sounded impatient almost urgent.

"Well, of course. Would you like to eat with me? You can even stay the night; I'd love the company. I've been away for three days, and the house seems empty."

"Okay. There's nothin' earth shatterin' to keep me here. I'll see ya'."

After the artist hung up, she paused to think about what the old man had said. *What did he leave here? I'd better go to the guest room and look.*

The guest room was on the lower level. Terry hurried down the steps and opened the door. It looked just as he had left it. The bed was made, and the door to the bathroom was closed. Opening the door, Terry remembered his towels were still in the laundry where she had washed and dried them. The laundry was in the same part of the house. She went to get them and returned. After putting them back into the bath, she looked around puzzled. There didn't seem to be anything different. The room was furnished in early American maple. Letty had purchased a beautiful Amoir for the television set, which also had drawers for guests. Terry opened each of them and found nothing. Then she looked into the night table drawers and under the bed and the big overstuffed armchair. There weren't many other places to look. After examining the room thoroughly, she thought he had to have been mistaken. Shrugging, she went back to the kitchen where the tea kettle was singing loudly.

During lunch Terry decided that her sojourn to the big city probably would pay off. Waxman, the agent, seemed thorough and well connected. If that were all she needed, everything could turn out fine. The goal wasn't to wind up in the Museum of Fine Art, but she would need some acceptance in the market place in order to continue. His encouragement certainly lifted her spirits, particularly, after that devastating experience in the Gallery Henry. Thinking of that brought a question to mind. *Who recommended me to that obnoxious man?* It was puzzling.

Baron barked. "Oh, okay boy, the mail is here. Let's go out to get it."

There were the usual bills, a letter from Adam regarding the telescope and another from Dan Levine. The last piece raised a small but noticeable smile as she ripped it open.

Dear Terry,

What a nice treat meeting you the other evening in San Francisco. I hope you had fun. Since you agreed to have dinner with me when I come to Crescent City, I decided to firm that up right away.

I'll be in town on the 17th for several days of meetings. I hope I can rely on you to spend time with this city boy.

I would like an escort to see the sights. I'll call shortly to confirm.

Regards, Dan

The letter seemed very friendly. Terry chewed her lower lip considering where they might go when he was here. Then, she realized there weren't any places to stay. It occurred to her to ask the housekeeper to stay over while he was in town. Having decided that, she made two calls: one to Marge and the second to the lawyer.

The housekeeper lived on social security and was always glad to make extra money. Terry thanked her and hung up. Then, she made a call to Sacramento and asked for Mr. Levine's office.

"Dan Levine," he said in an efficient, businesslike voice after the secretary rang through.

"Dan, this is Terry Hamilton. I just received your letter."

His voice changed becoming tense. "Well, don't keep me in suspense."

Terry's laughter rolled into the wires. "I'm just calling to offer you a place to stay. My housekeeper will be here, so you won't feel compromised. You see, the hotel went out to sea, and I'm afraid our one motel is filled with repair people. These aren't usual circumstances. Would you mind doing that?"

"Terry, that's really nice of you. Are you sure?"

"Yes, I'm in the northern part of town on Ocean Terrace. You have the address. Will you be here in time for dinner? I like to cook. Oh, and, Dan, are there any foods you hate?"

His relieved laughter sounded hearty. "Just turnips."

They confirmed everything, and Dan hung up.

Terry took a long shower before climbing into her comfortable gray sweat suit and tennis shoes. "There, that is more like it," she said out loud. "Now, I can take the dog for a run and then fix our dinner."

Around four the pair returned from the beach. Terry gave Baron a big bowl of water before preparing their meal. The kitchen seemed very alluring; after art, cooking was her favorite activity. It wasn't as much fun when there were no guests. The captain appreciated it, consuming the food with real gusto. Terry began to pull things out of the refrigerator in preparation.

By a quarter to six the pasta was awaiting a boiling pan, and the shrimps had been peeled and cleaned. The cheese broccoli was in the casserole, ready for the oven, and the French bread was cut and buttered. Terry decided to broil it tonight. The bell rang on the oven signaling the succulent baked apples were done. She took the Pyrex dish out, sniffed its spicy aroma, smiled and put it onto an iron rack to cool.

The stereo played softly in the background while Terry poured herself some white wine. "Well, Baron, our guest should be here shortly. Let's go up to the studio for a bit."

They went upstairs and entered the workroom. Terry merely stared at her recent work. After studying in one of the finest schools in the country, wondering about her work's authenticity was normal, and being hard on herself was a way of life. She knew how to be disciplined referring always to her training for reference. In fact, had she looked at those watercolors in someone's gallery, she would have admired them. It wasn't false pride – they were good. Shrugging, she moved toward the staircase after first collecting the painting she was going to give to the captain.

It occurred to her that the captain was extremely late. Immediately, she called the lighthouse and let the phone ring for a long time. "That's funny, Baron," she said frowning and feeling a premonition of fear. "Come on, boy, the old man might need us." Turning everything off in the kitchen, she snatched up the Jeep keys and ran outside.

It took five minutes to drive to the parking lot on A Street. The captain's truck was parked in its usual spot. Baron ran ahead as they tore across the spit. Terry was winded before they reached the other side. She stopped to catch her breath, then started up the curved path toward the promontory. Just at the top she saw the door was standing open. A chill seized her. The wind had come up and her voice, calling to the old seaman, was blown away.

The dog went inside and began to bark loudly. Terry approached cautiously.

"Captain, it's Terry. Can you hear me?"

Once inside it seemed too quiet. Sensing something ominous, she moved slowly into the parlor. Just ahead, in the radio alcove, she saw him slumped against the desk. He was dead; his head had been bashed in. Terry's scream rent the air. She ran to him and pulled him close. His eyes were wide open, staring ahead.

"Please, don't be dead. Oh, please, Captain."

Tears spilled down her young face as she rocked him in her arms, his blood spilling over her clothes. In a minute she realized there wasn't time to stay there. The tide would be coming in. The thought of spending the night alone with his dead body was impossible to comprehend. It also crossed her mind, the murderer might still be in the lighthouse. Momentarily frozen with fear, she stared at the old man until the dog licked her face.

"Okay, boy. I know – we have to go."

Getting up and gently laying him flat, she blew him a kiss. They ran out and hurried toward the cove.

Shortly, after they reached the cement ramp leading up to the parking lot, the tide began to seep onto the rocky crossing. Terry climbed into the Jeep and wept uncontrollably. Within a few minutes a realization grew; she needed to get help. Turning on the ignition, she drove into town toward the sheriff's office. It took only moments to go inside and tell the surprised deputy what had happened. He went to get some coffee; it was evident she was really distraught. Her shaking hands lifted the cup.

"It's hot," she mumbled blankly before taking a sip.

"Look, miss, I called the sheriff – he'll be here soon. I also called Mr. Delaney. Just relax if you can . . . you look pretty pale."

Just as the sheriff entered, Terry fainted. He ran to catch the woman before she hit the floor. Martin entered just behind them.

"Jesus! She has blood all over her," he shouted.

A deputy ran for some smelling salts. They broke an ampule, then waved it under her nostrils. There was a moan. The sheriff lifted her head and began to talk. The room was still swimming. Terry's eyes glanced around before she lost consciousness again.

"We'd better get her over to emergency," Cameron instructed. "Martin, go start your car. Charlie, come and help me carry her. Joe, you see to her dog; he's in the Jeep."

Later, at the hospital, a nurse helped them put her on a gurney and wheeled her away. Just then a voice called out.

"Sheriff," Martin demanded, running inside the emergency entrance after having parked his vehicle, "what the hell happened?"

They moved to the waiting room, and Cameron Ripley removed his ten-gallon hat, smoothing his white hair unconsciously before sitting down and motioning the lawyer to join him.

"I honestly don't know, except, she told the deputy the old man was late for dinner at her house. When he didn't answer the lighthouse phone, she and the dog hurried over there. His truck was still in the lot. They ran across to the island and the door was open. When she went in she found him, dead. I suppose she got pretty hysterical. They were good friends."

"Well, how the hell did she get so bloody? I don't like it one bit. Who is she, Lizzie Borden?"

Getting up off the hospital bench, he began to pace. It didn't make any sense.

"Every time we find a body, she's right there." The lawyer seemed frustrated, his look tightened, and his hands clenched. "Maybe, this woman is not who we think she is."

Sheriff Ripley's voice rose. He was nobody's fool. He imagined the lawyer was getting involved, otherwise, why would he be this upset?

"I think you'd better calm down, son. You don't have any information, and we can't get any until the tide goes out tomorrow morning. So, it seems you are jumping to a lot of conclusions."

Martin mumbled, "Son of a bitch."

"Look, Martin. That island is surrounded by rocks, above and below the water line. There is no dock, and I'm not going to jeopardize any of my men to get a body out of there. By morning, when the tide is out, we'll be ready to cross, and everybody will just have to work fast. Or, better yet, I'll leave the forensics guys over there for eight hours. Either way, it will get done and be a good job. Quit worrying."

The doctor came out shortly to tell them she was in shock. He was going to keep her overnight. He told them he had given her a sedative, and she would be sleeping for a long time. He asked Martin to go to her home and pick up some toiletries, a nightgown, robe and slippers. The lawyer agreed and left. The officer on duty seemed really relieved to see him.

"Hi, Mr. Delaney, I'm glad you came back. The sheriff asked me to get that shepherd out of Miss Hamilton's Jeep, but." He paused and looked embarrassed. "I don't know about them dogs, and that one is real agitated. I'm gonna catch it, I know, but frankly I was afraid to try to take him out."

Martin nodded. He certainly understood the man's concern.

Baron's mistress went into that building and didn't come out. The dog might be wanting to take a bite out of anybody wearing a uniform. "I'll take him with me, Charlie. I like dogs, and he will sense that."

Minutes later Martin opened the door to the Jeep and spoke reassuringly to the dog. "Okay, boy. She's okay, but for tonight, why don't you and I go to your house and get her some things?" The man rubbed the dog's head. Baron yipped. He seemed to understand. Martin took him out for a short walk, and then they climbed back into the vehicle.

At the house everything seemed normal. Martin unlocked the door just as the dog shot past him baring his teeth. There was no barking but rather a deep guttural sound until the animal was at the top of the staircase when his sound became unbelievably fierce. Martin froze. The animal stopped, listened for a second before leaping toward a room at the end of the hall. The prosecutor knew there was someone in the house. He heard a man's scream and a long stream of profanity. There was a loud bang. By now Martin had drawn his revolver and was bounding up the stairs. It took only seconds, but the intruder, who had had the seat and flesh ripped out of his pants, went out onto the deck and leaped to the ground. Outside Baron's barking was intense. The dog was up on the railing, trying to find a way to jump. Martin whistled and yelled, "Stay, boy." He could see a car waiting for the burglar. The lawyer spotted Terry's newly installed telescope. Fortunately, he had good eyes and was quick to assess the mechanism. He made a mental note of the license number. Within seconds the car sped away. The vehicle was a dark blue van with no apparent markings, and the license plate was from Oregon. Martin hurried to the phone. "Yes, this is Mr. Delaney. Put an APB out on a late model dark blue van license number Mary-Charlie-7026 – Oregon. Get some cars out immediately; he is headed toward town. Yes, I interrupted a burglary."

Martin calmed the dog. "Good fellow. What we have here," he said picking up the blood-spattered cloth, "is prima facie evidence. It's good as gold. All we need now is to find a guy wearing a brown jacket who can't sit down." He laughed hard.

The room had to be Terry's studio. Martin had never been in the house before. He glanced around admiring all the water-colors posted on the work board. "That lady is sincere and it's good. I've never seen so much work." He looked at the dog. "Okay. Let's go down to the kitchen and get a baggie to put this baby in. Forensics will want to examine it – flesh, cloth and blood. How nice, Baron, that he left a piece of his ass as evidence. No defense attorney can refute this one." Martin chuckled all the way down to the kitchen imagining his inter-rogation of the subject in a court room.

It seemed apparent the house had not been rifled. Martin took the time to find the kitchen and look for the baggies. He hunted in a drawer and found one, placing the evidence inside.

Realizing he was hungry, he helped himself to a few shrimps and, while nibbling, put the rest of the food back into the refrigerator. "Well, this does confirm her statement; she was preparing dinner for two. I'm really glad to see that." He rel-ished the food while casually admiring the carefully planned room. "Your mistress likes to cook, eh? Baron."

A siren was heard approaching as the sheriff's car rolled into the driveway. Martin went to open the door. He explained the whole matter to Cameron, and they began to move through the house.

"I haven't had time to search. I've only been in her studio where the dog apprehended the perp," Martin explained. "I also heard a shot. I imagine he fired at the dog before he was bitten." Leading the way, he pointed above them saying, "There seem to be three floors. I suggest we go up to her bed-room. He probably hit that room first." Martin led the way.

Cameron Ripley had admired the house for years and was anxious to look through it without interference. He whistled as they entered the big bedroom. "Pretty nice layout, eh? But, her grandmother was a genuine lady. The family had money." After saying that the big man moved toward a bay window that overlooked the ocean. Glancing out, he stared at the view. "My wife would get real excited over this place. Yes sir, it must be nice to be able to live like this."

"I think the guy went to her studio first. He must have been after something specific or he would have gone for the jewelry in the bedroom," Martin said, before going into the walk-in closet to select a robe and nightgown. There was an overnight bag on the shelf. He opened it to put the clothing inside and then looked around for her slippers. Everything was in order, and the closet smelled of expensive perfume, an appealing fragrance he recognized. Then, the blood stained sweat suit came to mind. He found another one and put it inside the suitcase with a pair of tennis shoes.

Cameron looked all about commenting on the French provincial furniture and the matching canopy and bed linens. He wasn't used to such finery. "Look at this chaise longue; it matches the bed. Yes, sir, my wife would sure like this place."

Shortly, the pair went down the hall to her studio. There was a trail of blood on the carpet leading out to the deck. They followed it and examined the route the burglar had taken.

"That's quite a leap," the sheriff said. "In fact, a guy would have to be in good shape to make it without breaking something."

Martin nodded adding, "Yes, but the lawn was pretty soggy after the rain. I imagine we can get good footprints from it. Why don't you get your boys out here right now for casts?"

Cameron agreed and went to the phone. He called out to Martin that he could see the entry spot of the slug. He hung up the phone and pulled out a penknife that he carried regularly. "I'm guessing it's a .38. Yep, there it is." The sheriff held it up for inspection; then, dropped it into a plastic bag.

It took about half an hour to search the house. Baron followed along calmly. It was obvious to both men that he considered it his job to protect these premises. Martin stopped to pet him. "Good boy. Your mistress is lucky to have you. I'd better go up to the bathroom and get her toiletries, Cameron. I'll just be a minute. Then I'll take the dog to the vet. He's stayed there before. I think that would be best. Maybe I'll take the Jeep and leave it at the hospital."

Sheriff Ripley agreed. It would be at least eight hours before they could talk to Terry or examine the murder scene.

In a few minutes the deputies arrived to take the casts and examine the crime scene for their reports. Martin led the way explaining everything. Later, they found a window on the lower level that had been cut at the lock area. Charlie called up the stairs for the photographer to come down to get a picture of it. They also dusted for prints. Martin passed the evidence he had over to them and left with the dog.

Chapter 8

Someone to Care

A thick fog blanketed the cove at 5:00 A.M. the following morning. Cameron, Martin, the coroner, the ambulance people and deputies waited silently on the ramp leading to the beach. The lighthouse was hidden from their view.

Martin, huddled in his all-weather coat, stood staring at the rocks below. *It seemed so doubtful that Terry killed Captain Tillman,* he thought, *but why was she always on the scene. Coincidence, not likely. Either someone wanted her framed for murder or she was damned unlucky.* In his mind's eye he saw her beautiful face across the table during dinner in San Francisco. If he had wanted to clone the perfect wife, he couldn't have done better. His plans did not include murder.

"It's rotten on this coast in the morning, Martin." Cameron approached and shivered noticeably. "Why the hell didn't someone do this in town? It would have been so much easier." He grunted.

The fog horn moaned. It always made Martin uneasy. Maybe it was from sailing for so long, but he hated that desolate sound. No one could imagine how insecure it made one feel to be sailing, hear it and not know exactly where the rocks or other ships were. A lot of people died hearing that noise. He realized he was definitely in a bad mood, and the weather wasn't helping.

"Sheriff," Charlie Stevens called. "I just got a reply from the Oregon State Police on that APB on the van. They located it at Medford Airport. It was a rental."

"Who rented it?" Cameron asked.

"A company in San Francisco." Charlie squinted trying to read his own writing. "Yeah, the City by the Bay Fish Corporation. How's that for a crazy name?" He grinned. "The driver was Olaf Czechof, a rather questionable character. Plenty of priors but no outstanding warrants. I been thinking, Sheriff. Why would a guy fly in from San Francisco, rent a van and come here to break into that girl's house? It don't make no sense. He wasn't there to get jewelry or silver. Hell, there's plenty of that stuff there, but he didn't take any of it?"

"You don't know that," Martin answered.

"Right. And we won't know until Ms. Hamilton gets out of the hospital. But, let's say I'm right. What did the guy want and who sent him? Also, who drove the getaway car?"

Cameron Ripley looked at the young deputy and smiled. "Very good thinking, Charlie. That's the kind of stuff that made your old man the best detective in California. Keep it up. You'll figure it out."

Charlie colored but smiled appreciatively. He wanted to achieve a reputation like his father's more than anything else. When he was a boy they had talked out his father's cases at night by the fire. He grew up intending to be a respected lawman; his father would have expected no less.

"Well, let's hope somebody does," Martin snarled.

Someone yelled, "Tide's going out. Let's get this show on the road."

The dampness penetrated everyone as they crossed. They were at the island before they could see it. Looking up, Martin strained to see the lighthouse, which was barely visible in the fog. The horn moaned constantly and the bell on the end of the jetty clanged. At that moment it seemed eerie.

The deputies entered first and secured the crime scene. Cameron and Martin were close behind. "What do you suppose she touched?" the sheriff asked.

"She touched him. That was obvious – she had blood all over her sweat suit and hands."

"Look! He was sitting up. Maybe she grabbed him and then laid him flat before leaving. From the trail of blood, I'd say he was sitting at the radio when someone hit him from behind. Either someone moved him or he fell, but he wasn't on the floor originally." Cameron moved toward the radio alcove to point to the blood trail.

"Something else, sheriff. He let the person who killed him in here," Martin stated. "This place is damned near impenetrable. No one broke in. It can't be done. Well, at least, if that had happened we'd see the evidence. Someone would have to have had a key or a battering ram. That door is too thick to break through."

The sheriff let the forensics people do their work. He instructed Charlie and Joe to search outside for a weapon. They left.

"I'm going up to the tower. I'll just look around and see if anything looks suspicious," Cameron said before entering the stairwell.

Martin followed saying he wanted to see the captain's personal effects for clues.

Cameron joined him in the captain's bedroom. The room was very orderly: bed made, clothes hung up or put away and all of his personal effects sitting in their proper places. They searched the footlocker, which contained old dairies and his papers. "Nothing here," Martin explained after reading over the contents. "Just insurance policies, his ship's masters papers, a birth certificate and bank books." Martin opened them and flipped through the small green books. "That's interesting," he said to the empty room. "Oh, Cameron went topside. I'll tell him later."

Within five minutes the sheriff returned. "Find anything?"

Martin's look penetrated Cameron's. "You won't believe this."

"What?"

"Captain Tillman just deposited $10,000 into his bank account. All of these bank books are registered to the Commercial Bank of San Francisco."

"When was the deposit made?"

Martin whistled. "Three weeks ago. That's when those guys from the National Ship Salvage Corporation were here for the big meeting with the Town Council. This was a wire transfer."

"Coincidence?" Cameron asked.

"There are no coincidences." Martin looked puzzled. He collected the bank books and took them for evidence. Both men went down to the lower level.

Charlie came in to tell the sheriff they had searched the grounds and found nothing.

"Okay." Cameron told them to let him know how long they would be. "We've got forty minutes to get out of this building. If you need more time I suggest you stay until tonight."

They agreed saying they would work fast. No one particularly relished the idea of spending all day in so lonely a spot, but they would probably have to do it. The tide took eight hours to change.

Martin announced he was leaving. He asked for a copy of the DR when they'd finished. He left and hurried down the path toward the beach. After crossing the spit, he went to the parking lot to get his car. Shortly, he drove to the hospital which was close by; then, he entered and asked for Terry Hamilton's room. The nurse pointed down the hall, "Room 12, Mr. Delaney. She is having breakfast," she said sweetly. Since the tidal wave Martin Delaney had become the local hero. He was also single and good looking. The young nurse looked after him longingly.

84

Terry had already dressed and packed. The bloodied sweat suit lay on the bed; she intended to discard it. The coffee they delivered with breakfast was too strong, and she put it back on the tray. The whole matter had become overwhelming; she wasn't hungry. Turning, she saw him in the doorway. "Martin!"

"Yes, how are you feeling?"

"Tired, confused, depressed. Do you want more?" Her eyes lowered away from the handsome face. She thought how good he looked in the suede hat and the turtleneck sweater under the brown tweed jacket. He laid his all-weather coat on the bed, then picked up the sweat suit and folded it.

"I just came from the lighthouse with the forensics people. It wasn't a pretty sight. I guess, it threw you, huh?"

"I don't want to think about it." Watching him finger the suit, she asked, "What do you want with that?"

"Well, it's not possible not to think about it. A murder has been committed, Terry. We'll have to interrogate you. You were the last person to see him. This suit is material evidence. I have to take it."

Terry turned to look up at him. She recognized suspicion when she saw it. "I suppose you think I killed him. Is that right?"

"I don't know what to think. Two murders and you are right there. What would you think if you were me? Besides, you must realize this is my job – I don't have a choice."

"Am I under arrest? If so, tell me." Her voice hardened. "I won't talk to you anymore until I get a lawyer."

"Now, wait. I didn't say that."

"You implied it, Martin. I don't like your attitude and, I believe, in a situation like this one, I have need of a defense attorney."

Martin already regretted his officiousness. Dammit, what made him do it again? "Look! I'm upset. I've got a serious

85

crime, and you're in the middle of it. I don't want to do this to you. Can't you see the predicament I'm in?"

She didn't answer. After a moment she said, "I've got to wait to be released. The doctor will be here shortly to examine me. Why don't you go."

"There is something else."

"More good news?" The barb hit the mark.

"I took your dog to your home yesterday to pick up your clothes as the doctor instructed."

At the mention of the dog she brightened. "Is he all right?"

"Better than that." Martin began to explain what happened. When he mentioned the shot fired at the dog she gasped.

"My God! Don't tell me he's dead too!"

"No! Nothing like that. He apprehended the guy." Martin relayed the story trying to evoke a smile with the detailed explanation.

The woman looked stoic. "Is he hurt?"

"No. He's a great dog. I don't wonder you feel the way you do about him. I took him to the vet for last night. If you like I'll go and pick him up for you."

"No. I can do that. Besides I want to see him soon." She expelled a breath feeling relief.

"Can you think of anything you have that someone wants?"

"What are you talking about? I think you're crazy. How the hell do I know what the burglar wanted? Why don't you catch him and ask?" Terry's hands were clenched and she turned away in disgust.

The doctor entered. He asked pleasantly how she was and if the good night's sleep had done her some good.

"Yes, thank you. I've never done that before. I'm embarrassed." She smiled softly hoping he hadn't heard them arguing.

"Here, let me feel your pulse. Uh huh. It's a little fast, but your color is good this morning. I think you can go. If you have any more episodes give me a call. You had a terrible shock; it was natural."

Terry thanked him, and he left.

Martin seemed to be waiting. Terry's eyes looked like glacial ice. "I won't be needing anymore help, Martin. Thank you for helping Baron and bringing my clothes. Goodbye." She picked up her purse and the overnight bag and left the room.

Suddenly, the prosecutor felt very alone.

* * * * *

Charlie Stevens had a thought when he returned from the murder scene. He dialed the Medford police station and identified himself. The dispatcher put him through to the detective branch where he spoke with a young officer. He explained his needs, and they struck up a good conversation. The officer asked if he was related to Chuck Stevens, the famous investigator. Charlie grinned broadly. That information expedited Charlie's request. He was promised a call shortly. Charlie whistled while he typed up the DR.

Martin entered the courthouse and went directly to his office. Within minutes he leafed through his messages and began to return calls. The first one was to the California State Capitol, the Attorney General's office.

Dan Levine picked up his phone and upon hearing Martin's voice greeted him cordially. "Hi, Martin. Thanks for returning my call so soon. I'll be up there tomorrow at around nine, and I'll need a good part of the day with you on the following day also."

Martin concurred saying he would make time. Then he asked where Dan was planning to stay.

"Well, as a matter of fact, I called Terry Hamilton to ask her for a dinner date and she invited me to stay there. She said the hotel had been destroyed during the tidal wave and the motel was filled with repair people. I thought her offer was quite generous, and I accepted it. I hope you don't mind."

Martin's face flushed red. He couldn't believe what he was hearing; the son of a bitch was moving in on his girl. "I must say I'm surprised." It sounded terse.

Dan laughed. "Listen, Martin, she's a real catch. I asked if you two were involved, and she said you'd just met. Was that wrong?"

Martin choked. His voice cracked as he answered. "No, that was true."

"I'm relieved. I wouldn't move in on your territory, but hey, all's fair and all that. Right?"

They concluded their business before hanging up. Martin banged the receiver down and swore. "Yes, sir," he shouted, "This is turning out to be a wonderful day."

* * * * *

Terry parked at the vet's office and hurried inside. Baron's greeting almost knocked her down. As sensitive as the dog was, she knew he had to be worried. Kneeling, she hugged him tight. "I'm okay, boy. And you are a big fat hero. I heard all about it." He licked her face and yipped.

The vet called out to her from his work room. He quickly washed his hands and came out to the reception area. "He sure missed you, Terry."

"I missed him too, Doc. Did they tell you that he captured a burglar?"

"I heard. Martin Delaney brought him in yesterday. He told me all about it. Also, I read about it this morning in the weekly rag." The old man held out the newspaper for her inspection. His wrinkled face evidenced the long standing love he had for his work. He smiled at the two of them, thinking how perfectly suited they were.

Terry took the paper and read the article. She shook her head. "So much for privacy, huh? Oh, how much do I owe you?"

Terry paid the bill, and they went out to the Jeep. They were both anxious to get home. It also occurred to her that whatever the thief was after was probably still there. She shuddered. Looking over at the dog she said, "Good old Baron, I'm sure lucky to have you."

The house looked fine. They examined it together. Up in her office she noted the bloodstains and put her finger into the hole in the doorjamb where the sheriff had extracted the bullet. Suddenly, Terry laughed out loud. "Say, Baron, do you think he was after my paintings? Ha! Ha!" The dog watched her intently. "Come on, boy. Let's go fix a good cup of coffee. I've got some serious thinking to do."

Downstairs, while the coffee was brewing, she relived all of the recent events. Why had the captain sounded so nervous when he called to come over? Whatever he left in her house obviously had some value. Of course, only she knew about that conversation, but if the people were looking for it and were using guns, it must be serious. *Grandfather had two guns in his study. As soon as I have my coffee, I'll go and look for them. I haven't shot one for years, but I damn well will have to learn. I'm getting mad. Who do these people think they are setting me up like this?*

The coffee tasted good. There were some bagels in the refrigerator and some fresh jam. She put the bagel in to toast while she poured the freshly brewed café au lait. It seemed normal to have the treat. Afterwards they went to the study. The room was adjacent to the living room. It was paneled and had floor to ceiling bookcases. The desk was walnut wood with a dark stained finish to match the bookcases. Sitting down in her grandfather's red leather swivel chair, she opened the side drawers. The one with the gun in it was locked. It took some rooting, but eventually she located the keys in a secret compartment where he always kept them. The .38 was in the bottom drawer. Letty had obviously thought it necessary to have it handy. It was loaded. "Good! I'll put this in the nightstand just in case." Then, reconsidering, she searched the closet for his shotgun. "No, I'll keep the

.38 on the refrigerator and the shotgun in the bedroom. I'm not going to be taken advantage of anymore." The determination rose in her look and her walk.

* * * * *

Charlie Stevens entered Martin's office after three. The young officer's manner evidenced his personal satisfaction.

Martin couldn't help but notice. "You look like you swallowed a canary."

Charlie laughed. "I got 'im."

"You got who?"

"The perp. The Oregon State Police are picking him up right now."

"Well, good for you, Charlie. That's the best news I've heard all day. How did you manage that?"

"I figured he was pretty bad off. That dog's teeth look like they're an inch long. Shepherds can exert fifty pounds of pressure with their mouths. I figured he was in a hospital, but even if he wasn't, he wasn't sitting on an airplane or in a car. He still had to be in Medford."

Martin whistled. "Brilliant deducting. Go on."

"Well, I called the police department and asked them to give me the telephone number of every doctor in Medford. There are at least fifty, and ten of those are vets. It didn't take but eight calls. He put the guy in the hospital, and that was where I started – in the emergency rooms. The state police arrested him forty minutes ago. Now, if you could get him extradited, you can try him yourself."

The prosecutor was already dialing Medford's State Police barracks. The conversation was fairly short. They really didn't want to extradite. Martin realized this was a capital case. He couldn't prove it, but he honestly believed the two matters were connected. He hung up and began to think about the problem. His district attorney, Frank Starbuck, was away in Europe with his wife. Martin knew the governor of Oregon and Frank Starbuck had been college fraternity brothers. Quickly, he buzzed his secretary. When she entered, he asked if she could impose on Frank's secretary to get his itinerary. She nodded and went to get it.

It took the rest of the night and far into the next morning before the matter was accomplished. By six the following day the perp was being put into a van to be delivered into Martin's hands.

When Charlie heard the news he yelled, "YES!" And began to dance around the squad room. This was a real bonus. The sheriff would be doing some evaluations for the city manager shortly. Charlie was due for a promotion.

* * * * *

Terry answered the door. "Martin, what are you doing here?" she asked with disdain.

"I came to tell you some good news. Can I please come in?"

The artist stepped back. Martin entered and petted Baron. "Hi, boy. I'll bet you're glad to have your mistress home," he said almost too pleasantly.

Terry invited him into the kitchen where she was working. The room was succulent with aromas from the oven. There was a freshly baked pie on a rack cooling near the stove top. The newly cooked clams, waiting to be shucked and cleaned, were lying in the strainer. Terry was currently making a marinade for a fresh piece of plump, pink salmon she had just cleaned.

Martin felt jealous. "I see you are cooking. It looks as if you are expecting company."

"Does it?"

"Well, I came to tell you we've found the burglar. He is being extradited as we speak. I hope to be able to interrogate him by tomorrow. Isn't that great?" He grinned, and it was forced.

"Am I supposed to jump up and down?"

"Well, I thought, I mean, surely you realized the murder

91

might be tied to your house being rifled. By the way, is there anything missing?"

"I don't think so. I've looked pretty thoroughly, but I can't find anything missing." Terry stared at him. *I wish I could trust you,* she thought.

"By the way, do you own a gun?" He appeared genuinely concerned.

"Yes, I have several, and I intend to use them if that becomes necessary."

"I'm relieved, Terry, I don't really feel good about you being here alone. Would you like me to sleep here for the next few nights?"

"No. That won't be necessary. Why do you ask?" It seemed strange that he would offer to do that. Terry wondered if he had spoken to Dan.

"Well, whatever they were after is still here or, at least, they think it is. What do you suppose that is?" He watched her carefully.

The water was running in the sink. She turned it off and picked up a hand towel to dry her hands. The anger she felt for this man creased her lips. It wasn't her norm to hide her feelings. This guy had crossed the line once too often. "Look, if you think I'm involved why don't you arrest me?"

Martin ignored the accusation. "You will keep everything locked up, won't you?" he said feigning concern.

"I hate to disillusion you Martin, but everything was locked up before. I suppose you knew they cut the window to gain entry. I've already made arrangements to have it repaired, but I don't suppose that would stop them from doing it again. Do you?" Her blue eyes froze as they watched him.

Martin didn't ever remember being so completely vanquished. The lady was pissed, and he guessed he wasn't accomplishing any peace. Suddenly, he remembered his adversary was coming here tomorrow. He sweated noticeably.

Taking out a handkerchief, he mopped his brow. "It's hot in here. Could I have some cold water?"

The tap sounded loud as she pushed it on. Filling the glass, she handed it him. "Will that do it?"

"Eh, yes. Thank you." He couldn't stall any longer. "I guess I ought to let you get on with your work."

Terry folded her arms. She was silent as she watched him exit into the hall. When the door closed, she broke out into peels of laughter. "Baron, that guy got exactly what he deserved. Ha! Ha! Ha!"

Dan Levine used a pool car from the attorney general's office for the trip. He loved to drive and was actually excited to go by way of the coast road. That coast line offered some spectacular scenery on a clear day. It was almost four by the time he reached Crescent City. The fog was still lying low and had barely dissipated. He was by nature optimistic. *I wonder*, he thought, *Is this a premonition of things to come?* Having thought that, he smiled and chided himself. There was no point in making assumptions.

The tidal wave had wreaked havoc. Dan was staggered by what he was seeing as he drove toward the courthouse. He parked, pulled his briefcase out of the back seat and headed up the stone steps. Inside the marble entry a security officer directed him to Martin Delaney's office.

Martin was cordial. Dan Levine was a colleague, and they were both working on the same case. However, Martin had been struggling with the matter at hand since last night. He'd finally decided he had to tell Dan before he went to Terry's house.

Once Dan was seated and Martin had instructed his secretary to bring coffee, he broached the subject.

"Dan, we have had a situation here that involves you." Putting up a palm, he halted Dan's questions. "Let me explain. It barely involves you, but nevertheless, I feel I must tell you."

Martin leaned against his desk casually. He started with the murder at the lighthouse. It took all of fifteen minutes to tell the lawyer the story. Martin hoped he hadn't left anything out. All the while he was watching Dan's face for some sign of resignation or anger. Dan was stoic until he concluded.

"Are you intending to charge her?"

"No! Did I give you that impression?"

"What's more important, Martin, is did you give Terry that impression?"

"Well, eh, I suppose I did talk about interrogation. I was trying to find out if she knew what they wanted?"

Dan stood and put the coffee cup on the desk. "I think I'll get over to the house. I think she might need a friend about now." It was said without rancor, but he was definitely making a point.

Martin felt unnerved. He was unraveling and wanted to yell.

"What time tomorrow?" Dan asked in a solemn voice.

"Oh, nine, is nine good for you?"

Dan nodded while putting on his London Fog raincoat. He stood buttoning the double-breasted garment while staring at the prosecutor. It was a very effective ploy. "Tell me, Martin, did you ever advise Terry of her rights?"

"No. There wasn't any need. She isn't under arrest."

"Is she under suspicion?"

The prosecutor waffled. "This is an early examination, Dan. At this point we barely know the facts."

"Well," he said with confidence, "you know the captain was given $10,000, probably by the people we're fighting. You know he stayed in her home overnight, and then, she was burglarized by someone who had a gun and who was looking for something of value. You know she is probably being set up. It seems to me you know a great deal. I think the lady needs a good lawyer, one who will protect her from a ruthless bastard like you."

Martin blanched. He stood mute as Dan exited his office.

After Dan left, Martin went to his drawer and took out a bottle of Scotch whisky. He opened it and poured himself a stiff shot, which he drank in one gulp.

* * * * *

Terry's long, hot shower at four offered her time to reflect. There was no doubt she needed help but from whom? Dan was on his way. He seemed smart and nice, but could she really trust him? Adam, the family lawyer in Boston, knew civil law inside out, but he wasn't knowledgeable in these matters. Of course, she could trust him. If she called he would get her a top flight criminal lawyer. *Maybe, I should just wait and see what transpires. Dan is definitely interested in me; therefore, he will want to give me good council. Then again, Dan is handling this case for California. He's really busy and might not want to get involved.* It was a puzzle. Shutting off the steam, Terry stepped out into the warmth of the bathroom and put on a towel robe. She went to the dressing table to put on some body lotion and brush out her hair. The act of brushing her hair felt good; it seemed a good time to reflect. There were so many questions. Glancing in the mirror, she saw her fear. "I don't like it. Why is this happening?"

Later, dressed in a pale pink sweat suit and matching tennis shoes, the girl set the table for their dinner. Marge had arrived around noon to clean. Terry could hear her talking to the handyman who was still finishing up the repair on the bedroom window in the guest room.

The dining room looked festive. On the table were fresh flowers and Letty's lovely bone china with silver. Terry liked entertaining. She placed each piece carefully until the table looked exactly right. The food was all prepared, and she had instructed Marge when to serve and what to serve.

At half past five Baron signaled that a car had pulled into the driveway.

Outside Dan whistled looking up at the house. The English

95

Tudor was quite eye appealing even if it seemed out of place in the beach setting. He saw her at the entry with the dog. He was right; she was as beautiful as he remembered. Climbing out, the lawyer waved. "Hi, Terry. Glad to see you."

Her smiled warmed him. It was very genuine.

"Dan, come on inside. It's so damp out here today."

He hadn't noticed. Immediately, he handed her the wine he'd brought.

The thank you faded quickly as she introduced him to her dog. "This is Baron, my friend and companion. I'd like you two to get along. He is quite amiable, but he won't tolerate anyone bothering me." She laughed lightly.

"So I hear. Hi, boy." Dan leaned down to pet the big dog. "I guess this fellow saved the day recently."

So, he talked to Martin. Well, this ought to be interesting, she thought while directing Dan to the guest room on the lower floor. "Here we are. Please, get settled and then, come up to the kitchen and we'll fix a drink. Do you have a preference? I have everything." Dan asked for hot tea. Terry went off to fix it.

Within minutes he appeared in the cozy room. "Well, I guess a real cook lives here," he said glancing around and sniffing generously. It didn't seem out of place for so grand a house to have a well-equipped kitchen. Although Dan knew little about cooking, he could see someone in this place used this room a lot. His eye caught a glimpse of the pie. "I hope that's apple. That's my favorite, and I can't remember the last time I had a piece of homemade?"

Terry laughed nodding. It felt good. "Listen, we can take the tea into the living room or go up to my studio. Which will it be?"

Dan wasn't particularly interested in art, but he wanted to see what she did. He told her that. She picked up the tray and handed it over to the lawyer. "You carry this, and Baron and I will lead the way."

The art work intrigued him. He spent a short time examining it and said, "These are very nice, Terry."

The fog was getting thicker outside her balcony obliterating the ocean just below. Dan followed the stains and remarked about the burglary. He opened the door and went outside while Terry filled their cups. Shortly he returned. "That's quite a drop. I see the bullet hole in the jam. Lucky dog, huh?"

Fear rose in the girl's look, "I don't think I could handle anything happening to him. I don't mean to whine, Dan, but this dog gives me real confidence. I've lost my family; I need him. Besides, I love him very much and he knows it." Terry's look washed over the dog lying nearby.

Dan sipped his tea. He felt completely comfortable in this house. She had a way of making that happen; he especially loved her honesty – if was like a breath of fresh air.

Chapter 9

This Is the One

Dan eagerly accepted her decision not to dress for dinner. He took off his tie and changed into jeans and a sweater. When he returned to the dining room, the candles were lit and Marge was serving their shrimp cold with horseradish and ketchup sauce. Terry had chilled his gift. They drank it with dinner, and she complimented him on the choice. During their pasta course, the lawyer elaborated on his life, which she was anxious to hear about.

"After I graduated from law school, I took a job in the criminal division of the California Attorney General's Office," he said while sipping the wine. "I've been there ever since. Now, I'm into civil work, which I find fascinating." He grinned modestly. "In fact, this shipwreck case is wonderful. I live, eat, sleep and breathe it. Just think, 50 million dollars in assets for the state, if I win. That would also be a feather in my career cap." His deep brown eyes sparkled. There was no doubt, he was enthused.

Terry smiled. "It's nice to see someone enjoying their work that much. I understand that, Dan. I feel that way about mine."

"I'm impressed, Terry. It looks quite professional. Of course, I'm not qualified to judge; I only know what I like. In fact, if you would allow it, I'd like to buy one. I have just the spot in my apartment where a lighthouse painting would fit perfectly."

"You can have one. We'll select it tomorrow, and I'll take it to the framers while you are working." She could see how appreciative he was.

"What about family?" she asked pleasantly.

"My parents live in upstate New York. My dad is a lawyer – private practice. My mother has a degree in clinical psychology and works in a downtown children's clinic part-time. She has had some health problems in recent years but seems better of late. I have two sisters, both married with children. I have never been married. How about you?"

"No. I've never found anyone I wanted to marry. Finding the right partner is very difficult. Don't you agree?"

Dan chuckled just as Marge came in to pick up their plates. Terry asked if he would have dessert and coffee. He nodded.

"Let's have it in the living room. I've got a terrific fire going on this damp, foggy night. I'd really like you to share it with me."

"You are a great cook, Terry. I enjoyed that meal very much. I get tired of restaurants, and I don't cook. So, what happens is, after awhile, you really don't care if you eat or not."

"I have time, Dan," she explained. "When my grandmother was alive, we used to cook together. At least once a week we'd concoct something really delicious and then critique it. We didn't always succeed, but we learned a lot. After she died I just kept on with the exercise." Looking temporarily wistful, she said, "The captain loved to come here for dinner. I think he must have felt the same way you do."

The fire was blazing. Marge brought in a tray with their dessert. After she poured the coffee, Terry thanked her and told her they wouldn't be needing anything else. The woman said she would be going out to the maid's quarters and would see them in the morning. Dan sat down on the floor nearby, rubbing his hands together near the flames.

100

"This is a treat. I won't want to go home." He laughed.

"It's nice to have you here, Dan. I hope we can do it again. I feel very comfortable with you." Her glance seemed sensual.

There it was again. That complete honesty that would make her vulnerable, but she obviously didn't mind. Dan's gaze caressed her. This woman was so beautiful in the firelight, he was having trouble not going over to grab her. They were actually strangers, and yet, it felt so right.

"Terry, I think there is something we need to talk about."

The artist smiled at him as if she knew. "Okay."

"I don't know if you are aware of what's been happening or not."

"You mean the murders and my 'so called' involvement?"

"Yes, I don't think you realize these people have been over-stepping their bounds. I want you to allow me to get you some good legal advice. I don't want you to talk to them any-more without a lawyer present. I think sometimes people are so anxious to make a name for themselves that they take advantage of witnesses."

"Thank you. I've been thinking the same thing. I even told Martin that in the hospital. I mean, he keeps denying I'm under arrest, but he acts as if I am. He knows damn well I didn't kill anybody. If he doesn't, he's stupid. I'm pretty mad at him anyway."

"I'll call San Francisco tomorrow. I think I know just the right guy for you. He is expensive, Terry, but you need some-one good. Maybe, nothing will come of this. If so, fine. In the interim you need good advice, and these guys need to know they can't pull this baloney."

"Listen, Dan, I'll follow your advice. Meantime, I know you have to get up in the morning for business. I can stay up, but I'll bet you are tired after that long drive."

Dan admitted he was. He yawned and stretched not wanting to leave the cozy setting.

"Oh," she said in a hesitant voice. "You are sleeping in the room they broke into. I'd feel better if you took my .38 Smith & Wesson downstairs with you – just in case. I have Baron and a shotgun. I'm not taking any more chances."

"Do you think they'll come back?" he seemed surprised.

"Martin Delaney thinks they will. He even offered to sleep here tonight."

Dan laughed. "I wonder if that was because of burglars or me?"

They both laughed. Terry led him into the kitchen and handed him the gun before she went upstairs.

The lawyer was really tired. He always had trouble sleeping in strange places but fell asleep almost immediately. Later, he heard a noise just outside the window. It sounded like glass being cut. He thought he was dreaming until he opened his eyes. It was very dark outside. He couldn't see out but knew there was someone there. He fingered the gun and remembered the law. As much as he wanted to shoot whoever was cutting the glass, he would have to let them get inside and threaten him first. Slowly, he slid out of bed and crouched beside it just out of sight. Adjusting to the darkness, his eyes found the subject who was at the moment unlocking the window and sliding it up. Dan stood up and went closer to it just as the intruder climbed in. Dan put the barrel next to his skull and said, "Move and you're a dead man."

A hand came up, knocked the barrel toward the ceiling just as an elbow crashed into Dan's midsection. A moan escaped. There was a scuffle; the gun went off. Dan was knocked to the floor, and the man went out the window.

Terry heard the shot and jumped up screaming. Baron began to rage until she let him out of the room. They both heard the car race away. Running downstairs, she yelled, "Dan, are you okay? Dan, please, answer me!"

"I'm fine," he yelled back, just as Baron bounded through his open door. "It's okay, boy. The guy is gone." He turned on the light and picked up the gun, which had fallen to the floor. There was a hole in the ceiling.

Terry hurried downstairs to the guest room. Appearing in the doorway, she breathed a sigh of relief. "Oh, I can't stand this, Dan. What do they want?"

"Why don't you tell me?" He said it so simply.

Surprise registered. "What do you mean?"

He took her hand and led her upstairs to the kitchen. He was concerned about the housekeeper. Terry told him Mrs. Jennings always took sleeping pills and probably didn't hear the shot. Terry put on the tea kettle. "I think you know something you haven't told me. Am I correct?"

Her hair was completely disheveled. The blue eyes showed signs of sleep deprivation, but she looked suspect. Dan stared at her, waiting.

"Look, I wasn't sure I could trust you. I think I can, now." Putting her head down, she remembered. "Just before he was killed, the captain called me and said he left something here the night he stayed after the tidal wave. He sounded as if it was urgent that he come and retrieve it. Of course, I invited him back that evening. When he didn't show up, the dog and I went scurrying over to the lighthouse. He was dead – murdered. The rest you know." Terry eyed him waiting for some sign of acceptance.

He nodded. "Have you searched this place?"

"I searched your room. That's where he slept. I found nothing."

Dan was serious and very quiet while Terry put the tea things on the counter.

Finally, he spoke. "Tell me what happened the night of the tidal wave."

She began slowly and built up until the first wave hit. He instructed her not to leave anything out. When she told him that the water disappeared and the captain started marking the charts, Dan reacted. "How did he act?"

"What do you mean?"

"What was his manner?"

Terry smiled. "He was happy. I thought that was very odd, but I was so frightened. I also thought, maybe, that was part of his job. I didn't want to interrupt him."

"I think we should turn off that kettle and do a thorough search. Do you mind?"

"No. Of course not. But, you will have to move all of the heavy stuff."

Downstairs, they moved everything. They looked on the back of the Amoir, between the mattress and box springs, under the drawers, behind the pictures, under the Amoir, on the shelf in the closet and behind the sink. The room was clean. "What else is on this floor?" Dan asked.

"Just the laundry and the storage room. Come on, I'll show you. I didn't think to look there. I guess I wouldn't make a very good detective – would I?"

Dan began a thorough search of the laundry. When he had exhausted all other options, he pulled out the dryer, put it back, and then, pulled out the washer. "Bingo," he shouted. "Come and see."

Looking over his shoulder, she saw a nautical map taped to the side of the washer that had been flush with the wall. "I don't believe it. What do you think it is?"

Dan's laughter was deep and satisfying. "It is the location of the wreck. This baby shows where the *Brother Jonathan* went down."

Terry gasped. "No wonder they're willing to kill for it."

Dan pulled the tape loose and removed the map. Under it he found an envelope. "Here, Terry, it's addressed to you."

She took it and opened the envelope. "Come on upstairs. Let's read it together."

Terry poured their tea and sat down beside of Dan. "It's a letter from the captain."

Dear Terry,

You have been real sweet to me. I appreciate that. I found this location the night of the tidal wave. When the ocean sucked back so far I seen the old *Brother Jonathan* resting on the bottom. They want it real bad, honey, it's worth a bundle. If something happens to me, Terry, you take this to the law.

Them guys paid me $10,000 in advance in case I could give them directions. They probably figured out by now that I seen something the night of the tidal wave. Terry, I ain't got no kin to speak of, so, if you read this I'll be gone. I'd like you to have my belongings. I got some insurance and some money in the bank. The bank books are in the footlocker in my room. I taped a key to the washer so you can get in. Be careful, honey, them guys is mean. You was real nice to me, and I thank you.

Captain Tillman

Dan saw the tears roll down her cheeks. He put his arms around her. "Go ahead and cry. I guess you deserve a good cry after all you've been through." He held her for a long time, and when she looked up at him, he kissed her lightly, and in a second they fell into a passionate embrace. They stayed that way for a long time. Finally, she pushed him back until she could see his face clearly. "You are wonderful, Dan. Thank you for being here with me tonight. It felt delicious to be safe in your arms, and I want more. I imagine you do too, but for now, we need to proceed cautiously. Don't you agree?" Her eyes were wide, the look expectant as she waited for his answer.

Dan stared into the blue pools; he ran his hand through her

auburn curls – just touching her gave him chills. "Terry, I think I'm falling in love with you. If that's the way you want it, that's the way it'll be." He encircled her shoulders with his arm and led her to the staircase where they kissed for a long time. He watched her longingly as she climbed the stairs.

Dan was awake early. There were many issues that needed deciding. Jumping up, he went to his coat to get his address book. Shortly he dialed San Francisco. He knew the office was closed but decided to leave a message. "Yes, the call is for Jess Timeron. This is Dan Levine, Jess. I'm in Crescent City at the home of Terry Hamilton. I want you to represent her. Please call at your earliest convenience." Dan instructed the lawyer on how to reach her and hung up. Shortly he got into the shower while his brain was processing the information. He would need to think this through very carefully.

At 7:30 A.M. Terry rapped lightly on his door. "Hey, sleepy head, want some breakfast?"

Dan opened the door. He was fully dressed and ready to come up. He kissed her gently. "I missed you."

Terry grinned and, looking a trifle embarrassed, said, "Me too."

"Listen! I called Jess Timeron in San Francisco. He'll be calling you this morning. You tell him everything, and Terry, you do exactly what he tells you to do."

She agreed and they went to the kitchen where breakfast was already in progress.

The phone rang. Terry answered it and handed it to Dan. "Yes, un huh. Okay, Martin, I'll await your call. Thank you." After replacing the receiver Dan said, "Martin's at the jail. The Oregon State Police just brought in the guy who broke in here. They are going to interrogate him right now." Dan grunted. "If I'm right, they won't get a thing out of him."

"Are you going to tell them about last night?" she asked.

"Yes, in due time. I've still got some thinking to do. I don't want you in any more jeopardy. As far as I can see the only way to stop that is to set it up."

"Dan, you be careful. I don't want anything to happen to you."

He smiled broadly. "Hey, that sounds nice. I like that."

The phone pealed. Terry answered. It was Jess Timeron. Handing the phone to Dan, she listened while he explained the situation. They talked for a long time; finally Dan turned the phone over to Terry.

After she hung up, Dan put his arms around her. "Now, you do exactly what he told you to do."

"He sounds confident. I liked that in him. I will do what you both said. It's nice, Dan; I'm not alone anymore. Now, let's you and I take Baron down to the beach."

At 9:15 A.M. Dan entered the sheriff's office. Martin, who had just interrogated the suspect, came out of the holding area to greet him.

"Did you get anything?" Dan asked.

Martin shook his head. "This guy's a pro. He won't crack. I think Cameron is wasting his time." Moving toward the coffee machine, he lifted a cup and held it up to his guest.

Dan shook his head before asking, "Did you tell him how much time he'll do if you connect him to the murder?"

"No dice. This is going to be very difficult."

"I want to see him," Dan said in a somber tone.

"This is my turf," Martin came back at him quickly.

"Martin, I'm not asking. If you want to play hard ball, I'll just call the attorney general. So, let's quit wasting time – shall we?" Dan's scowl deepened. "And I don't want any company."

The prosecutor flushed. His anger surged just beneath the surface. "What the hell business is it of yours?"

"Are you denying this is connected to the state's case against the National Ship Salvage Corporation? I'm not here to make any headlines, Martin, but I have a vested interest. That's all I'm going to say. Now arrange it."

Martin left for a few moments and returned with the sheriff.

"Dan Levine is trying the state's case, Cameron. He wants a few minutes with the prisoner."

Cameron was plainly angry. He'd spent two hours with the intruder and hadn't gotten a thing out of him. He swore and banged his fist on the desk. "That bastard is connected, and he's going to tell me why they are after that girl!"

Dan stiffened. It was personal now. "I suggest you two put some security on Terry Hamilton."

"I haven't got the manpower," Cameron shouted.

"Then get some. They made another attempt last night." Dan's voice became sharp. He meant business, and they both knew it.

Both men reacted instantly. "What do you mean?"

"I mean I caught a guy breaking in. He got inside, knocked the gun up and sent me sprawling. I shot a hole in the ceiling."

"Why didn't you call? You know the law. If she needed help, I would have come immediately." Martin's face was flushed. This guy was besting him all the way around.

"I hate to tell you young bucks, but it's my job to catch criminals. What the hell is going on here?" Cameron demanded. Both lawyers turned to face the big man whose eyes were protruding slightly above a white, angry mouth. But, exhibiting his anger didn't frighten either one of them.

"I'd like to see the prisoner now," Dan said calmly. His eyes turned cold and seeing them, Martin decided he would oblige.

The cell was damp. It had a musty smell. Dan entered and waited until the guard locked the door and retreated. Doing criminal work was unpleasant at best, but he knew this was necessary for Terry's sake.

Olaf Czechof looked bored. Dan knew by his size and eyes,

he was dangerous. Killing was probably a lucrative pastime; he had the look of a man with no scruples and brute strength.

"My name is Chief Attorney General Dan Levine. I am here for just one moment to tell you something, Mr. Czechof. Tell your friends to call off the dogs. What you are looking for is no longer in that house. I have it." Dan turned and rapped loudly on the cage. The guard returned immediately and unlocked the door. The lawyer knew Czechof had stopped looking bored, but he never glanced back.

Dan left the holding area and looked for Charlie Stevens. He was told that Charlie was at the morgue. A deputy drove him over to the building. Dan told him to wait. Inside he called to Charlie. The police artist continued to work while Charlie and the lawyer chatted quietly. "I understand you're good at detective work, Charlie." The deputy grinned. "Well, I just gave Mr. Czechof some powerful information. If you were to run a trace on any calls he makes in the near future, I'd be very grateful." Dan handed him a card and said, "Please call me if you get anything. Oh, and Charlie it's between you and me."

* * * * *

At three o'clock Terry, dressed in a black suit, carried some flowers to the cemetery just south of town. There were a handful of people there. From the hillside burial ground she could see the ocean off in the distance. Down below were dunes where the reeds and grasses were blowing in the wind. A minister, whose robes were flapping as he spoke, stood over the grave site. Terry listened stoically to the patent eulogy. After he finished and blessed the ground, everyone left except the young woman still holding the flowers.

The wind caressed her. "Captain," she said dry eyed. "I am so sorry about this. I found your note, and now I understand a little better. It was sweet of you to leave me your money. I don't need it, so I thought I'd do something good with it. I hope you'll approve. God bless you, and I'll miss you." Bending she laid the flowers on the top of the casket waiting to be

109

lowered into the open grave. Turning, Terry started to walk to the edge of the grounds bordered by a silver-colored, low, antique fence. There seemed to be an irony about this funeral. This was the graveyard where the victims of the *Brother Jonathan*, whose bodies floated to shore, were buried.

Suddenly, she had a premonition to look back. Turning, she gaped. Standing beside the grave were three transparent figures – Captain DeWolfe, the woman Captain Tillman described and a small child. They appeared to be praying. A low frustrated moan escaped as she fled to the Jeep. Once inside she wept. Captain Tillman said the ghost never did anything without a reason. He wanted her to see him paying homage to the old sea captain. "I suppose I should be honored," she said out loud. "I have the feeling this is not the end of it."

All the way back to town Terry wondered if she should love Dan. The fact that something happened to everyone she loved scared her. "Maybe I'm cursed." The matter was weighing heavily. Perhaps, he was sent to help her. Why not? Her eyes drifted to the art folio laying on the seat. "I'll get that framed for him and every time he passes it, he'll think of me." She grinned broadly.

It was almost five when she returned. Changing her clothes took only a few minutes, and she hurried down to the beach for a run. The weather had cleared. Sunshine glistened on the Pacific rolling gently into the shoreline. Terry stopped and stared out. "It's so beautiful until it decides to rage, and then, look out." The lighthouse sparkled near the tower with the bright sun reflecting on the glass. Its red roof offered a neat contrast to the white walls and green grass and trees. She smiled. It was still her favorite place. The smile faded and she knew she would never see it again without thinking of the captain.

* * * * *

Charlie Stevens had spent all day with a police artist who

happened to come down to Crescent City once in awhile to fish. Prevailing on his good nature, Charlie took him over to the morgue to see the dead man they fished out of the cove. They were almost finished. "That's got it. You are really good. Now, Joe, maybe I can find out who this guy is. It don't make any sense at all that I can't I.D. him. How about if I buy you a beer for that favor?"

The artist laughed. "Sure, Charlie, but not today. I got a date in town at six, and I'm not fit without a shower. Catch you on my next trip."

Shortly, Charlie put the sketch under the scanner in the sheriff's office and made a copy. Within minutes he had run off 50 copies and was whistling his way out the door.

The docks were still a mess after the tidal wave. A makeshift meeting shed had been set up for fishermen, the night watchman and the packing people. The fish were running and anyone who could beg, borrow or steal a boat was out trying to use his permit. It was nearly supper. The trollers were heading home through the jetty followed by the indomitable gulls screeching after the heads and innards being dumped into their wake. It was a comforting sight and sound.

Charlie parked the patrol car and walked slowly toward the dock. He wanted to watch the dinghies being sent out to the buoys to ferry the incoming fishermen after they anchored for the evening. The fish were being processed on a tender anchored in the channel. It was working out pretty well considering all that had happened. Eventually, each crew was brought in. Charlie was waiting to give them a photo of the dead man. Most of them said they would ask around. It was a long shot but worth a try.

After he ran out of fishermen, Charlie went to the shed to talk to the packers. When he was finished with that he was meeting the guy from the telephone company for coffee. If all went as planned, they would have the information for the assistant attorney general by lights out.

Chapter 10

The Search

Dan was still at the meeting with the historical society when Charlie returned from the coffee shop. It was late in the day. Climbing upstairs to the third floor meeting room winded the deputy. Charlie took a deep breath before rapping lightly on the frosted glass door. A security officer came out.

"I've got some important information for Mr. Levine. Would you please ask him to come out here for a moment."

The officer nodded and went back to retrieve the lawyer.

Shortly, Dan appeared. "I hope this is what I think it is?"

"Yes, sir. That telephone repair man is my cousin. It was a piece of cake. Here is the number and the tape with the conversation on it." He passed it to the lawyer grinning. The officer's humbleness surfaced; he twisted his hat and looked down.

"Good man. We could use somebody like you in Sacramento, Charlie. I'll pass the word along." Dan's smile broadened as he extended his hand.

The officer hesitated before putting his hand out. "Look, Mr. Levine, that sounds terrific, but I wouldn't want to mislead anybody. This is my place; I grew up here. I'd miss it – you understand?"

Dan's head bobbed. "Certainly. Thank you very much; you

have been an immense help. I'll see that it's not forgotten. By the way, Charlie, the attorney general of California is quite interested in this case. If any other information should surface that you feel we might be interested in, please, call my office. You have my number and my assistant will track me down. I'd certainly appreciate your cooperation."

"Sure, Mr. Levine, why not. The way I see it, we're all on the same team." The young officer's look brightened noticeably. Whistling, he went down the wide staircase.

Returning to the meeting, Dan was pleased to see it was breaking up. While he gathered his papers and put them into the leather briefcase, the sheriff approached. The group noise subsided as the members of Crescent City's Historical Society and its town council moved out into the hallway and started downstairs.

"Dan – good meeting, don't you agree?" Cameron slapped his shoulder in a friendly gesture.

"Oh, yes. I think their decision to have the wreck declared a California Historical Site is a good one. That was to have been my next move."

"How about if we go out together?" Cameron offered.

Dan picked up his attaché case and coat. They moved in tandem toward the stairs.

"Were you able to get anything out of Czechof?"

"No, he's mute. I would guess sustained torture wouldn't open that guy up; however, I felt my boss would expect no less. I definitely believe that these two matters are connected."

The sheriff appeared thoughtful. Dan waited for the next question.

"Do you think Terry Hamilton has told us everything she knows?"

"I think, Sheriff Ripley, that Terry's decision to hire legal council was a good one."

Cameron looked as if he'd been hit with a sledge hammer. "Oh, it that so?" It sounded brusque. "Who'd she hire?"

"The best criminal lawyer in San Francisco. So, I suggest that you and Martin back off. Jess Timeron will be calling you shortly." Dan forced the big brass doors to the building open and moved quickly down the stone steps toward the pool car. He grinned without looking back.

Ripley stood motionless at the top of the staircase, his look reflecting grave concern.

Terry heard Dan's car and ran downstairs to greet him. Once he was inside and the door closed, she kissed him tenderly. He put the case down on the rug and took off his coat, tossing it onto a nearby chair, then took her into his arms. "I missed you. All day I couldn't think about anything else but, honey, we have to talk."

Her plump lips slid into a seductive grin. "Yes, I know."

He drew her into the living room, and they sat together on the sofa. "I want you to give me that nautical map."

Terry nodded. "What would I do with it? Certainly, you can take it." She looked disappointed.

"What's wrong?"

"I have been hungering for you all day, and all you can talk about is that damned map." She pouted and turned away.

Dan grabbed her face and drew her back. They were eye to eye. "I love you, do you hear me?"

The auburn hair shook as she answered in the affirmative.

"Two people have been murdered over that thing, and by God, I don't want you hurt." He was sweating. It was evident he felt strongly about the matter. "In fact, I've got to call Sacramento right now. You wait right here in this very spot." He kissed her hard and then went to the phone.

"Yes, operator I want Sacramento 274-8602 extension 314 please, and reverse the charges. Yes, I'll wait." He looked over at her and winked. "Wynn, this is Dan. Yes. Get the attorney general, both chief councils and the chief of detectives on a conference call immediately. Yes, it's urgent. There have been two murders here and a burglary. I'm sitting on the reason for all three." He gave the lawyer the number and hung up.

"Darling," Terry said softly, "I just got a chill when you said that."

Dan got up and came over to her. "Honey, this is very serious. I've set things in motion now, so you shouldn't have any more trouble. I've also told Ripley I want protection for this place and that you have good legal council. Ripley became very concerned when I said that. Those two birds won't be giving you any more trouble."

Terry nuzzled her face into his neck. "Hold me, Dan. Oh, it feels so good and so safe. I've been scared, and I didn't realize it until I had you here protecting me." Her daunting gaze lifted to his. Putting two hands on his head she pulled him closer. "If something were to happen to you . . . I wouldn't be able to survive." She looked distraught and he clutched her to him.

"It's going to be all right now, hon; I'm going to take care of it. I promise. Let's go make some tea." He laughed, hoping to lighten her spirits. "I think we both need it, and I need some of that great pie." Standing, he pulled her up, kissed her lightly, encircled her shoulders and drew her toward the kitchen.

Dan's attitude broke the tension. He was chatty while she pulled things out of the refrigerator, secretly wishing he never had to leave. "You sure are beautiful. Did I tell you that?"

Looking up, she smiled softly. "Tell me that often. I need to hear it."

While the kettle boiled, Terry put the tea things on the counter. Then, she went to the pie cover, lifted it, cut a piece and put it onto a plate. "Here you are. The forks are in that drawer," she pointed to the place near his chair.

"How could I get so smart as to fall in love with a twentieth-century woman who can cook? This is great apple pie."

116

"Good, I'll send the rest of it with you when you leave." She looked sad.

"What's the matter?"

"I just realized you will be leaving soon. Oh, Dan, I don't want you to leave. I sound like a child, I know."

"Actually, I feel the same. So, next weekend you fly up to San Francisco, and we'll have a great time. How's that?"

"Yes, I accept."

The phone rang. Dan picked it up. "Yes, operator, I'll wait. Okay put them on."

Terry listened as Dan explained the murders and her involvement. Then he continued telling them what he had told the prisoner and how he had the deputy tape the calls he made and to whom. She was astounded. Of course, she also realized what jeopardy he put himself into by doing that. Her innards tightened. This was real; it was all happening.

"You're sending the chopper today? Okay. It could land on the parking lot near the lighthouse. The state police can ferry the pool car to Sacramento. Okay, I understand. Yes, have a car waiting to pick me up to get control of this evidence. Uh huh. I want someone to get on these calls immediately. We've got to find out who's masterminding this stuff. Oh, by the way, they've agreed to have us go into court making the wreck a historical site. Yes, sir, I agree. Good. I'll see you all when I return. Thank you."

After he hung up he glanced at his watch. "It's just four o'clock, Terry. The chopper will be here at six. I've got to leave you, hon." His voice was laced with regret. Unconsciously he ate the pie, staring at her. They were both feeling the loss, and it hadn't occurred yet.

"I miss you already. You know, Dan, I've been alone for a long time. Baron and I have been depending on each other for support. I didn't realize until I heard you on the phone to Sacramento just how much jeopardy I've been in. The captain, God love him, didn't do me any favor hiding his map

117

here. I could have been killed." Her look sobered into incredulous disbelief. "I was so busy being angry with Martin, it didn't really sink in."

"Honey, I honestly believe this fight will move out of here now."

"Yes, that may be, Dan. But, now, I have to worry about you. They aren't going to take this lightly. Whoever did this has nothing to lose now. What's one more murder? I mean they can only give you one lethal injection if you're convicted. These people will stop at nothing to get at that treasure. And, of course, you have to prove it first. That isn't going to be easy."

"Is there anything you haven't told me?"

The woman became introspective. "I don't think so." She refilled her cup and put the kettle back. "Oh, wait a minute. There is one thing, Dan. I don't know if it means anything." She glanced at him thinking how wonderful he was to be so concerned.

"Tell me."

"Well, someone in this town recommended me to an art gallery in San Francisco. I don't know who it could be. When I went there, the day we met, the owners treated me so badly it was unbelievable. None of it made sense. I mean, maybe it had nothing to do with this whole matter. But, when I tried to leave the shop, this Mr. Henry tried in the worst way to convince me that he didn't mean it. I was so mad I told him a big fat lie about other galleries wanting my work. I don't know if it's relevant, but he's called here three times since. I don't trust him, but he wants something, and it isn't my art work."

"I'll think about it, Terry. Who knows? Maybe all the pieces will fall into place soon." Dan's face broadened into a smile. He got up and went to her, clutching her to him. "You know, I've never held anyone who felt better in my arms. I can't believe how happy you make me. It is a wonder." They kissed for a long time.

Terry glanced up at him. "Take me to bed, darling."

"Terry, darling, I want you more than anything ever before but not like this. When you come next week, we'll do it right. I want flowers and champagne, I want to take you to bed and make you mine. I want to do the town and show you off. Do you understand?" He watched her face for acceptance. Her smile warmed him.

"Yes, darling. I'll spend all week preparing."

He laughed and picked her up in his arms, swinging her around and making satisfied noises.

"I hate to say this, hon, but you'd better pack. Look at the time."

At 5:40 P.M. she drove him to the parking lot, and they just sat in the Jeep feeling forlorn.

"I'll call you every night. How about if I call around eight. I'm just getting into the apartment about then. I usually pull off my tie and open a beer before reading my mail. Does that sound good?"

She reached for him and pulled him close. The dog yipped.

"You take good care of her, Baron. I'm expecting big things from you. Okay, boy?" Dan reached into the back and rubbed his head.

"He's probably wondering how come I'm so close to you. It'll take some time before he gets used to us."

Dan snickered. Then, they heard the plane's rotor blades. He opened the door of the Jeep, and they both climbed out to watch its descent. The wind blustered. Dan pulled her to him, sheltering her from the downdraft. He yelled into her ear, "I love you." The transfer was too quick. Dan climbed in and closed the door. The big machine, lumbering into the wind, rose and crossed toward the lighthouse, circled and disappeared. Terry watched for a long time. She really couldn't believe he was gone.

She and Baron drove home in silence. For once in her life

she actually knew real love, and being without him frightened her.

It didn't take long for the helicopter to reach the Medford, Oregon, airport.

Dan's thoughts were completely on the woman he loved, and leaving made him uneasy. Knowing that someone wanted to harm her lingered, raising fear. He watched the scenery down below with passive acceptance. *It won't be long,* he thought. *Today is Tuesday. As soon as I get home, I'll order plane tickets for her for Friday. We can have a whole weekend.* The thought of planning that time together rather enthralled the lawyer. He spent time thinking of places she might like. Fortunately, the time passed quickly. The plane started down, and Dan realized he could see California's jet waiting on the runway. Within minutes he thanked the state police pilot and climbed out. They had been in radio contact, and the jet was already operational. They were airborne within minutes.

The flight to Sacramento gave him ample time to reflect on the crimes. He was more than anxious to play the tapes to find out who the Russian fisherman called from the jail. There were some good investigators in the criminal division. Dan knew his office had probably already prepared the people who would do the work. There was some suspicion that someone in Crescent City was involved, but who and why was another matter. By the time they landed, he was experiencing growing excitement.

A pool car waited on the runway with two investigators in it. Dan used the time to brief them on all the information he had. They were from the criminal division and had excellent track records; besides he knew both of them from past cases. They asked all the right questions. It was a quick, productive trip.

By seven Dan was fatigued. Their meeting at the office had just broken up. It was wonderful to have such an experienced team pooling their efforts. The tapes hadn't produced as much as he hoped. However, he knew shortly the investigators would have taps on the phones in San Francisco. There was already a plan in motion to put somebody on the inside of the City by the Bay Fish Packing Company. Dan parked in the underground garage and took the elevator up to his apartment on the tenth floor. Once he started down the hall he realized the door was ajar. He raced back to the elevator and pulled out his phone. The police arrived shortly. The apartment had been ransacked. Everything was turned upside down and disheveled. Dan cursed, "Son of a bitch." Pulling out the phone, he called his office and told the agent in charge what had happened. They agreed to contact the investigators and have them over there shortly.

* * * * *

Being a deputy in the Crescent City Sheriff's Department meant a great deal to Charlie Stevens. His norm was to check his calls morning and night. This evening he wandered into his office and picked up the pink slips. There was a call from Josephe Nicharo, the night watchman at the docks. Charlie winked. This could be a good piece of information. Picking up his ten-gallon hat, he gingerly flipped it onto his head and hurried out to the squad car. The drive to the docks lasted only a few minutes. Parking near the temporary tin packing shed, Charlie climbed out. He saw the old man checking the moorings on a few trollers still in their berths. "Hey, Josephe." Charlie waved and hurried across the compound.

The old man's wrinkled face creased into a genuine smile. Everyone knew the deputy was a good man.

"Charlie – it's good to see you. I got something you want."

"Really? Well, how about that?"

"Yeah, you know that picture you showed me. I got it right here." He fumbled in his dirty trousers for the paper. "See, I remember some guy he come here awhile back. He come in a big fancy black car. I seen him go down the dock and meet that guy in the picture. Only I didn't remember because he was wearing a seaman's cap. You know the kind?"

121

Charlie nodded.

"The fisherman was from somewhere else. I remember his troller looked different." Josephe's hands automatically waved as he spoke. "I mean it had things I ain't never seen."

"Like what?"

"You know, Charlie, all the big, new boats have special fishing stuff to find the fish."

"Oh, yeah – radar."

"Yeah, but much more. I got curious when he left the dock with the guy who owned the big black car. I climbed on board. It was fancy. I mean – I ain't never seen a boat in this harbor with equipment like that stuff."

"Huh," Charlie looked puzzled. "What else? Is there anything else you can tell me?"

"It was late when they went out. The guy in the car was with him. The boat came in at dawn only he wasn't on it. I thought that was strange. I mean it was real clear he was the skipper. The guy in the black car didn't even know how to tie her up. He left her almost adrift. Of course, then, the wave came and she broke loose. Hell, Charlie, I don't even know where that troller went?"

The deputy was busy writing in his notebook. It looked as if the captain might have been murdered at sea and tossed overboard. This was really terrific. "Thanks, Josephe. I don't think you realize how much you've helped me? I've been looking for just one clue. I owe you one."

The old man's color deepened. "No, you are good for Crescent City. Besides," he winked, "you scared me out of here the night of the big wave. I would have been dead. My wife says you gotta' come for her homemade noodles and raviolis."

Charlie slapped his back. "That's a deal, Josephe. You name it, I'll be there." He waved and left. *There it is – a tie to someone who is connected to this case. I'll make sure that Mr.*

122

Levine gets this information, and the sheriff will be really pleased.

The drive back to the office was short. Charlie climbed out of his squad car just as Cameron Ripley was hurrying out of the building. There wasn't time to get his attention. The deputy decided to fill out the report and send a copy to the attorney general's office before he left for the evening.

Chapter 11

In Jeopardy

Charlie Stevens, excited over the new information, was disappointed to return to an almost empty station. There was one hitch. The description the Italian watchman had given was a bit sketchy. He fixed himself some coffee before sitting down at his desk to think. Suddenly, it occurred to him – the answer was staring him in the face. The computer, why not? He turned it on and went directly to cyberspace using Netscape. Charlie's smiled broadened as he typed in Coast Guard, United States. The selections soon became obvious. Within the next forty minutes, the deputy had not only secured the information he needed, but he had downloaded photographs of the equipment using the scanner. His dark eyes flashed at the coup. Now, he could go to the old man, show him pictures and get some identification on the electronics he saw on board the ship. If it was what the deputy thought it was, it all made sense. Getting up, Charlie made copies of the information and photographs before going out to his car.

The watchman had less to do now that the boats were moored on buoys out in the bay. Usually, he went into the shed and read or listened to the radio his children had given him for Christmas. Charlie found him there and called a greeting from the doorway.

"You back soon. I was about to have some dinner. You want some?" The hoary skinned face wrinkled into genuine appeal as Josephe held out his homemade pasta to the lawman.

After a polite refusal, the officer said he had some photos for the old man to look at. He pulled up a chair and laid them out on the desk side by side. "Oh, just a minute. I'll get the old specs on. I can't see much without them." A shaking hand lifted the pictures which Josephe examined for a long time, mumbling occasionally and saying, "Uh huh, un huh. Sure, sure that's it." A wide grin exposed yellow stained teeth as he looked up saying, "It's just like the stuff on the troller. What is it?"

"It's called sonar, Josephe. I got the pictures from the coast guard over the computer screen. I'm really glad you could identify it."

"What they do with that?"

"I think they were trying to locate the wreck."

Josephe's silver hair rotated. "I don't think they did."

"Why? What makes you say that?"

"Because they were arguing about that. And, when they came back or that big guy came back, he was real mad. I even heard him talking to himself about the stupid skipper who couldn't make all that expensive stuff work. I figured he must have paid a lot and got nothing out of it. Oh, and, Charlie, there is one thing I forgot to tell you."

Charlie perked up immediately. "What?"

"I got the number off that boat when she first come in. I always do that because these guys try to cheat about berth rentals. I go every night and record those numbers in my little book." He held the dirty, well-worn, leather book up for Charlie's inspection. "See, here it is on page 52. There's the date, the description and the troller's name and number. Will that help you?"

"Will it? Josephe you are a genius. Hot dog! I got em' now."

The watchman agreed to let Charlie take the journal and photograph the page of entries. Charlie said he'd be gone about twenty minutes. Josephe said if it had been anyone else he wouldn't have done it.

Charlie sped to the office, completed his task and returned with the precious record. It was a sweet victory. There was no doubt about it, just as his father had always told him, doggedness paid off. For now, at least, he had a motive and a suspect. There was one more thing to do, but it would have to wait until morning.

* * * * *

Dan's call wasn't until almost news time. Terry was nearly frantic when the phone rang. "Are you okay? I've been worried sick for the last hour. I imagined all sort of skullduggery."

He heard the fear in her voice and apologized. By the time he explained what had happened, she was more frightened. "Honey, I wasn't going to tell you, but there isn't any use to start that. I won't lie to you, but you'll have to be patient. This isn't going to be easy or quick."

"Oh, Dan, I miss you. At least, when we were together I felt safe. Honestly, hon, the only good thing about all this is that we met."

Dan chuckled. "I guess, you're right." He went on to explain some of the things they were going to do to protect him. Deciding to change the subject, the lawyer told her he had purchased airline tickets for the upcoming weekend which she could pick up in Medford at the airline counter. He began to outline the things he'd planned for them. Momentarily, it all sounded normal and thrilling. "Terry, darling, I've looked for you for a long time. Let me show you how much you mean to me?"

He heard her sigh. "If I'm with you, I won't worry so much. Okay, I'll just dwell on the good stuff." She faked a laugh.

"Will you drive over to Medford?"

"Yes, I'll take Baron to the vet, and then I'll go directly to the airport. It is a terrific drive through the giant redwoods. The Smith River is full of rapids and snakes right along the road. It is so beautiful. The next time you come we'll do it together."

They agreed that Dan would meet her flight. They were both lonely as only new lovers can be when they are separated.

Terry suddenly remembered something she hadn't told him. "Dan, I almost forgot. That gallery owner, Mr. Henry? Remember my telling you about him? Well, he called again. This time, when I refused to see him, he asked if I had sold my grandmother's art collection. I couldn't believe he knew about it. Anyway, I told him to call my grandmother's lawyer in Boston. Adam is an old family friend."

"Why?"

"I'm going to teach that smart aleck a lesson."

Dan started to laugh. "Good for you."

"I called Adam and told him the whole story. We agreed that he would encourage that piranha to come to Boston on the pretext of seeing the collection. Then, when he gets to Adam's office, he'll be told that a third party had made us an offer he can't refuse."

The lawyer's quick mind was reeling. "Are you certain you want to do that?"

"Yes. Adam thinks we ought to find out what this guy is really up to. I'll be well out of it. Maybe we can find out who put him up to this?"

"Is it valuable? I don't mean to pry, Terry, but what does this actually mean? Can this be connected in any way?"

"I think the only way to find out is to have Adam give him the third degree. He might talk to a stranger more easily than he would me. At least, I know he wasn't interested in my art work." She sounded caustic.

"I love you. I wish you were here with me. I'm feeling really detached tonight."

"Me to. It seems so long since you were here holding me in your arms. It's only been two days. Gosh, Dan, I was better off alone."

"Don't say that."

"Forgive me! I was just feeling sorry for myself. I'll be good, and I'll see you Friday. I love you too, hon. Good night."

* * * * *

The sun was barely up before Charlie was putting on the coffee pot. His pulse raced. Just thinking about solving the murders excited the man. While he scrubbed his teeth, he detailed the day. *First, I'll hit the newspaper office and get a photo of those men from the National Ship Salvage Corporation. Then, I'll take it over to the sheriff's photographer for a blow up. After that, I'll get a positive I.D. from Josephe and find out who the guy was.* The deputy whistled softly while he buttoned his clean shirt. Quickly, he moved to the kitchen of the small apartment to pour a cup of coffee. Then, as he sipped it, flipped on the television to the San Francisco station. A photograph of the City by the Bay Fish Company flashed on the screen. Charlie grabbed at the knob to turn up the sound. "This morning Alfred Jablonski, chairman of the board of the National Ship Salvage Corporation, announced his intention to launch an all out effort to locate the *Brother Jonathan*." Charlie raced across the room to grab a pencil and paper from alongside his telephone. There was much more to the story. William Le Baron, president of the company, who had spent 12 years looking for the wreck, had been forced out of the company. The newscaster recapped the entire legal battle including the fact that Congress had passed a Federal Abandoned Shipwreck Act which, in essence, gave California title to certain shipwrecks. The story concluded by saying Le Baron was unavailable for comment. Charlie shook his head. *It's such a puzzle*, he thought. Apparently, Jablonski was also connected to the fish company, but he'd turned up the sound too late. That phone call could be added to the list.

By noon Charlie had completed most of his tasks. It was gloomy. A light drizzle beaded on the patrol car as he pulled into the parking area just in front of Josephe's trailer. The old man's wife opened the door to welcome him.

"Ha, you come at last," she said exposing a welcoming smile. "I get Josephe. He is just getting up."

Maria made coffee and put out some Italian cookies she'd just baked. The scent, permeating the small enclosure, was enticing. Charlie picked one up and took a good-sized bite. He made suitable satisfying sounds and watched the woman's growing pleasure.

Josephe scuffed in old slippers as he joined them. He reached for the photographs that Charlie took out of the brown envelope he was carrying, put on the glasses with shaking hands and sat studying them. "Here," he said pointing to the big dark man in the center of the picture. "That's him. I am sure. He's a tough man, I think."

Charlie refused lunch but asked if he could take a few cookies along to the car. Maria was gracious, quickly collecting some cookies and a plastic bag for her homemade treats.

Shortly, Charlie whistled softly and headed back to the office munching contentedly on the gift.

Cameron Ripley wasn't in the office. It had been two days since the deputy had actually spoken to his boss. After inquiring of the secretary, Charlie learned that Cameron had been invited to a meeting in another county and wouldn't be back for several days. He shrugged. The office was unusually busy. Closing the door to his work room, Charlie placed a call. "Yes, this is Deputy Charlie Stevens in Crescent City. Yes, ma'am, I'm trying to locate Chief Deputy Attorney General Dan Levine. Uh huh. Sure, I'll wait." Charlie swung his chair around, seeing the activity outside his door and grinning at his privacy. Eventually, he heard the lawyer's voice and sat straight up.

"Hi. Mr. Levine, this is Charlie. I got some good information for you. Do you want it faxed?"

They talked for fifteen minutes. Dan was extremely interested in the data. For the first time they could actually tie a murder to one of the group. It also seemed pretty clear that there was a rift going on and somebody was being shoved out. Dan felt certain these were excellent motives. At least these were motives a jury would buy. When the conversation was concluded Dan had a thought. "Charlie, I'd like to ask a favor?"

"Sure, Mr. Levine."

"I'm very close to Terry Hamilton."

The deputy sounded surprised.

"I'd appreciate you kind of keeping a check on her without her knowing it. You see, she still might be in danger and I'm pretty far away. I know you understand."

Charlie admitted he did. He smiled knowingly.

Dan asked him to keep it quiet. He said, under the circumstances, it might be misunderstood. They left it that Charlie would phone if anything unusual seemed to be happening.

Dan called the investigative division as soon as he hung up the phone. This was as close as they'd come to having real connections to criminals involved in a very big case. Dan had actually done just about everything he could to protect Terry, but he would continue to worry until she was with him.

* * * * *

It was Thursday. Terry decided early on to pack for her trip. Baron whined when she withdrew the suitcases from the closet. Putting them on the bed, she drew him close and hugged the thick, furry neck. "Hey, boy. It's just for a few days. I love you, and now I love Dan. I can't take you on the plane. Please, try to understand." The dog licked her face. Terry smoothed his coat. "You are my best friend. How lucky I was that Letty bought you for me. She must have known I would really need you." Baron yipped then barked loudly as he accepted her words.

Suddenly, as she closed the case, it occurred to her that she could go to the city early and surprise Dan. "Yep, I'll call Doc and see if he can take you, boy. But, first, I'll call Medford and see if they have an afternoon flight to Portland. I know I can get all kinds of service out of there for San Fran. Ha, Ha," . . . she danced around the room and went directly to the shower, humming all the while.

At 11:00 A.M. Baron went to the vet. Terry drove up to the art supply shop to get the painting she'd had matted and framed for Dan. It was wrapped, and after paying for it, she put it into the back of the Jeep. Shortly, she was driving into the deep caverns of the redwood forest. The road twisted and turned past tree trunks so wide they seemed unbelievable walls of slowly darkening bark. The rain had turned the tar black and the green glades of lacy ferns and long-stemmed grasses into an eclectic, fantasy world. Just past the redwoods, she emerged onto the river whose torturous route followed the road. The water roared over rocks and boulders, its tumultuous chorus filling the canyons. After about an hour she stopped for coffee at a redwood inn. Although the drive had been demanding, Terry was exhilarated and anxious to see the man she loved. Medford was probably an hour away. It was just one o'clock; she had two hours before the plane left.

* * * * *

The investigators were seated in Dan's office when he returned from lunch. They were going over the information he'd given them earlier. "Hello, you two. What have you got for me?"

The older of the two, Bert Maxmillian, spoke deliberately while reading from his notebook. "We've got a man on the inside of the fish packing company. He's putting a tap on the line in Jablonski's office. I imagine that will pay off. It took some doing to convince the judge we had enough to warrant a tap. The listening equipment is in a van on the docks parked inconspicuously near a load of crates. I really don't think it'll be detected. There is a tremendous amount of activity there day and night. Oh, and Dan, the information from the deputy in Crescent City was invaluable. Please, tell Charlie Stevens how much we appreciate his efforts."

Bert's partner, Ted Blumenthal, concurred. "I was able to contact the maritime commission and learned that the troller was registered to Soto Melendez. He is apparently missing. The troller was leased to the fish company for some months. There is no record of it returning to this harbor. We are getting a set of prints from the maritime office. They require fingerprinting for all captains. It might be a good idea to contact Crescent City and ask Charlie to send us a set up so we can do an I.D. comparison."

Dan turned his swivel chair to face the wide glass spans behind his desk. "Do you think that Soto Melendez was murdered?"

"I'm betting the corpse they have in Crescent City Morgue is Melendez," Bert offered. "In fact, I honestly believe that the old lighthouse keeper located the wreck, and before he could give them what they paid for, someone tried to squeeze him and failed. If that is true, that's why Captain Tillman was murdered."

"But, what had Terry Hamilton to do with it?"

Ted pulled out his book. He flipped through some pages until he located the proper one. "Here it is. Someone has been keeping really close tabs on her. We got that off the wiretap. Jablonski said he was surprised to learn that the map was found in her home."

That statement brought Dan out of his chair. He was sweating and mopped at his head with a handkerchief. "Have you been watching her too?"

Ted grinned. "Listen, Dan, we aren't going to let anything

happen to your girl. You got that?" The pair gave him a smug smile.

Dan was pacing now. His thoughts were racing. *Suppose they have a tap on my phone.* The swarthy looks paled.

"Hey, Dan. Cool it. We have the resources of the entire state and a lot of good minds, including yours. But, I do have a suggestion."

"What?"

"Well, you two want to be alone this weekend, right?"

"Yes. Of course. And, I don't want you two hanging around."

Bert's fat face colored. He squirmed in the chair and coughed. "Would we do that?"

The statement made Dan laugh hard. "Yes, I'm afraid you would."

"We found a really nice bed and breakfast down the coast about fifty miles. It's right on the ocean and it's safe. I know it'll queer your plans but, Dan, better safe than sorry. These guys mean business and they are real mad at you."

Silence abounded. Dan moved back and forth his quick mind assessing the situation. "All right, I agree. It does seem the expedient thing to do. They probably are watching my place."

Both of the investigators seemed relieved. They agreed to go make the arrangements and get back to him but not until they told him not to discuss that information on any of his phones.

* * * * *

Portland's airport was crowded. Terry sat quietly reading a magazine awaiting the second leg of her flight. Since she had not discussed the trip with anyone, she felt safe. Just after the preflight announcement on the loudspeaker, she noticed a man watching her. It was as if a warning bell had gone off in her brain. The sunglasses refused him knowledge of her feelings, but her hands became clammy. There was a moment when she decided not to board but she discounted the idea. She told herself she was probably safe on the airplane, but it would be dangerous after they landed in San Francisco. The man got up and entered the line. Terry waited until he was in the boarding tube before she contacted the gate attendant. "Please, get a message to Chief Deputy Attorney General Dan Levine in Sacramento. Tell him there is someone watching me, and he boarded this airplane. Tell him to have someone meet me. It is urgent." The attendant wanted to call the police. Terry refused. "Please, do as I ask. It is extremely important; someone's life may depend on it."

* * * * *

Dan was working on a brief when the call came in. He broke out into a cold sweat before he dialed the investigative division. "Blumenthal, please, yes. This is Levine. It's urgent, find him!"

They were in his office within minutes. After he gave them the information, they raced to the parking garage. The flight was due in San Francisco in an hour. They had the time. Dan wanted to go along, but they refused and insisted he pay heed. They told him this was what they were trained to do, and he should stay out of it. He became angry but, reluctantly, agreed. They were right, but the waiting killed him. He wasn't sure he could stand much more of this. He was also pretty certain that life would never be good again if he lost her. Dan knew he was what they called a one-woman man. All through college and law school he dated when the occasion dictated. There had been many women who were attracted to him, even here in the office, but there just wasn't anything to it. In his mind he'd always thought there would be one outstanding one; the one he would spend his life with. The night he met Terry with Martin Delaney it was like a volcanic eruption. One look at her was all it took. He hoped he hadn't been obvious. In fact, he was scared that she might really be connected to Martin Delaney. Not that he could picture those two together; Martin was an obvious opportunist. Dan was a good lawyer. Work came easily, and the tougher the fight the better he liked it. What would life be without a challenge? But, this thing was consuming them. What did they want with her? How far would they go to hurt her. The whole puzzle was keeping him up nights. He glanced at his watch and paced some more. It was taking a long time, and he was really frightened. That's what Terry meant when she said she was better off alone. Once you are connected you lose all control and there is no safety. He couldn't even imagine life without her. The realization of the pain and fear was overwhelming. It had been forty minutes. "God," he yelled out in his office, "What is happening?"

* * * * *

Blumenthal and Maxmillian left the car in the street, doors open, motor running. Ted flashed a badge at the officer at the door, waved back at the car and dashed into the airport. Bert was right behind him. Fortunately, they knew the location of most of the airlines. Terry was booked on Alaska Airlines which was due in five minutes at gate E-17 in the south rotunda. They were both out of breath when they reached the gate. Bert stopped and drew several deep breaths. Ted's eyes fled to the ceiling as he leaned against the wall and mumbled, "I'm too old for this shit."

A flight announcement gave them the correct time of arrival. Shortly, the door to the tube was being prepared by a gate attendant. They both spotted the men waiting in the lounge and agreed to a plan.

Ted went to a counter phone and asked for police to join them immediately at the gate. It took all of one minute. As Terry emerged from the gate, a uniformed officer approached her. "Miss Hamilton?"

"Yes. I'm Terry Hamilton."

"We've been advised to take you into custody, ma'am. Please, come with us."

Terry was only too happy to comply. While she was led away by two officers, the three interlopers were being secretly photographed and followed.

* * * * *

The phone rang. Dan jumped to pick it up. He smiled softly. Their words were music to his ears. "Okay, bring her here."

Dan was waiting by the elevator when she stepped off. He grabbed her and gave her the tightest hug she'd ever received. Once he let her go she laughed hard.

"What's so funny?" Dan looked offended.

"Nothing is funny, Dan, but if I don't laugh I'm going to cry."

Dan hugged her again.

"I'm so glad to be in your arms. Don't you dare let me go," she whispered into his ear. He encircled her shoulder and drew her into the privacy of his office and shut the door.

Chapter 12

The Hideaway

A brunette from the secretarial pool, standing just behind Terry and the investigators on the elevator, went into shock when that good looking attorney, Dan Levine, snatched the redhead with the investigators and almost crushed her. The woman watched the entire scene, gasping. Then, suddenly realizing what a coup she'd witnessed, rushed down the hall toward the pool. This juicy bit of gossip would be good for, at least, a whole lunchtime. And, the blonde secretary in the civil division, who was so snotty because Dan had taken her to the office Christmas party, would be the first to know.

Dan spent fifteen minutes with Terry before he called the investigators back into his inner sanctum. "All right. We're in agreement. Someone will have to go to my apartment to pack personal items. Here's the key." He pulled it off the key ring and handed it to Bert. "I've already packed my clothes, I intended to take Terry to a hotel, and my suitcase is sitting on the bed. I suppose you've also arranged for transportation?"

Ted spoke up immediately. "Yes, sir. The state police will ferry you both to the arranged place. When you are ready to leave, they will pick you up and ferry you back to the city where an unmarked car will be waiting. Here's the number to call if you need help or a ride. There are several restaurants nearby for your pleasure." He winked.

Dan looked at her with regret. "Sorry, hon. It should have been so grand, and now, I don't know."

"Dan, listen! If we are killed, there won't be any moments. Let's be grateful for all this help." The artist sobered and glanced out at the city. Crossing her arms, she walked toward the windows and stood staring out.

"Smart lady. See, Dan, even your girl knows what's right."

They agreed on a time for the pickup and the investigators left.

"Want some coffee?" he asked gently, his voice sounding soulful with a trace of bitterness.

Terry approached touching the back of his suit coat. She leaned down and kissed him lightly on the mouth. "I know you wanted it to be so special. You must be very disappointed." She kissed him again. "Well, Mr. Levine, I promise you it will be special." Her plump lips parted seductively while she caressed him with her limpid eyes. "We can be just as happy, just as in love, just as alone, there as anywhere. No one will bother us. We won't have to be looking over our shoulder or wary. We can just be us."

Dan grabbed her, and pulling her onto his lap, he crushed her to him and kissed her hard. "Oh, I think if I don't get you alone pretty soon I'm going to burst."

She hugged him tight, laughing lyrically.

The door flew open. A very embarrassed, red-faced Bert Maxmillian said, "Oh, shit! Sorry." Turning, the man ran out, banging the door behind him.

It broke the tension; they both roared with laughter. Terry jumped up, smoothing her suit coat, she assumed a dignified stance. "I suppose, Mr. Levine, that this is not normal behavior in so prestigious an office."

Dan sat staring at her; he was seething. Suddenly, his fist punched the desk top. "Dammit, I cannot believe the way this is playing out. You would be better off with Martin."

"Oh, no! Not now, not ever. You must be mad, darling."

The phone rang. Dan answered. It was Ted begging his pardon. He gave it. Then Ted said, "Those three guys in the airport went to the fish packing company. Believe it or not, our guy already had the tap in the office and on the phone. Whoever answered the phone was fit to be tied that she got away. He raised hell with them. But, are you ready for this?"

Dan bellowed. "TELL ME . . . NOW!"

"Guess who he called later? I won't make you wait. It was Martin Delaney. He was really hot under the collar because Delaney hadn't called him. Unfortunately, they did not discuss the matter further."

Dan told him to stay on it and to keep him posted. He was very angry. Terry saw it in his eyes. "I want these bastards caught. I want no stone unturned. Do you hear me?"

"Yes, sir – boss. Got ya'. Go have fun. We'll take care of it. I gotta feeling we're getting close."

Dan left Terry making phone calls at his desk while he took care of some last minute details.

Terry phoned her lawyer to keep him appraised of the latest events. He told her it sounded like a dime novel and was twice as frightening; then, he insisted that she call his office daily. He advised her to keep a diary of every little shred of evidence. He said he had been in touch with the sheriff and Assistant District Attorney Delaney. His laughter became caustic. "I think I scared the pants off those two, Terry. You won't have any more trouble with them and, furthermore, I told them you'd better be fully protected or else they'd be looking at a pretty hefty civil suit."

Terry snickered. She was picturing Martin being told off by someone who could back it up. There was definite determination in Jess's voice and, if what Dan reported was true, this man's reputation preceded him. After agreeing to call him upon her return, Terry hung up.

The following call was to Alex Waxman. It was short but

very informative. He said he'd had a call from the Gallery Henry. It seemed that Mr. Henry had heard she was being represented and was interested in securing a watercolor for an upcoming show. Terry wanted time to talk to Dan about it and promised to call Alex within a few days to firm a meeting.

Minutes later Dan returned. He was brimming. "We're ready, my lady. Let's get the hell out of here before anything else happens."

At 6:30 P.M. they were in a state police car rolling across the bridge headed for the lower coast. The night was cool, and as the sun began to dip into the western sky, the colors of the landscape turned to purple. Terry leaned back against Dan's shoulder sighing heavily. He reached for her hand and squeezed it.

The day was waning by the time the car turned off the highway and headed down a sandy road toward the cliffs overlooking the sea. The anxious pair, poised on the edge of their seats, stared ahead to see just what their destination looked like. Upon seeing it they both looked surprised. Up ahead, nestled in a grove of eucalyptus trees, was a three-storied stucco hacienda with a red-tiled roof surrounded by an adobe wall. It seemed to be a re-creation of a Spanish movie set complete with a gurgling fountain that sounded cool and musical as they climbed out of the car in the circular driveway. The officer removed their cases and handed them to a bellman who disappeared behind huge wooden gates which were slightly ajar. Inside was a garden filled with mature olive trees and a riot of flowers in every color. It was extraordinary. The windows were covered with brightly colored wooden spindles, and the entry door was open. Inside the tiled lobby a middle-aged woman waited to greet them. She handed them a key and requested they follow. She was pleasant, chatting amiably about the weather and their wise choice of accommodations. Winking, she said, "I have reserved the special guest cottage for you. You will not be disturbed unless you wish service. Please, call for drinks, room service, the maid or

142

phone calls." Eventually they arrived at an old adobe house. It was so charming they both extolled its virtues at once. "Everyone says that. I always have pleasure bringing guests here. It is beautiful – please, enjoy. Your luggage will be outside your door shortly." Having said that she disappeared.

They went inside where it was cool and shaded. Dan went to the glass doors and opened them. The sea was just below, and they could hear its roar. Terry gasped. Dan curled her into his arms and kissed her passionately. They stayed that way for a long time. It seemed impossible but they were actually alone. "I can't believe we are here," he said, astonished, looking around at the adobe room. Overhead there were carved wooden beams, the walls were painted a soft sandstone color, there were navy blue linen sofas and white wrought-iron tables and lamps. Against the far wall was a stucco bar behind which was a small refrigerator, glasses and assorted wines and liquors. A huge fruit basket wrapped in cellophane rested on the counter. On another wall was a beautiful fireplace with wrought iron andirons and a carved mantle. A fire had been laid. They walked around admiring the place.

Terry followed Dan into the bedroom. "It's so beautiful. I'm just overwhelmed. Oh, Dan, honey . . . it is perfect. We are going to enjoy every moment. We have three glorious, uninterrupted days just to play and love and sleep and eat. I'm in heaven." Turning, she moved back to the living room and walked through the open doors.

Outside was a brick terrace where chaise longues covered in colorful woolen blankets sat here and there between wrought-iron tables. The vast ocean seemed at peace and yet it raised large waves at regular intervals, creating a harmonious chorus as it thundered onto the beach far below.

Terry took his hand and drew him outside, inhaling deeply as she did. "Oh, Dan, I could never want anything any better than this."

"I must admit it would be hard to beat. I can't believe those two gum shoes had this much soul. I was afraid it would be a cheap motel with a beach."

They laughed hard.

"Dan, order us some margaritas. I'll bet they are great here, and I love them." She was grinning from ear to ear.

"Your wish is my command." He went to the phone and called the desk. "They'll be here shortly. Now, what would you like to do? Would you like to go for a swim first? Would you like to lie on the terrace and get smashed? Would you like to have dinner or go for a walk or?"

Terry came close and put her finger on his lips. "Shush, darling. I think our drinks have arrived." She giggled, "They anticipated us."

Dan went to the door and took the tray. Then, he carried it to the terrace where Terry was already stretched out on a chaise. "This is exquisite. I've never been so happy."

Dan poured them both a drink and brought her one. "I guess we ought to have a toast?" He was smiling broadly and for the first time seemed relaxed.

Terry sat up and kicked off her shoes while sipping the iced drink through the salted rim. "Oooh . . . magnificent. I've never tasted one this good."

Dan came over and sat down alongside her, and taking a sip, he agreed. He put the glass down and clutched her to him. "I need you . . . NOW."

Terry put her arms around him and drew him into her shoulder. "I have chills, Dan. I love you so much. How could we be so lucky?"

He undressed her slowly on the terrace. He could not believe how beautiful she was. He looked at her longingly, running his eager hands over the flesh and nipples before pulling off his clothes and climbing back onto the chaise. There was no reluctance, only passion – the passion he'd dreamed about for weeks since he'd met her. He found her breasts with his hands and then his lips and thrilled as she moaned. He kissed her over and over and moved down kissing her waist and womanhood until he was drunk with her scent. Terry opened her legs to receive him, raising her hips, pleading with him to love her fully, her voice addictive in his willing ears. His fingers curled into the vulva, feeling the moist lubricant awaiting him as he massaged her, his passion rising until he sweated but not wanting to rush this moment. Then, as he pushed his manhood into her trembling body, their longing rose into some kind of delirium, and she cried out in ecstasy as they plummeted into the oblivion where all thought is lost and blindness overtakes the human soul. When at last it was complete, they lay exhausted against each other. It was silent for a long time until Terry, dry mouthed and barely able to speak, whispered, "Do it again."

At half past seven Dan suggested they needed sustenance. They both became hysterical at the suggestion. It broke the tension. "My God, woman, you are insatiable."

"And you're not?"

Dan's chortle followed. Getting up, he went naked to the front door to bring in their luggage, then he returned to the terrace carrying their bags.

A giggle filled the evening breeze.

"What's so funny?"

"I've never seen a naked bellman before. I like it."

"Get up, wench. We need some dinner."

Terry unpacked and pulled out the long, white crepe evening skirt. She laid it on the bed while Dan showered. Her new pale pink beaded top looked inviting lying next to it. She lifted it and went to the mirror holding it against her chest. The pink neatly contrasted her auburn curls, and she realized the color in her eyes and skin was enhanced as never before. "Wow!" she said out loud, "he certainly lit you up." Dan called, distracting her thoughts.

The bathroom was red Spanish tile and had a step-down

shower with a glass wall that overlooked a garden patio. There were rubber plants, cacti and red flowers everywhere. Terry's throaty voice cooed, "Oh, Dan, this place is unbelievable," as she stepped down into the steam.

"You'd better climb in here with me. It is so wonderful, and I need my back scrubbed."

It was another hour before they dressed for dinner. They just couldn't get enough of each other. By ten o'clock they were beautifully dressed and ready for dinner. Dan crooked his arm and bent from the waist saying, "Dinner awaits, madam." Terry curtsied, took his arm, and giggled as they glided out into the stillness of the night. Somehow, they had actually forgotten the trauma. Their love had overcome all the pain, at least for the moment.

The dining room was almost full. Strains of a flamenco guitarist floated about them as the maitre d' directed their route. Terry honestly thought she was dreaming. It was almost too good to be true. He led them to a table by the open terrace where they could hear a fountain cascading over rocks. Dan ordered wine and hors d'oeuvres of shrimp, hot avocado and cheese chips and a bean paste. They were both starving. They drank and ate and loved each other with their eyes. They amused each other with stories about their childhoods, all the while passing information which was new and interesting. In fact, it soon became evident that they knew relatively little about each other.

"Terry," he said suddenly during the salad course, "Are you as happy as I am?"

"Dan, darling, I've waited so long for you. And, after this afternoon, how can you even question it? I hope you don't think I behave that way with just anybody."

Dan's grunt startled her. "I certainly hope not!"

He stared at her. She looked so beautiful in the candlelight. It seemed staggering to have found her at last. The thrill of their love and the sheer power of it overwhelmed him, but he knew they deserved this time. It had been an ugly mess up until now. And, how was he going to protect her? His eyes washed over the perfection he saw across the table. If anything happened to her, he wouldn't be able to handle it, not now, not after this.

"Dan, you are frowning. What is it? You're scaring me."

The swarthy looks softened. "Sorry, honey. I was just thinking how beautiful you look and how perfect this is. I just don't want anything to spoil it."

"Dan, relax. We're safe here. No one knows we're here. That was the whole idea, wasn't it?" Her smile enticed him while lowering her eyelids at him over her wine glass. "Besides, we promised each other we wouldn't talk about it while we were here."

"Would you like to dance, hon?"

Terry nodded. They got up and Dan drew her onto the dance floor where the other couples seemed to part leaving a spot for them. Terry clung to him. Her head leaned into his, and they floated across the tile to the strains of Estralita. Dan hummed.

"You dance beautifully, darling."

"Hmm, I don't even dance. I must be besotted," he said into her ear.

They danced for a long time, and then went back to the table where their meal was waiting under silver covers to keep it warm.

Later, they clung to each other walking slowly down the vine-covered, softly lit paths to their cottage. "Oh, Dan, what a perfectly gorgeous evening. I've never had one better. Thank you, honey; I loved it."

"Terry, I love you."

"I love you too, darling. I'm just going to enjoy you. I'm not going to question the fates. I figure we deserve it. So, let's not

147

do any what ifs; let's just enjoy every precious moment while we have it."

Dan picked her up in his arms and carried her into the bedroom where he undressed her slowly, deliberately and kissed her constantly.

The sun was high in the sky when they awoke. Dan was already up once. He ordered fruit, coffee and sweet rolls delivered. The tray was sitting by the bedside when she opened her eyes. Dan was curled up next to her, leaning on an elbow, staring at her face. She reached for him, pulling him close and kissing his eyelids. "I thought it might have all been just a beautiful dream."

"No, my sweet. It's real, and it's late. Let's get up and get going. I'd like to go down to the beach for a swim."

Terry was savoring the coffee. "Okay, but first I need some of this coffee and some fruit. I'll be ready shortly, promise."

They took their time getting down to the beach. It was late, and the sun was high. Dan rubbed lotion on her back, and she returned the favor. Neither one of them relished a sunburn. Later, they swam for a long time, riding the incoming waves and back stroking in the gully that was formed as the tide went out. They slept in the shade of the cliffs as the sun slowly moved away, and when they awoke clung together talking about their love and the magic they were experiencing. At five Dan suggested they go get a shower and make it an early night.

The desk made reservations for them at a nearby restaurant. It was a seafood place that sat high on the cliff overlooking the sea. It was rustic and the decorations were nautical. They both really liked it. On the wall under a wide window were life preservers and nets held together by crossed oars. The waiter, assuming they were newlyweds, led them to a quiet table overlooking the blue-gray Pacific. They ate quietly, and their mood was one of complete peace. Over dessert, Dan asked if she was still content.

Terry yawned. "Oh, like a kitten. If I get anymore relaxed I'll pass out."

"I've never enjoyed being with anyone like this before. It's as if we've been together all our lives."

"You seem so surprised, Dan. I guess I knew it that night at the Top of the Mark. I was sick when you said you were leaving."

Dan's grin broadened. "Martin was sick because you were enjoying my jokes so much. Hell, I had to leave, no telling what he would have done if I had stayed."

They both chuckled.

By Sunday they were both starting to feel uncomfortable. Neither one of them wanted it to end, but they knew it would. They also knew they were going back to that awful uncertainty which meant danger. Dan knew he had her covered as best he could without going to her home and watching every move. Terry was feeling real fear that she might lose him. He had set himself up without a doubt. These people were killers, and there wasn't any way to tell what they would pull next.

By evening they were packed, and the car came to pick them up. Dan went to the desk to pay the bill. He told the manager how pleased they were and asked if they could return sometime. The manager, Mrs. Bloodworth, gave him her card and assured him they would be just as welcome. There was a flurry of goodbyes before they climbed into the waiting patrol car. They were both quiet on the way back to town.

* * * * *

Bert Maxmillian had spent the last twenty years of his life chasing criminals. He was astute where it counted. The entire story had to be right in front of him, but there were still a few missing pieces. He worked for Dan Levine, but he also liked the man, and now, he even liked his girl. It wasn't going to be easy to prevent any problems, but he was working overtime trying to protect both of them. He had electronic surveillance

149

on Dan's apartment and on Terry's house. The taps were all in place. The team in the van had picked up some good stuff while the lovers were at the beach. He wished he had been there to see their faces when they entered that beautiful cottage. He guessed they thought he was an unromantic slob who wouldn't know a good place from a bad one; he chuckled in his car as he drove into San Francisco. He wasn't about to tell them the place was owned by a cousin of his first wife. It so happened that she liked him and would do pretty much whatever he asked. And, he had to admit it was pretty spectacular. He stopped for a light in the deuce area near Chinatown. It was a long light and he glanced all around with deliberate attention to detail, a habit of long standing which had saved his life a time or two. It was just a brief glance, but he thought he saw that Henry guy going into a gay bar. Glancing at his watch, he pulled out a cellular phone and dialed quickly. "Ted, yeah – guess what?"

At six o'clock the two detectives entered the bar. It was quite dark inside and took more than a few seconds to adjust to the dimness. They split up and Ted went to the bar while Bert roamed the room ostensibly looking for the men's room. He saw Henry in a corner booth holding hands with a man. It was too dark. Bert swore. They stayed for a half an hour then left. Just as they got into their cars, the pair emerged. It was late. The street lights were on, but their faces were obscured. Mr. Henry and his companion kissed and parted. Bert followed Henry as they'd planned, while Ted took the other one. Within an hour Bert parked at the airport, went in and waited until Henry checked in and then left. *So, old Henry is headed to Boston. I guess he is going to see Terry's grandmother's lawyer. Well, if we are right he is after the art work. I'll be interested to see what this lawyer can find out.*

Ted was doing fine following the other car. He had the plate number and was running a make on it as they drove. He still hadn't seen the guy, but he was damned curious. Once they hit the bridge, there was a traffic snarl and a small fender bender. "Son of a Bitch," Ted yelled in the closed car, "I lost him." Just then his radio blared. "Yeah, this is 620, come in."

"Ted, the car is registered to the City by the Bay Fish Company."

"Thanks . . . call later."

By half past seven the two detectives entered Dan's office where he and Terry waited. They were greeted cordially.

Bert grinned smugly. "I'll bet you two didn't think I had it in me, huh?"

Terry laughed out loud. "Boy, were we wrong. That place was so wonderful, we can never thank you enough. We owe you one, Bert."

Dan blushed and mumbled his approval and appreciation.

"We just happened onto a bit of luck, Dan."

As Bert explained, Terry left to freshen up. She guessed they would fly her home in the state plane because Ted had said they were definitely watching the airport. All the time that had passed without incident was a bonus, but now, she told herself, it was back to normal. The only problem was they were both vulnerable. Her love for Dan would certainly make her so. Terry stood gazing into the mirror. She suddenly realized she was glowing and said aloud, "I guess love did that to me." She shivered before leaving the room, and it made her smile.

Ted had told Dan that there were numerous calls between Martin Delaney and Alfred Jablonski. Unfortunately, they weren't explicit. And, as Dan explained later, they could be in regard to the trial of the guy who worked for them. "Somebody paid his bail, and somebody hired that lawyer who is defending him. They aren't dumb enough to do it themselves, but the check may have come from the fish company." He then instructed them to check the bank.

"Oh, I forgot to tell you, Dan. We got a make on that body Terry found floating in the ocean. It was Soto Melendez, the skipper of that troller that disappeared in the tidal wave. In fact, I want to commend that young Charlie Stevens, the officer in Crescent City; he has been invaluable. I'd love to get that kid up here with us."

"That won't work. I already tried that. He said he was real happy there; it's his home," Dan offered.

Terry entered and the men told her what they had learned. She was really puzzled by the whole thing. "Oh, and I just learned before we left Friday that Mr. Henry called my agent to tell him he wanted to buy one of my paintings for a show. I didn't give an answer because I wanted Dan to decide if I should. Then it occurred to me that he had no way of knowing that unless my phone is tapped."

Both detectives agreed it was. "It is pretty stupid of Henry to assume no one would catch that," Bert said. Then he suggested they give her one of their phones. "If you want to make any calls which deal with Dan or the case or your movements use this one and it won't be traceable."

Terry accepted agreeably.

They concluded the meeting. Ted said they would take them to a restaurant and leave them. They would be picked up by the state police at 9:00 P.M. and taken to the private air terminal where Terry would be put onto the state plane. At Medford she was to be driven to her home and a state police agent would follow with the Jeep.

Dan thought that was a sound plan. He thanked them both for everything they had done and then instructed Terry to call her housekeeper to ask her to pick up the dog and take him to her house. "That way, hon, you won't be alone when they drop you off tonight late."

The detectives left after telling them to meet shortly in the parking garage.

Terry came close; she reached for him and he clutched her against his shoulder. "I love you, my darling, I can't say it

152

enough." Her sad eyes misted over quivering lips. "My God, Dan, I cannot lose you."

"Don't do that, Terry. I won't be able to let you leave if you cry. We have covered every avenue we can think of, honey. Let's hope fate is on our side." He caressed her with a dismal look. He pressed his lips against her cheek and squeezed her until she gasped. "I know you know my love goes with you. Be extra careful. If anything looks wrong call the police, promise me?"

"I will. You do the same."

They kissed each other ardently, each wondering if it were for the last time.

Chapter 13

Exposing Chicanery

Dan's night had been sleepless. Reliving the wonder of their weekend kept him awake coupled with the fear that it could all end abruptly if the chicanery persisted. At 5:00 A.M. he showered and dressed for the office. The air was always clearer in the early morning. There was little or no traffic, and he loved cruising across the bridge with the windows down listening to the fog horns' incessant moaning warning tugs and steamers passing beneath the great span. By the time he reached his office he felt refreshed; the ride had cleared his head. There was no doubt of it, he was excited, eager to solve the problems.

It was too early to call Terry. He decided to postpone that treat until later. He would spend the time outlining what he knew about this whole fiasco. Pulling out the yellow pad, he began to write. It took about an hour before he had accomplished his graph. There were definitely some missing pieces. *Well, I'll call Terry's grandmother's lawyer. What was his name? I have it here somewhere.* Dan rooted in his desk drawer. *Yes, here it is, Adam Linquist.* Glancing at his watch and calculating the time difference, Dan figured it would be just about right for a call to Boston. He picked up his phone and punched into an outside line. "Operator, yes, can you give me information for Boston. Thank you." Within five minutes

Dan was listening to the phone into the law office ring. "Hello, Adam. Yes, this is Dan Levine, Terry's friend."

The conversation lasted for fifteen minutes. Dan was pleased with the results. Adam Linquist definitely had Terry's best interests at heart and would cooperate. They had formed a good strategy for the conversation with Mr. Henry. Adam had agreed to have someone follow him to the airport to find out what plane he would be returning on. Dan decided to have Ted or Bert meet the plane and get a photo of anyone he met and follow him from there. It was time to find out who he was in bed with. Dan laughed at the analogy.

Realizing he was hungry, Dan went down to the cafeteria for a cup of coffee and some sweet rolls.

"Hey, Dan. You are a sight for sore eyes," Bert called from the coffee line.

"What?"

"Just an expression – forget it. I wanted to talk to you because I've got a couple of theories that need sounding out." The fat man looked agitated. Rolling his eyes, he grinned before sitting down and tearing into a plate of scrambled eggs, bacon and toast.

Their table was in a quiet corner and Bert proceeded. "There is a big piece of this thing missing," he mumbled while chewing heartily. Dan nodded. "Maybe Jablonski isn't our man. I mean what about this guy Soto? I pulled the corporation papers on that fish company, and his name is on them along with Jablonski. Now, Soto buys the farm and his boat disappears. I checked the maritime commission records, and the boat was registered to Soto Melendez and Jesus Melendez. I also checked with the insurance company, and a claim has been made by Jesus for the full policy limits which was $500,000."

Dan whistled. "That's quite a sum."

"Yeah, a guy might even get murdered for that much money,

huh?" Bert had finished the breakfast and was swilling the last of his coffee.

Dan frowned. "I don't follow. How do you get from point A to point B?"

"I'm not there yet. First, I got to find out who Henry is meeting with. I honestly think those two things are tied together, and I can't explain it. It's just a hunch." Standing, Bert lifted his cup. "You want seconds on coffee?" Dan nodded and the big man took both cups and hurried over to the coffee stand.

When he returned, Dan told Bert about the call to Boston. "I'll call you as soon as we find out what Adam Linquist learns and what airplane our Mr. Henry is coming back on."

Bert grinned. "I got a feeling, boss. I can always feel it when we are getting close."

"You'd better be right, Bert. We're running out of options."

At 9:00 A.M. Dan went to see Attorney General Steven Landry, who greeted him cordially and asked him to sit down. "Janice, please bring us both some coffee and hold all my calls until we are finished," he instructed his secretary. They watched her leave.

"I'm glad you have some time this morning, Steve. I don't think this can wait." Dan pulled his chair closer to the desk.

Steve Landry looked interested. He had great faith in his chief deputy, and the case involving the sunken treasure was intrinsic to his political future. He had been busy when Dan returned from Crescent City and was extremely curious about the particulars.

"I suppose Bert told you I brought a map back. It's the actual location of the wreck."

Steve grinned broadly and made a winning gesture with his fists. "That was the best news I've heard since election night. I hope you don't think I didn't appreciate all your efforts, Dan. It's just that I've been snowed, and I knew you'd handle it."

The young lawyer shook his head. "No, no problem. I just

really think we have to finalize the effort to retrieve, and it is complicated. Most of it cannot be done without your expressed approval and help. You will have to call in some favors, but for 50 million, I imagine, you won't mind." Both men laughed.

Landry was nothing if not pragmatic. He sat up, poured some coffee and prepared to do business. "Perhaps, I need to be informed. Are you having problems – that is to say – more than the usual matters?"

"Yes, but look, Steve, we've got to proceed with real caution. There have been two murders and sundry burglary attempts. My life has been threatened, my apartment broken into and Terry's life is in danger. I might just as well tell you, sir, I intend to marry her, if she'll have me. This is really serious."

"Have everyone who is involved into my office within two hours, and we will plan our strategy. I'll clear my calendar and keep the rest of the day open."

Dan left and went to his office. His secretary began to make the calls, and while that was being done, he phoned Terry. "Hello, Miss Hamilton, this is Assistant Attorney General Dan Levine. I'd appreciate you getting in touch with me, later."

Terry almost forgot the phone instructions. "Oh, yes. I'll be going into town shortly and, after I get what you asked for, I'll call. Goodbye."

The phone rang almost immediately. "Hi, hon," he said grinning. "Is everything okay?"

Terry cooed. "It would be if you were here with me."

"Don't I wish. Look! I've contacted your friend in Boston, and I'll have that information later today. Someone will be on him from start to finish. Maybe, just maybe, we can find out who is doing exactly what to whom."

Terry sounded scared. "Are you sure you are okay?"

Dan's other lines were both lit. "Gotta go, hon. I love you, I'll call later. Oh, one other thing. I hung the gift, and it looks terrific . . . thanks again."

* * * * *

Adam Linquist's office was in the financial district of old Boston on the twelfth floor of the Matlin Building. His secretary ushered Mr. Henry into Adam's private office that overlooked the harbor. The woman regarded this excellent specimen with a critically approving eye before leaving to get him some coffee. Later, she would tell the other secretaries what a handsome client was with her boss. She would describe in detail his camel-hair overcoat, Italian shoes, pinstriped suit and silk shirt down to the solid gold cuff links and tie tack.

"Hello, Mr. Henry, sorry to keep you. I was detained on another matter. Did my girl bring you some coffee?" Adam asked extending his hand.

Mr. Henry was pleasant, he gushed, assuring Adam he was well taken care of and turning reluctantly away from the spectacular view. "You are quite fortunate to have that view. I wouldn't be able to get any work done," he said moving closer to the desk.

Adam wanted to laugh. The man reeked of San Francisco, which the lawyer figured wouldn't be acceptable in staid old Boston. "Shall we get right down to business?"

"Yes. I am interested, as you know, in bidding on Mrs. Hamilton's art collection, which I understand you are handling for the estate," he said sitting down in a leather chair opposite Adam's desk and crossing his legs.

Adam smiled pleasantly. "I don't feel good about your having come all of this way for nothing, but we have had an offer which cannot be refused." The lawyer's thin face contracted, his green eyes narrowed as he prepared for Mr. Henry's growing wrath.

The beautiful features drew up into a livid mask. Adam felt the anger building. "That is not possible. I haven't officially made a bid yet. Surely, in good conscience you cannot accept a bid until all takers have been heard." The blond hair seemed more fake gold against the man's paling skin. His eyes became stark and his pink mouth turned ashen and taut. Nervously, he ran a hand against his hair.

The lawyer's charm had been well honed during his long years at the bar. "Oh, Mr. Henry. I know that a man of your experience would surely realize that the collection has been appraised many times by all of the major appraisers. Naturally, we will accept the highest bidder. Your intention to bid at $500,000 was fully considered and did not come close to the one offered by our European bidder. It isn't a question of being unfair at all."

Mr. Henry stood and walked back to the window. He needed time to think, but his fury was overtaking him. Adam saw his hands shaking. Turning, he eyed the lawyer with a cold stare. "I'll increase the bid."

"Look, perhaps there is one piece in which you are particularly interested. I would be most happy to pass the information along to my purchaser. They might entertain the idea of selling." Adam poured some more coffee from a silver pot and held it out in offering. Mr. Henry declined shaking the golden hair vehemently.

"I hadn't thought of that," he said softly almost to himself.

"I didn't hear you."

"I said, I hadn't thought of that. Perhaps, you could put me together with the purchaser?" It sounded apprehensive and impatient.

Adam Linquist was approaching fifty. He played racquetball twice a week and golfed when the weather allowed. He ate simply, avoiding fat and sugar and only accepted coffee with clients. He drank very little, almost never lost his cool and was always in command, but at this moment his blood pressure was rising. He wanted to punch this fake bastard in his pretty face. He was reminded of Terry's explanation of the day she took her paintings into his gallery. Taking a deep breath, he answered in his best court room demeanor. "This is a prestigious law firm, Mr. Henry. We are nothing if not discreet. All matters occurring here are held in the strictest confidence. I couldn't possibly breach that; besides, why wouldn't you want me to pass on your request? It isn't a secret . . . is it?" Adam could hardly contain his laughter. He remained stoic watching his adversary squirm.

Mr. Henry's tactic changed. He obviously didn't want to leave without trying, but he was afraid to give himself away. "I'd like some time to think about this matter. Is the collection still housed at the estate?"

"No. It has been vaulted for protection. One can never be too careful, now can one?" Adam's features relaxed as he smiled. The look had appeal; he evoked real sympathy for the man's plight.

"Oh, of course. I'm certain it is a big responsibility having such matters to take care of. Your clients are very fortunate, Mr. Linquist." Mr. Henry forced a smile.

"We do our very best. It has certainly kept us at the top for many, many years." Adam glanced at his watch, a ploy he often used to conclude an unpleasant situation.

"I hope I'm not keeping you?" Mr. Henry said sarcastically.

"No. I do have a pretty heavy schedule today, but if you need more time, I'd naturally try to accommodate you." Adam stood up signaling the end of the meeting, which completely unnerved Mr. Henry.

"I'd like to bid a million dollars. Will that offer suffice?" It sounded condescending.

Adam Linquist shook his salt and pepper hair, a small grin replaced his stoic look, his manner softened becoming full of regret. "I'm sorry. I honestly feel bad that you've come so far and I am unable to help you. That is not close to our bid." He approached Henry and held out his hand. "Look, you think over what I suggested and if you have a partner or client you want to defer to – just let me know. I'd be more than happy to do some further investigating with our client." Adam winked and smiled pleasantly. "Who knows, it might just work out for both of you?"

Mr. Henry was ashen. He left without saying goodbye. It was obvious he was completely shaken by what had occurred. He never noticed the office law student getting into the elevator alongside him or saw him enter a cab at the curb. Within an hour Dan Levine was telling Bert what plane to meet.

* * * * *

The meeting in Attorney General Landry's office turned into a large gathering. There were lawyers, financial advisors, secretaries, investigators and liaison people who would make the contacts with the coast guard, navy, port authority, captains, archaeology specialists and fishermen. Dan was asked to fill in everyone. They were all sworn to secrecy even though the matter was expected. Dan let them know there were lives at stake, his included.

After an hour it was evident they had a pretty efficient team. The liaison people left to find the fishermen in Crescent City who would be hired to sail within a mile of the site when it was located. They were to be armed and deputized so they could protect the treasure site. There was a decision to hire the archaeological team from the University of Southern California to send two capable people up under contract to be on site at all times until the treasure was brought up and the artifacts identified. The Crescent City Historical Society was to be notified and asked to set up a collection area for sorting artifacts. Everyone decided that was a very politic thing to do when and if they actually located the wreck. The coast guard divers, who were offered before, were going to be paid to dive and locate the wreck under special contract and for a negotiated salary. Upon location, the area would be marked, and the fishing boats would protect the site for the duration. Four captains would be hired and two boats would be on site simultaneously and continuously until the job was completed. It seemed a really efficient plan. Dan suggested that extra police, military or frogman types be hired from the coast guard, if that was possible, because of the trouble already in progress. It was agreed. Attorney General Landry said absolutely no interviews, no press whatsoever, would be tolerated. "So, keep quiet." They all agreed but knew someone would see them out in the ocean or become curious or whatever. Each of them hoped there would be no bloodshed.

Dan talked to the lawyers about the fact that the court ruling said that National Ship Salvage Corporation had the right to search. "The judge did not say we couldn't search nor did he say we cannot have the find. I think we are home free if we locate and can get it established legally once and for all. Also, Congress has just passed the Federal Abandoned Shipwreck Law, but it doesn't go into effect until January of next year." It looked solid. The attorney general was hopeful and offered Dan full cooperation for his lady friend and his own safety.

"I don't want anyone hurt or killed. Be careful, Dan, and have Terry be very careful. Once we locate and it becomes a legal issue, some of the problems will stop. Let's face it, what they want is the gold."

Steve Landry was pleased with the entire meeting. He called Dan back as the meeting was breaking up. "Dan, if you want to go to Crescent City during the dives, I'd sanction that. You've done a bang-up job for us. I'd offer that to you as a bonus."

"Thanks, Steve. That is great news. I'm certain my lady will be glad to hear it." Dan waved and left the office feeling tired but exhilarated.

* * * * *

Bert and Ted were leaning against opposite counters in the San Francisco airline terminal at 9:00 P.M. that evening. Mr. Henry was met by a swarthy Mexican man dressed in an expensive navy and maroon sweat suit and jogging shoes. The pair greeted each other warmly. They went arm and arm to the luggage area where Henry picked up his expensive luggage while his friend went to get his car. Bert followed the man in order to get a license number, make and model on the car and also to place a transponder under the bumper in case they lost him in traffic. Ted stayed on Henry until he got into the car at the terminal entrance. The police, who had been notified, stopped the pair as planned. They were polite asking them to get out and answer a few questions. Mr. Henry became incensed. While they argued, an investigator from their office placed a bug in the front of the Mercedes under the dash. Ted whistled as he watched. "Oh, baby, that was smooth," he said to the air. Within twenty minutes the van with the listening equipment was following the Mercedes to Mr. Henry's apartment. Fortunately, they had already bugged the place. They didn't know who the other man was and were desperately hoping the conversation in the car would give them the information they needed or that these two would go directly to Henry's apartment.

Dan was pacing up and down in his office awaiting Bert's call. When it came, he realized he was sweating. "We're coming in, boss. We got photos, tape and a good make on this whole thing. Get some dinner sent in. We're all starved, okay?"

Dan laughed. "You name it, Bert. I'll buy with pleasure."

The team came into the investigation office within fifteen minutes. The photos were sent to their lab where the boys were waiting to develop them immediately. Bert instructed they fax a scan to San Francisco's Police Department for identification as soon as they had a print.

Someone yelled that a guy was in the parking garage demanding to be paid for eight pizzas. Dan yelled, "Tell him the money is on its way down with a big tip for his trouble." He handed his aide $120 and sent him flying out the door.

Everyone was excited. It took awhile to set up the tapes and put them onto a speaker. Dan paced. Bert gobbled pizza with Ted. The others ran around setting up equipment. It was evidence, and they wanted everything to be right.

"Okay, we're ready," the electronics specialist yelled. The room got very quiet. The tape started to whir. They heard Henry's voice.

"Oh, hon, what a trip. I'm just exhausted."

"Quit stalling, vat happened?"

"We lost the deal." His voice sounded quaky, as if he were afraid.

"Yesus Christ . . . vat are jou saying? Jou mean after I murdered my brother and sunk his son of a bitchen boat, dat ve didn't get the Madonna?"

Bert was picturing Henry's whitewashed face.

"Yes. Oh, hon, I'm so sorry. I did everything you told me to do. This lawyer was incredible. So sure of himself, the bastard just kept patronizing me. I wanted to scratch his eyes out. Don't get so furious. I couldn't help it; they have a solid bid. I even offered a million."

"A million! Are jou insane? I haven't got dat kind of money."

"We were going to make it selling the Madonna to the Catholic Church. I figured if they would go that high they would pay more. I know the art world, darling; they will always go for more. Besides, it is worth twice that." They could hear Henry sniveling.

Ted raised his hands in the air, he looked up and yelled. "That bastard is crying. I'd like to make him cry."

"QUIET," everyone yelled simultaneously.

Henry's pithy voice continued in between sobs. "Wait, Jesus, I did get him to agree to ask his buyer if they would sell the one piece. Maybe we haven't lost yet."

By now everyone in the office was on the edge of their seats.

Dan recognized the name immediately. Jesus was Soto's

brother, and they had a legitimate tap and a confession. Bert was right. They were after the wrong guy all along. There were a lot of questions still unanswered. They would need to let this thing run on awhile longer. How else were they going to find out who was connected and what else they were willing to do?

Henry stopped crying. He sounded indignant. "Is that the thanks I get for running myself ragged all over this damned country trying to help you. You don't appreciate anything. I ought to . . ."

Suddenly there was a crack. It sounded as though someone was punched. Mr. Henry was screaming. "You bastard! You split my lip." The sobbing increased until they heard the brakes squeal.

"Get out. Jou piece of trash, get out of my car."

A door slammed. The only other thing that was heard was the squeal of tires accelerating and a voice saying, "Jou, bitch, I fix jou."

* * * * *

Terry crossed the parking lot toward the art store. She was carrying her large art case and her purse. Upon entering the store she happened to glance back toward her Jeep. Baron was inside and she could see his head. He was barking loudly. Dropping the case on the counter, she flew outside toward the Jeep. Martin Delaney was just on the other side out of sight.

"What are you doing?" she demanded.

"Terry! I thought that was your car. I was just passing and decided I'd stop to say hello. I haven't seen you for quite awhile." He smiled and tipped his suede hat.

"You've upset my dog. I thought you'd know better than that."

"I know Baron. What's better, is he knows me. I like him, he's a great dog and very protective of you. You aren't having any more problems are you?"

She frowned. "What an odd question, Martin. If I were having problems you'd be the first to know. Now, if you'll excuse me, I have some business to take care of." She turned and started back toward the art store.

"Wait! I was wondering if we could have lunch or dinner sometime soon?"

"Why?"

"Oh, give me a break, Terry. I'm trying to make amends. I'm sincere, please."

Terry's laughter had a caustic ring. "All right, lunch . . . tomorrow at the seafood place near the bay, at noon."

Martin brightened, but he was obviously surprised. "Great. I'll be there . . . thanks."

Terry went back into the store chuckling. She wanted to have two of her paintings matted and shipped to the two investigators in Dan's office. They had been wonderful to arrange so nice a weekend for them. She hummed as she picked out the mats.

* * * * *

Dan was too tired to think by 10:00 P.M. He had forgotten how early he started the day. He stretched and yawned, "Oh, it's almost ten o'clock. I'd better be getting home. Terry will be worried if we don't speak, and I'm bone tired.

Once in the apartment Dan sat down on his couch. He intended to have just one beer, watch the news, hit the shower, call Terry and then, sleep. He closed his eyes, leaned back against the divan and fell into a deep sleep. The phone rang at 11:30 P.M. Dan tried to awaken, he couldn't and began to believe he was dreaming. It wasn't until it didn't stop that he finally shook himself awake.

"Dan, just tell me you're all right."

"Un huh. Sleepy, sleepy and tired. Please, I'll get back to you when I'm more coherent. Love ya'."

He fell back into the same deep sleep as before. At 3:30 A.M.

Bert called. Dan reacted in much the same manner. Finally, he reached for the cellular, which they'd all agreed to use. "Yes?"

Bert's voice was sharp. It was obvious he was excited. "Wake up, Dan. I've got real news."

Dan shook himself and sat up. "Okay. I'm trying to get coherent. Talk to me, and it better be good; it's three thirty in the morning."

"I decided to camp out at Henry's. We still got the place bugged. So, I sat in my car and put the tape on. He had a couple of calls from Jesus. They had a wow of a fight on the phone, and Mr. Henry told him off in no uncertain terms. I guess Jesus had given him a fat lip in the car, and Mr. Beautiful was pissed. I think his quote was, "I've never looked this bad in my life." Bert's cackling crowded onto the line.

Dan laughed. He was exhausted but that sight really tickled him. "Okay, so they fought on the phone, so what?"

"So, I'm still parked here when I see the Mercedes pull up an hour later and Jesus or someone who looked like Jesus unlocked the front door and went in. I'm still listening and these two get into a shouting match. I loved it, boss. What a fight."

"It is almost four in the morning, Bert . . . get on with it."

"Well, so in the middle of this shouting match it sounds as if Mr. Henry throws something really heavy at Jesus. The next sound is this great crash and then a thud. I perked right up. I mean, I guessed something bad happened. I didn't want to run in there just yet because I didn't have a search warrant, and you like everything nice and legal like."

Dan was nearly crazy. "BERT, WHAT THE HELL HAPPENED?" he shouted.

"Well, just then I see this guy running out of the building. It looks like Jesus, so I let him go. I went inside and I found Jesus crumpled into a ball, and he is dead as a doornail. And, Mr. Henry is no where in sight. There is plenty of blood all over the place because he hit him with a piece of sculpture,

HELEN CORBIN

maybe soapstone. You know, that heavy stuff the Eskimos use to carve with. It weighs a ton."

"Are you serious?"

"I know, boss, it's crazy. I can't figure it out. All I can think is that Mr. Henry had been making plans to do Jesus in – either a frame or something like it. He must have had clothes and a wig and makeup. He also must have been suspicious that someone was onto him."

"But how?"

"Well, it might be that he found the bug in the apartment. It happens. If that's so, our boy is headed to South America."

"Well, call the police and put out an APB. I want that bastard caught."

"I knew you'd say that, boss. I already did all of that, and they got him at San Fran' trying to board a plane for Brazil. I'm feeling really good. Oh, and, boss, he was wearing a wig and makeup. Damn, if he didn't look a whole lot like Jesus. He was even carrying his passport."

Dan was absolutely awake by now. "Bert, old man, I gotta hand it to you. This was one terrific piece of work the whole damn day. I'm going to see to it that you get a commendation from the governor. You are a genius." He could hear Bert purring on the other end of the line.

Chapter 14

The Analyst

Bert Maxmillian's ego had been given quite a boast from Dan's compliments. He knew he did a good job, but it certainly felt good to have one of his superiors say so. This case had been crazy. Everyone in the office was putting massive man-hours into it trying to solve the problem. There was an extra push because the woman involved was the chief deputy's girl and, also, because Attorney General Landry wanted to win the fight for the bullion.

Bert had gotten four hours sleep after they arrested Mr. Henry. He awoke tired and plagued by the still unanswered questions. Their search warrants were being processed while he slept and now, he decided, it was time for some serious investigating. First, he would ransack Jesus's place. Some piece of evidence would show up in that guy's office or apartment.

He grabbed some coffee at a diner and ate two pieces of stale Danish heated with butter. Once that emptiness was satisfied, he was ready to go to work. He burped, took the last swallow of coffee and left.

Jesus lived in a remodeled warehouse near the wharf. Bert pushed the freight elevator's buttons and watched the gate clanging shut before it rose with such heaviness it caused apprehension. Up on top he opened the metal door and faced a large living room furnished in expensive black leather couches and chairs. It was definitely modern decor. He could see Mr. Henry's artistic hand in every bit of the place. Bert scrunched his nose. The brick walls were appealing, but the purple and black paintings and accessory pieces were a bit much. "Oh, well, to each his own," he said out loud.

Off to one side was an alcove that contained a black lacquered desk and chair. There were plants and statuary nearby. Bert figured that would be the best place to start. He opened one drawer after another, examining the bank books, papers, notes and a telephone directory. Being thorough took a long time. Obviously, Jesus needed the $500,000 insurance money from the boat he and his brother jointly owned. The bank books showed low balances. His checking account had $800 in it. "Old Jesus was running on empty," Bert exclaimed. There were a few pieces of paper with notations that didn't really mean very much, a title to the boat, a title to the Mercedes and a lease for the apartment. The rent was due. Bert shook his head. "Not much here." He was disappointed. Getting up, he went into the bedroom. He found the king-sized bed unmade and clothes all over the floor. There were women's clothes hanging in the bathroom and closet and expensive toiletries covered the counter as if a cyclone had been made up there. Surplus jogging clothes piled up in the corner reeked of sweat. "Not too tidy, Jesus." It looked as if Mr. Henry spent quite a bit of time there. Bert laughed thinking about the pair. He continued searching the closet. In a leather coat pocket he found a notebook. Picking it out, he went back to the living room and sat down. It was dark inside the loft; he flipped on a floor lamp. The book was leather, small and filled with small white perforated pages. The notes contained addresses and some names. There were notations regarding certain dates and places. Most were in Spanish. Bert pocketed the book thinking that someone in his office could interpret later. He got up and looked around; disgust laced his face. "This was a waste of time. What I need is a snitch." He grinned. "And, I know just who it is." He hummed as he headed back to the freight elevator.

By early afternoon he was in the office of the San Francisco Chief of Police. They greeted each other cordially and Bert made reference to his old police force detective days. Chief Marshall pointed toward a chair. Bert sat down eyeing the aging lawman whom he had known for ten years.

"Chief, you incarcerated one Mr. Henry, a San Francisco art dealer, on murder charges at four this morning."

"Yes, we did. I heard the press is having a field day. I've only just come in. I had a function this morning and missed most of the commotion."

"Well, he is involved with one of our major cases. What I need is a snitch like Jessie to be put into the cell with him. We need information that only he can give us. Outside of thumb screws, which I know you won't use, I don't know how else to get information from this guy. The attorney general would be very grateful." Bert stared at the chief. "I was hoping you would cooperate with me, and I need to talk to Jessie without anyone in here knowing I did it."

Chief Marshall nodded. "Okay. I'll have Jessie brought to the infirmary for an exam. You can go down there and put on a white coat, which the doc will give you. You know the drill. Go ahead and I'll take care of having Jessie put into Henry's holding cell later."

"Chief, we won't forget this," Bert said grinning. "This Henry is the key to a case involving a great deal of money for the state." *It might be a good day after all,* he thought. He was finally going to get a chance to find out what the hell this whole deal was about.

Jessie Lark was a drug addict who Bert had arrested years ago. Their paths crossed regularly while the detective worked for P.D.'s drug detail. Bert gave him a break a time or two, and Jessie remembered it. Without anyone knowing it, the druggie began to sell information to Bert for small sums. Occasionally

Jessie had big stuff to sell. The relationship involved trust, and it took a long time before either of them actually believed it.

Bert put on the white coat and went into the examining room. Fortunately, there were hardly any inmates or guards in that area at that time of day. Bert hated the smell of disinfectant, which permeated the sterile looking, antiquated room. He made a face and walked around idly fingering the assortment of bottles, tongue depressors and cotton balls available. Waiting was part of his job, but he abhorred this kind of waiting. Eventually he heard the outer door open and someone enter who came directly to the examining room. The door opened slowly, and a man poked his head inside.

"Bert! What a surprise. I guess you'll be needin' info', huh?"

The investigator stared at him. Drugs and jails were taking their toll. Jessie might have been only forty-two, but he looked well over fifty. His hair was steel gray, what was left after it had been shaved, and his face, which had the usual prison pallor, was wrinkled into a permanent scowl. Bert tried to ignore his shock. "You got it. You'll be bunking with a homo named Mr. Henry. He killed his boyfriend last night with a big piece of sculpture. Bashed his head in."

"Yeah. I heard. It's all over the joint. The cons can't wait to get him into the shower."

"Okay. It's worth a reduced sentence and $500 if you get what I want."

" Five hundred clams. Wow, Bert, this must be big." Jessie perked right up, his face became animated as he sat straighter in the chair.

It took a long time to tell the story. Jessie always loved being privy to information. After all, someone told him once that information was power. Besides, if Bert could get him out with $500 bucks, he'd be in clover.

"Jessie, listen, while I outline exactly what you need to ask."

Bert left the inmate after forty minutes. He dumped the

174

white coat, carefully scanned the corridor and hurried out. He decided to call Dan. This information was too good to keep.

Ted Blumenthal had agreed to cover the art gallery and the apartment. The art gallery was closed. He took the keys he'd been given and entered. It was dark inside, and he went looking for the light switch. Once the lights were on Ted whistled. This was really a classy place. He even took some time to look at the paintings that were carefully hung all around the studio. In the back he found the cherry wood desk. It was just used for business, nothing of interest. Inside the back office he found Mr. Henry's private papers and a filing cabinet. It took over an hour to search through the documents. In one drawer under M he found a file of news clippings from a newspaper in Mexico City. He couldn't read them but felt they might be relevant and pulled the file. In Mr. Henry's desk he found a bank book with $300,000 in it. The largest deposit, $250,000, had been made that month. Ted hummed pleasantly. "Oooh, I think we might just have a little something here." He was about to close the drawer when he was accosted by an angry, well-dressed, middle-aged woman.

"Who are you? How dare you come in here and rifle through my son's things?" she yelled.

Ted pulled out his badge. "I'm an investigator with the attorney general's office, madam. Your son committed a murder this morning. I assume you already know that. Did you think we wouldn't show up here?"

"GET OUT!" she screamed. "I hate all of you. You ruined our lives." She was getting hysterical, yelling and waving her fists.

Ted wondered if she might also be violent. He was finished anyway. He closed the drawer, bowed politely and left, eager to be out of her range, all the while listening to her still raging voice as he closed the door to the gallery.

The two men met in their favorite coffee house at four. Both of them were excited to compare notes. They pulled out the evidence, careful not to get mayonnaise or coffee on anything, and began to talk at once. Laughing, they finally flipped a coin to see who would go first.

* * * * *

Dan had spent the entire day on the phone. He managed to get Terry to go to her housekeeper's apartment to call him. At last he was able to explain all the latest developments. It wasn't surprising how she reacted. Everyone thought this was a really smarmy twist of fate. Who would have ever guessed that the art dealer and the killer were connected. A fisherman and an art dealer, now that was different, especially one like Henry, who acted as if he owned the world.

Terry wanted to meet with Martin Delaney to ask if she could go through the captain's trunk. She asked Dan about it and was really surprised at his reaction. He was actually angry at her saying abruptly, "I told you not to do anything without calling your lawyer. Didn't you understand me?"

Terry's sensitivity surfaced. She held the receiver out in disbelief; then, putting it against her ear she said in a curt tone, "Do I need your permission?"

There was silence between them momentarily.

"Sorry, Terry. I just can't imagine that you don't realize how serious this is. This matter isn't over. We still don't know who killed the captain and why everything has happened. On the surface it looks as if it is half solved, but it isn't."

"Dan, forgive me. I'm being naive. I promise I'll behave. I miss you very much. In fact, all of the things I've loved here seem empty without you. And, honey, the last thing I want to do is fight with you."

Dan's remorse surfaced. "Terry, I need you. Don't take risks. If you understand that every move must be calculated, then I won't have to worry so much."

"You're right. It'll be done – I promise."

His voice brightened. "I have some good news for a change."

She grunted. "God, that would be nice."

"My boss said I'm free to come down there for the dives while they search for the wreck. He even said he wanted you safe, and he thought we had earned it."

Terry was delighted. "That's wonderful. WHEN?"

He could tell how much she needed him; it was very pleasing. "I'll call as soon as everything is firmed, but I would think no more than two days."

"Oh, darling, how great. Baron and I will be waiting anxiously."

After he hung up, he grinned. He always felt better after they spoke. He hoped she wasn't mad at him over the terse words, but he thought, *Dammit, she'd better realize someone is after her and that probably hasn't changed.*

When the investigators arrived, they were ushered right into Dan's office. He had been expecting them for hours and was tense waiting to know what they'd learned.

It took all of an hour to reveal each bit of their information. They had set up a flow chart with evidence, witnesses, suspects, time frames and equipment. Bert proceeded to put all of it on the cork board, and then he called in the intelligence analysts.

Meantime, Ted went into the secretarial pool to find one of their Spanish interpreters. He returned with Maria Simone Wheeler whose help had been invaluable to them in the past.

Ted took Maria out to the anteroom and spread out the newspapers and clippings from the file. He also gave her the leather notebook. She told him she'd buzz when she was finished. Everyone decided at half past six they would go get some dinner. It looked like a long night. They took Maria with them to the local Chinese eatery. Nearly everyone had either sweet-and-sour chicken or rice cakes with shrimp, the restaurant's special. At a quarter after seven they arrived back in the office where Dan had a call from San Francisco's Police Department.

177

The call turned out to be from Jessie for Bert, and it was marked urgent.

Ted and Bert literally flew out of the office. Within forty minutes they were both inside the jail infirmary with the drug addict.

Jessie was almost salivating. "I did it, Bert. You ain't gonna believe this."

Bert told him to hold it until he turned on his tape. Having done that, he waved at Jessie.

"Mr. Henry wanted to shower. I told you them cons was waiting for him. I guess it got pretty bad in there, and he was screaming by the time the cops brought him back. They gave him a shot to calm him down." Jessie looked sheepish. "I think he was raped a lot. Anyway, he was half out of it, and I could smell that $500, so, I kinda took advantage of the situation, figuring you'd appreciate it."

Bert laughed. "Good boy, Jessie."

"Well, it seems Mr. Henry met Jesus when Mr. Henry was on a buying trip in Mexico City. Jesus was just a thief who had contacts in the big hotels. Anyway, Jesus and his brother Soto were stealing art for anybody who would buy it. Most collectors don't ask no questions. This time, however, they stole a Madonna from the big cathedral in Mexico City worth – are you ready for this? – two million dollars." Jessie stopped talking. He wanted to watch their faces. They were suitably impressed.

"Holy shit," Ted said.

"They were afraid to be connected to it, so Mr. Henry sold it to a businessman as a gift for his wife. The guy's name was Baldwin, and he lived in Boston. He paid four thousand, and he said he wouldn't be giving it to his wife until the following Christmas, when it would be put into her collection. Mr. Baldwin had unknowingly accommodated them. The painting was hotter than an oil drum fire, couldn't be taken out of Mexico, but no one would suspect if a multi-millionaire took it. Their plan was to steal it back whenever they felt the time was right. They did this with a lot of art and artifacts.

"Well, somebody got wise to Soto and tried to put him away. They fled Mexico and with the stash they had bought fishing boats, one at a time, trading up. Eventually, they met Jablonski and talked him into bankrolling a fish plant. They had a bunch of illegals working on their boats for chicken feed, and they put the catch into Jablonski's plant. Unfortunately, Jesus was in bed with Mr. Henry, literally," he chuckled. "Soto hated Mr. Henry, and the boys fought pretty hard. Finally, Mr. Henry talked Jesus into killing his brother and sinking the boat for the insurance money. It was really equipped and expensive, but they were figuring they could locate the gold on the sunken ship first. Jablonski hired Soto to use the sonar to find the wreck. It was new equipment, and Soto didn't know how to use it. They had a real battle. Jesus followed them out in another boat to the spot where they thought the wreck was. He was gonna claim jump. Soto saw him and boarded the other boat. They had a hell of a fight. Jablonski brought the other boat back in and tied it up. End of story."

"No," Bert said. "There's more to this, and you've got to get it."

Jessie laughed. "Oops I almost forgot. There was a little more. Mr. Henry was really in bad shape. Whatever they gave him made him crazy fuzzy. I thought it seemed better than the stuff I buy." He laughed hard.

"Anyway, I asked Henry how they planned to get the painting back? He said the old man died, and they tried to buy it from the widow, but she refused to sell because it was a gift from her husband. They figured she couldn't live forever and then, they would buy it from the estate. Just as Mr. Henry was fading away and between sobs he said, 'Olaf better get those wets busy. Now, I won't get Jesus's insurance money or the Madonna, and Mama and I won't be able to go and live in Buenos Aires.'"

"That's it?"

Jessie snarled. "Shit. That's plenty. Don't you guys ever say thank you?"

They all heard it – it was the alarm bells. Jessie jumped up startled and shouted, "That's something serious."

Bert went to the phone. He called the main office. "What's happening?" His face turned ashen.

Ted grabbed his arm. "What the hell is it?"

"Mr. Henry was found hanging in his cell. He's dead."

Bert's first call was to Dan.

Entering the attorney general's office, the pair went directly to the conference room where the entire team was working. Dan was in shock.

"Have you ever worked on a case more bizarre than this one?"

"Only once," Ted said. "We won't go into it now."

"Okay, let's get the information from the snitch." Ted began slowly. Bert filled in whenever he stopped. By the time he'd finished someone explained what Maria had found in the clippings and put the information up on the cork board.

"They were all about the theft of the Madonna. Which, incidentally, has never been found."

"It has now," Dan said.

"Maria also gave us information from Jesus's notebook on illegals who are working for Olaf Czechof. I think he is either the ring leader, or he is working with someone else. It has to do with the wreck. They probably got the information out of Jablonski's office or have it tapped. Somebody is giving them information on actual events, sometimes before it happens."

"Okay," Dan said. "We know who killed Soto, who killed Jesus, who killed Mr. Henry, and now we have to find out who killed the captain. We also have a complete setup for the search. Bert and I will be going to Crescent City day after tomorrow for an undisclosed amount of time. I will post telephone numbers, and I want to be kept informed at all times – day or night."

The meeting began to break up. Bert walked over to Dan looking dumbfounded. "Thanks, Dan. What a coup. I'm really surprised."

Dan grinned. "You've earned it. Besides, I need a chauffeur while I'm there, and my girl needs protection from some of the locals. I thought it would be good for all of us."

Bert hummed all the way to the car. He thought he would swing by his apartment real quick and take some of his sports jackets to the overnight cleaner. "Yes, sir," he said out loud, "a guy ought to look good on assignment." He laughed hard feeling a definite exhilaration. He checked his watch, thinking he was late. He had promised Ted they would meet at Mr. Henry's apartment within the hour.

* * * * *

Charlie Stevens listened to the news religiously. He often took notes and just put them on a bulletin board in his kitchen over the sink. This morning he was surprised to learn that a San Francisco art dealer had killed Jesus Melendez. He realized the names were identical and had called the maritime commission. Of course, there he learned that the body they had in the morgue was related to the guy killed the night before. It was absolutely fascinating. Charlie wanted to call Dan Levine in the attorney general's office. He poured a second cup of coffee, sat down at his small kitchen table and gave himself ample time to think about the matter. They should be having the coroner's inquest pretty soon on the first murder. The coroner was really mad because the body was still in the morgue. The sheriff didn't want to talk about it, and Mr. Delaney had been busy. Charlie's brow wrinkled. Right then and there he decided to call Mr. Levine even if it was just to tell him he had been keeping a good eye on his girl. *Who knows*, Charlie thought, *maybe, just maybe, I'll get some little shred of information from Dan Levine. It couldn't hurt.*

Chapter 15

A Murder Scene

Mr. Henry's apartment looked immaculate except for the police yellow tape, a chalk outline of the place where the body was found and the blood splattered drapes and rug. The furnishings were European and obviously expensive. Bert whistled when he saw the bedroom. The bed was a copy of a Louis XIV gold leaf carved canopy and headboard draped with brocade fabrics in red and gold and had a spread to match. Bert really impressed Ted when he explained what it was.

"How the hell do you know a thing like that?" Ted snarled.

Bert laughed. "I didn't, but I had you goin' there for a minute. Didn't I?" The fat man's jowls jiggled when he laughed. "It's up there on the wall. See, there's the picture of the bed in the Louvre in Paris. It says in the news article from the *San Francisco Examiner* that it's a copy. I just thought you'd be impressed. Mr. Henry sure knew how to get publicity for his gallery."

Ted ignored him, moving around searching things that looked interesting. He was a little miffed because Dan was taking Bert to Crescent City. He knew his partner deserved it, but it still bothered him. They had worked the case together.

"Well, well . . ." Bert said, "Now, here's an interesting item."

He held up an open telephone directory. "There's a number here for the Crescent City Sheriff's Office. Who do you suppose Mr. Henry was calling there?"

"It probably was to check up on the perp who broke into Terry Hamilton's house. The snitch definitely named Czechof as one of Henry's buddies." Ted moved away from the vanity and went into the bathroom.

Bert went back out into the living room to retrieve their bug. "Hey, that's funny. It's gone. I was right, Mr. Henry knew the bug was there. That's why he raced out of here pretending to be Jesus."

Ted came into the room. "We'd better search this place good. I still feel as if there are a lot of unanswered questions. After all, Bert, how many people would have a wig, makeup and clothes handy to look like someone else?"

"Well, it is possible that Mr. Henry was waiting for Jesus to get the insurance money and then planned to just take off for South America pretending to be Jesus. Mr. Henry would just fade from sight. That way he could start a new life as either person or just evade the law wherever he was. I sure don't think he and Jesus were getting along, not from the conversation on that tape after he got back from Boston. Henry had already talked Jesus into killing Soto. What was one more body? Henry was diabolical."

They spent another hour and came up empty. Bert was troubled when he drove away from the apartment. He thought Ted felt the same way. Something wasn't right. It was probably staring them both in the face, but they missed it. That thought would keep him up nights until he got a handle on it.

Terry's call to Dan changed his plans. Martin Delaney had called the coroner's inquest for the next day. Dan decided he should be there with her. He put in a call to her lawyer and learned that Jess was in court until Friday. Dan left a message at the law office saying he was free to attend and would represent her during the inquest. He also said he would be in touch with Jess by the following evening to fill him in on all pertinent matters.

The two investigators returned to the office at noon. Dan asked them to follow up on some leads the analyst had requested. Ted left. Dan asked Bert to stay behind for a few minutes.

"Look, I've just learned that Martin Delaney has called a coroner's inquest for tomorrow. I called the terminal and one of our planes is going to Seattle at three o'clock. I intend to be on it. They can drop me at Medford and I'll get the state police to ferry me or Terry can pick me up. I want you to drive the pool car down tomorrow and stay until we are finished. Bring some old clothes because we will be out on the boats and it probably will be cold."

Bert's smile widened. "Yes, sir, sounds good to me."

Dan's look relaxed. It was pleasant to think about being with Terry again even under these circumstances. "Oh, by the way, Bert, I'll ask Terry if you can stay at the house. I really don't think she would mind." He winked. "I think she needs protecting, don't you?"

Bert assured him she did. They both laughed and the investigator left humming all the way to the parking garage. This was the part of the job he loved best. He also liked the idea of being friends with the chief deputy.

Dan left instructions with his secretary before driving to his apartment. It was almost two o'clock by the time he arrived. He pushed the packing, hurried to the parking garage and then drove quickly out into traffic. Fortunately, he had his cellular with him. Dialing, he listened to the line purring.

"Hey, beautiful, what are you doing this afternoon?" he said in answer to her "Hello."

"Why don't you tell me?"

"Picking me up in Medford at the airport."

"Oh, Dan that's great. I'll be there. What time?"

Dan scanned his watch. "We leave here at three. I guess, five would be good. We can stop at some fun place and have dinner on the way back to your house. Okay?"

"Wonderful!" she sounded excited. "See you, darling. I can't wait."

The plane was being gassed when Dan parked in the private terminal parking lot. He pulled the luggage out of his trunk and carried it to the steps where the pilot loaded it into the cargo compartment for him. They exchanged greetings and Dan boarded quickly and strapped himself into a seat. Shortly, he heard the distinctive whine of the jet's engines starting. He leaned back, grinned and closed his eyes, they would be together again in just a few hours, and the lawyer couldn't wait to hold her.

* * * * *

Terry took Baron everywhere with her. Dan wanted it that way. She definitely thought it was for her own protection and capitulated easily. Since they talked about the case involving the captain not having been solved, Terry began to be more observant. The drive to Medford took several hours giving her ample time to review the facts. She wanted to talk to Dan about a number of things, some of which had nothing to do with the case. But, the case was really puzzling. For instance, who killed the captain? Why was he killed, and were they really after her or was she just at the wrong place at the wrong time? It would all be explained in the future, she imagined, but in the meantime she was going to be with the man she loved. That thought made Terry grin appreciatively. He was wonderful. "Yes sir, Baron," she said out loud in the Jeep, "he is wonderful."

At the airport Terry left the dog in the car and walked out to the tarmac in front of the terminal. Squinting, she cupped her eyes with her hand to watch the jet land and taxi toward her. The door popped before he climbed down and reached for the luggage being offered by the co-pilot. Terry run out to greet him. He kissed her, and they walked arm in arm toward the waiting Jeep.

"Hi, hon."

"I'm so glad to see you." She glanced over and admired his open necked pale blue shirt and tan slacks. Against his dark coloring, he looked very sophisticated, which raised a satisfied smile. "I missed you," she said climbing into the Jeep and turning on the engine before driving out onto the nearby highway.

"Oh, Terry, it's great to be here. Where are we going for dinner? I want it to be special." Dan leaned against the headrest, relaxed and took off his dark glasses.

"You sure are in a good mood."

"I certainly am. I'm free for awhile and I'm going to be with the woman I love and her great dog. I'd say, I'm a lucky man." He smiled pleasantly. The dog yipped and they both laughed. Dan reached back and petted him.

"Well, there is a really nice inn by the Smith River in the woods. I know you'll like it. It sounds as if you want our dinner to be somewhere rustic but cozy. We'll be there in about an hour. So . . . sit back and rest, Mr. Levine, and tell me all your news."

Terry was quiet driving while Dan filled her in on the murder, Bert's snitch and Mr. Henry's untimely demise.

Terry shuddered as he explained the whole ugly story.

"Your friend Adam was a big help, hon. It was actually because of his astute questioning that we were able to find out what was behind it all. They were willing to wait all this time to get that painting out of your grandmother's estate. By now it is worth so much more and, of course, you've got to decide what you want Adam to do about it."

"Funny, Dan, that they didn't just steal it?"

"Oh, you might think so, but they didn't want to bring attention to it. One good news story and the cat would have been out of the bag. It would have been front page in many countries. It's worth over two million dollars, darling. But, getting back to the painting – What do you want Adam to do about it?"

"Umm, I've been thinking a lot about that, Dan. I think it would be best if Adam contacts the Catholic Bishop in Mexico City and relates the story. I want them to pay me exactly what grandfather paid them . . . no more. I don't want to make money from their loss."

Dan looked over at her with an admiring glance. "That's very big of you. They would probably pay a great deal to get it back. It is one of their icons. The news clippings that Maria Wheeler deciphered for us said the painting came from Spain and was extremely valuable, but it had a very deep religious significance. It belonged to Pope Pius V."

"I wanted to talk to you first, Dan, but that is what I really want to do with it."

"Okay. We'll call Adam first thing tomorrow and get that matter out of the way."

He saw Terry relaxing as they talked. It pleased him that what he thought actually mattered to her.

"Dan, there's a place up ahead where I like to stop. I can let Baron run, and you and I can just visit. It is quite beautiful." She pulled off the snaking, ribboned tar and parked.

Looking out, his mouth dropped open. They were in the midst of the giant redwood trees. After opening the door he exclaimed. "Terry, this is magnificent. I've never seen them before." The lawyer's mouth gaped as he twisted to look high above them at what appeared to be unending trees.

They climbed out, and the dog bounded off into the forest. Terry led the way into a deepening glade. There were downed giant trunks, too large to see over, deep green ferns, moss and the silent forest.

"I feel as if I'm in a cathedral," Dan said in awe.

The enormity of the trees totally captivated them. They stood together in that silent world gazing up without speaking. Dan curled her into his arms and whispered. "I hadn't planned this to happen here, but it seems very right."

"What darling?" She looked up into his eyes and absorbed the love waiting there.

He reached into his pocket and withdrew a velvet box. "Terry, will you be my wife?" he said handing it to her.

She was really surprised. "Oh, Dan! What a wonderful place to ask me. I'll never forget it as long as I live." Her expressive eyes sparkled in the darkness of the glade. She laughed feeling a tingle in the pit of her stomach as she opened the box.

Dan watched, subverting his mounting excitement, he looked somber, expectant.

Terry gasped gazing at the sparkling, blue white stone. "It is beautiful. I love you." She clutched him close with her hands folding the box against them. "Put it on me, please."

"You didn't answer my question." he said hopefully.

"I'd be proud to be your wife, Dan. I can't believe this is happening. In the midst of all of this turmoil and pain and chicanery that something so wonderful could happen. I'm delirious."

Dan slid the ring onto her finger. She stretched out her hand to admire it. "It is the most beautiful ring I've ever seen. How did you know my size?"

He chuckled. "I put a string around your finger while you were asleep. Simple, huh?"

They kissed passionately in that wondrous forest. "I'll love you forever," he said in a soft, sensuous voice.

"Don't ever stop, Dan. I need you more than life itself."

They called the dog and walked arm in arm toward the Jeep. Once inside he kissed her again.

"Do you have any idea how happy you've made me? I keep

thinking this is not real. It is too perfect and, sometimes, it seems a little frightening."

"I know how you feel. I was afraid to love you, because everyone I love is taken away. I need you, and I always will. It is wonderful to know I have you to turn to." Her gaze softened and a tear slid down her cheek.

"Terry, honey, don't cry. We're supposed to be happy." He cradled her in his arms, and she smiled softly. "I know. I am silly, huh? I guess, I'm crying because I'm so happy. You forget, darling, I'm an artist – we are all sensitive. That's what it takes to create."

"Turn on the engine, and let's go to that inn. We need some wine to toast each other."

At half past seven they went into the Hidden Forest Inn. Terry led the way to a place on the glassed-in porch. They could see and hear the tumultuous water cascading over the boulders in the Smith River. Overhead were the giant redwood trees and the late, setting sunlight slowly turning from deep red to purple had settled in shafts into the forest. The candles were lit and Dan poured their wine before he proposed the toast.

"To my beautiful Terry, forever."

"Forever," she said softly smiling wistfully.

He took her hand admiring the ring he had just placed on her third finger, left hand. "It looks good on you. I tried to pick out something you'd like. I knew you had such good taste, and I wanted it to be special."

"Dan, listen to me. You are special. The ring is special and our love is special. I also need to ask you some things."

"What?" He seemed surprised.

"Do you love children?"

"Certainly. What a question."

"Well, I mean, I want children, Dan, maybe three or four. I grew up alone, and that's not good. After all I have no one," she blushed. "Sorry, I had no one . . . Now, darling, I have you, and I want my children to have someone always."

"That's understandable. I do want children, Terry. But, could we have some time first? I don't want to share you with anyone right now or in the near future."

Terry began to laugh. "I must sound ridiculous. Honey, I just needed to know how you felt about that. It matters, and I won't bring it up again. Well, not for a long time . . . okay?"

"Terry, honey, I haven't thought about a lot of things, but there is one thing." He looked serious. "I know you know where I work. Can you live there? I mean, would it bother you to leave here?"

"No, I'd just sell the house, Dan. There are a lot of memories, but it's time to start fresh. We can get a house near some water or in the mountains with a view. I'd like that."

He grinned. "Gosh, I haven't thought about a lot of things yet." He seemed surprised. "I don't like apartment living anyway. It was just somewhere to live while I waited."

"Waited! Waited for what?"

"While I waited to find you. I knew you'd come along someday." He chuckled. "I still can't believe how it happened. Life is unbelievable."

They ordered steaks and all of the trimmings. Then afterwards they had the bones wrapped for Baron. It had been a night they wouldn't forget. Baron wouldn't forget it either – they gave him the bones from two steaks, and they sat on a downed log laughing as he devoured both of them.

It was late when they returned to the house. Mrs. Gordon, the housekeeper, had pinned a note on the refrigerator saying she had gone to bed at ten. Terry offered Dan a cup of tea, which he declined.

"I just want to go up to our room and make love."

They put out the light and climbed up the stairs. Once inside he undressed her slowly. They kissed each other ardently, passionately repeating their promises over and over. The sex was gratifying, and although they were madly in love, they knew they were completely compatible. The love making renewed them and was just as arduous as it had been on the coast. It lasted for a long time.

At 9:00 A.M. the next day they were both at the courthouse suitably dressed and glad to be getting this matter out of the way. Terry eyed Martin Delaney from under her dark glasses. He hadn't noticed Dan yet; she subverted a smirk when he finally did as Martin did a double take. Dan looked very proper in a dark suit, a white shirt and a red and blue striped tie, which she selected for him that morning from among the three in his suitcase.

He had explained the entire procedure to her while she brushed out her long auburn hair and rolled it into a top knot at the dressing table. She was struggling to put the hair pins into her hair and caught Dan actually pausing from tying his necktie to watch. Looking up she said, "What?"

"I was just thinking that we are acting like married people must act."

Terry laughed. She put her hunter green pant suit on and buttoned up the white blouse. Dan was already dressed. He whistled. "You look beautiful, soon-to-be-Mrs. Levine."

"I like that, Dan. Mrs. Terry Levine. Uh huh . . . it sounds just right."

Later, sitting in the court room, Terry remembered Dan's words, *soon-to-be-Mrs. Dan Levine*. They had a nice ring. She glanced at him sideways. He was handsome and there was no question about it, she loved him more than she could ever have imagined.

The judge was quite old. He seemed tired as he entered, sat down and banged his gavel. The bailiff had introduced him as Judge Rosco Emery. There were only about twenty people in the room. Dan had told her it wouldn't be a long procedure.

She wasn't even apprehensive. Martin wouldn't try anything with Dan at her side.

Shortly, the bailiff called Sid Brown, the county coroner, to the stand. He was sworn in and began to testify. He said he examined the body of a Mexican man, approximately fifty years of age, five foot nine inches tall, weighing 180 pounds that had been found floating in the bay near Battery Point on the fifth of June in 1996. He stated the cause of death was a severe trauma to the back of the skull from a blunt instrument probably a heavy metal rod. He said the body had been in the water a long time and the exact time of death was unknown but his educated assessment was probably around nine hours. The judge excused the coroner. He got up and left the court room.

The next witness called was Terry Hamilton. Dan patted her hand before she got up to go to the examining table.

"Will the bailiff please swear in this witness?"

Terry was sworn in and then, the bailiff said, "State your name, please."

"Terry Hamilton, your honor."

"Would you please tell this court exactly what took place on June fifth of this year regarding this matter."

It only took minutes. It was very simple, and Terry didn't mind at all. Just a few feet away, smiling at her was her future husband. She marveled at the fact of the matter and how reassuring it felt. Dan's look was pleasant and proper, but she felt his warmth. After she'd finished, the judge thanked her and told her she was excused. Terry stood up and walked toward Dan who was waiting to lead her out into the hallway.

"Hello to both of you." Martin was waiting outside. "I was wondering if you would be my guests for lunch?"

Dan reacted pleasantly. "If it's all right with Terry." He glanced at her and, seeing her nod, accepted.

"I've got some matters to clear up here. Why don't you meet

me at the Seafood House on the dock? Terry knows where it is."

"That's fine, Martin. What time?"

Glancing at his watch, Martin said, "Oh, how about noon? I should be finished by then."

Dan led Terry toward the Jeep. "What happens now?" she asked.

"Well, they will sign papers releasing the body to the next of kin. If there isn't anyone here to claim the body, then, the county will arrange a burial in potter's field. In fact, the real reason for this hearing is just to establish the cause of death certified by someone official and then to arrange to dispose of the body."

Terry had to admit it was interesting. "Now, why are we having lunch with Martin?" She grinned. "The real reason."

"Well, darling, we are going to start to search tomorrow. I need the cooperation of the county attorney and the sheriff. I don't really like telling anyone, but it is necessary; we are on their turf. It saves a lot of trouble later if we are up front with them now." He glanced over before squeezing her hands and saying, "Besides, I want to tell him my good news." Dan beamed all the way back to the Jeep.

Chapter 16

The Investigator's Search

The drive from Sacramento to Crescent City in the pool car was a rare treat for Bert. He got up early. Today, eager to get started for the long, beautiful drive along the coast road, he hurried out of his condo overlooking the Sacramento River at 4:00 A.M. The fog lifted considerably after he crossed the Golden Gate Bridge. He grinned, and taking a deep breath, sat back and relaxed against the headrest after first putting the car on cruise control. There was never any traffic on the road this early in the morning. Anyone needing to get to Frisco wouldn't take the chance that the fog might be bad and would have used the inland highway. Other than that, it was mostly used by tourists who were still asleep. Bert's smile reflected the view up ahead of twisted coves and mountains surging from above to the vast Pacific down below on the left. The highway he was viewing sliced in and out on its way to Seattle via upper California and the jagged Oregon coast line. This drive, especially at this time of day when the fog was down, was the stuff travel agents used for documentaries. The fat man's face broadened into a contented grin.

Reaching into the bag at his side, he extracted a plastic cup. The fresh brew tasted especially good. It was handy to know about the old newsstand on Market Street where hot coffee and fresh bagels were available twenty-four hours daily.

He sipped thoughtfully while his orderly mind began to channel the facts. Now he would have time to sort through the pieces of the puzzle. Bert's deep voice cut through the silence in the vehicle. "Okay . . . Mr. Henry contracted Terry Hamilton to show one of her paintings. Uh huh. Now, someone had to have informed him that she was living in Crescent City. The fact that she was an artist only enhanced the deal. It was the perfect foil. Terry goes to San Fran' and that bastard put her through a lot of hell just because he enjoyed it. She wasn't used to being badgered and walked out, leaving Henry with egg all over his dumb face."

Bert chuckled sarcastically. "I'd like to have seen that. Now, Henry and Jesus are left without entry to the art works. Big question? Who was the initiator? Who would have known a lot about the grandmother, the fact that she was dead and that her stuff would be sold? Okay, I'll put that aside for the moment.

Jesus was in bed with Henry, and they weren't getting along. Boy, is that the understatement of the year?" He cackled remembering the fight he overheard from the apartment bug the night of the murder. They were obviously planning to steal the bouillon from the salvage operation either for someone else or for Jablonski. "So, let's say Jablonski is innocent . . . hypothetically. That means someone else organized the plan to do both. That is to get Terry's grandmother's painting, sell it back to the Church for a couple of million and make off with the sunken treasure. Wow! These guys are enterprising. It's a pretty neat plan. Either way they get rich. They can split and if there are more than two . . . there is plenty to go around. Of course, they just kill anybody who gets in the way. That's easy.

Okay, now, if it's Jablonski, that makes more sense. I mean he is pissed because he has spent a couple of mill' and the state is shutting him out. He, or someone close to him, already knows the state has the locator map. Well, let's say Czechof has already told someone in the fish company about the map. That would explain Dan's apartment being burglarized; that would also explain the phone taps and the two attempts to break into Terry's house."

Bert took a long swig of the now-cooled coffee. He made a face – it tasted bitter. "Okay, there has to be someone close by who knows every move. It is a small town. I'm guessing everybody knows everybody's business. Of course, it would be easy since Terry has a housekeeper to pay her off. Terry said she needed money. Dan said she wasn't the type. Oh, hell, what's a type? Ain't many people who aren't for sale, but this narrows the field. If Terry let's me stay there, I can root around. Dan said she had a handy man, but he said the guy was straight as a stick."

Bert frowned again. "Czechof was a seaman – twenty years experience. He probably ran the wets for Soto. Okay, they were fishing regularly, selling the catch to the fish plant. If the wets complained, they'd just dump them overboard. I could see that. They were making money. That means they got boats, knowledge and people to sabotage this upcoming deal. If I'm right," he laughed out loud, "and I usually am. When we send the trollers out to salvage, we are gonna have a problem because whoever is feeding the information back to San Fran' is still in Crescent City. And, that brings up another problem. Captain Tillman was killed there. Czechof was in jail . . . so, it wasn't him. Since you can't break into that lighthouse, it is a good bet that he knew his killer or the killer had a key. Wow! This bears real thinking. I think this whole deal is extremely dangerous. Yes sir, I'll bet I'm right, and Czechof is out on bail. Son of a bitch. These damn judges don't get it. They let the perp out, screaming about civil rights, and they seem to forget there are innocents out there just waiting to be preyed upon. And, that guy wouldn't hesitate, if I'm any judge of character."

Bert had five hours to sort out every scenario. He played it back over and over in his fertile mind. If there was anything awry a bell sounded in his brain. There was still a killer loose.

197

The big boys were about to hone in on Crescent City. Whoever was guilty would know that. It was only a question of time until they made a move. Bert remembered Dan saying Terry needed protection. Was Dan being facetious or extra careful? Dan was nobody's fool. Bert put his foot to the pedal. It was time to get this show on the road, and his panic alert was working overtime.

* * * * *

Terry looked lovingly at Dan as he ordered coffee. Martin was late for their lunch date. She slid her hand through his arm in the booth, enjoying the warmth of his body and the feeling of stability the fabric of his suit gave her. He was a quality human being – a gentleman; he was loving and kind; he was here to protect her, and she felt safe at long last.

Dan looked over and squeezed her hand. "I forgot to ask you, hon. Do you mind if Bert stays at your house while we are here?"

"No. Not at all. He can stay down in your old room." Her gaze cast over him seductively and she cooed, "I've got other plans for you."

Dan's laughter sounded provocative. He leaned against her and gave her a quick kiss on the cheek. "You know, Terry, being in love is very" . . . he paused and looked away then said, "uplifting."

"Among other things." They both chuckled softly.

"Seriously, though, hon, I'll be out on the boats all day, and I want you to be very vigilant. Remember, we still have a killer loose. And, I think that person is still here."

Terry shuddered.

Dan put his arm around her shoulder and squeezed her. "Don't be afraid, just be careful."

They looked up and saw Martin approaching. He seemed harried.

"Bad day, counselor?" Dan inquired as the prosecutor sat

down, unbuttoned his suit jacket and spread out in the seat before sighing.

Martin's frown was immediately replaced with a fixed smile. "Oh, just the usual stuff. The coroner has been raising hell because that body was here for so long. There is no next of kin." Martin shrugged picking up a menu. "So, I guess, we'll just do potter's field the way we did with the captain."

"That reminds me. Terry received a letter from the captain. It is, in effect, a last will and testament leaving his worldly possessions to her," Dan explained.

Surprise registered, Martin said, "REALLY?"

Terry felt chilled. That was the same voice he used on the beach that morning . . . accusing.

Dan continued. "I'd like for you to arrange for us to go and examine his personal effects. I doubt if there is anything she wants, but we need to go. Then the matter can be finalized."

"What do you have to do with this, Dan? After all she has retained council, and he seems quite adequate."

"He is." Dan picked up Terry's left hand and exhibited it. "Terry has agreed to be my wife." Dan smiled. "I know you will want to congratulate me."

The man blanched. The news had obviously taken him completely off guard. Forcing a smile, he said, "Of course. My gosh, that was quick wasn't it? What's the hurry?"

Dan's smile broadened as he clutched her hand. Looking at the woman who returned his smile he said, "We are in love. Aren't we, hon?"

Terry became effusive. "Yes, we are in love and just want to be together. It is the most wonderful feeling." They made eye contact, and jealousy surged through the prosecutor.

"Oh, well, in that case I'll arrange it, soon. Of course, you must realize since the captain was murdered we have confiscated a few things that cannot be released until the trial. If there ever is one?"

"Surely you have some suspects?"

Martin coughed, his color deepened looking at her. "Just one."

Dan stood up and pulled Terry up after him. "My fiancée and I will be leaving – now."

"Wait. I'm really sorry. Let's be realistic here, Dan. Terry found the body. There isn't anyone else, and now, you tell me he left her all of his possessions. There is about $50,000 in that bank account. It is circumstantial, but it is a motive. Right?"

Dan's mouth was tight, his face turned ashen, and Terry couldn't believe the color of his eyes. Rage laced the look. He turned to her saying sternly, "Terry, please wait for me in the car."

"Dan," she pleaded, "don't, honey. It isn't worth it."

"Terry," he demanded. "WAIT IN THE CAR!"

She left and did not look back.

Martin's obsessive reaction had done it again. He already regretted the move. "Look, Dan, let's not be hasty. I know she probably didn't do it . . . it just looks bad."

"Like someone is trying to set her up," Dan said through clenched teeth.

"Maybe, but I'm the prosecutor. I have to consider every angle. You know that's true."

"What I know is," Dan said leaning into Martin's face, "you have unmitigating gall. You are a jealous, son of a bitch and you wanted to spoil our happiness. Now, you listen to me. If she is harassed in any way, I will make your life a living hell. I came here to tell you what was going to take place shortly, but, since you behaved in such an insensitive manner, forget it – you can get your information secondhand. There is one other thing, Martin. You even try to frame Terry for this murder, and I won't be responsible for what I'll do. I am a very resourceful man, and don't you forget it."

Martin felt the sweat rise beneath his shirt. He had just made an enemy, a powerful enemy, who would not go away – ever.

Terry was crying when Dan jumped into the Jeep. He was still seething and his hands shook. He had wanted to punch Martin's face in, but he was here representing the Attorney General of California and the headlines he pictured made him cringe. Suddenly, he heard her crying. "Oh! Terry, I'm sorry, honey. Don't cry – that jealous bastard isn't worth it."

She put her head onto his willing shoulder and sobbed. He pulled out a handkerchief and handed it to her. "Oh, Dan, it was all so perfect, and now it is spoiled. I don't want to lose you. My God, Dan, what did I ever do to deserve all of this? They have to know I didn't murder anybody. Besides, I loved that old man. He was my friend."

Dan sobered. "Come on, stop crying. Where can we go to eat? You need some food, and I need to call Jess."

It was late afternoon when they finally arrived at Terry's home. Their lunch had been toasted cheese sandwiches and ice tea prepared at the diner near the highway to Medford where they finally settled down and had a good talk.

Dan asked her if she would mind going to the sheriff's office with him while he informed Ripley of the plan to bring in the boats to search on the following morning. Although Terry didn't mind, she waited in the car. Deputy Stevens drove in and saw her there. He got out of his car and came over to say hello. Removing his hat first, he leaned into the passenger side window and was cordial.

"Hello," she answered. "How are you?"

"I'm fine, ma'am. Are you here alone?"

"No. Dan Levine is here with me. He went in to see Sheriff Ripley on business. He'll be right out. Why don't you wait and say hello?"

Charlie thanked her and said he would.

Shortly, Dan exited the building and waved to Charlie. "Hi.

Glad to see you, Charlie." Dan extended a hand. After that Dan explained what was happening the next day.

Charlie seemed surprised. "That's great, Mr. Levine. I hope you are successful."

"Look, Charlie, why don't you call me Dan? I'd like that much better."

The deputy glanced down at his boots and grinned. "Okay, Dan."

"Terry and I are having one of my investigators here this evening. Why don't you come by and have a beer with us? I think it would be helpful if you two met. He is quite impressed with your work."

Charlie's grin widened; he was proud that they would invite him. "Hey, I'd like that. It always helps to know people in your field. We can all use some help now and again."

Terry smiled. "Dan, why don't you invite Charlie for dinner. I'll have Marge set another plate. It will be nice, and you boys can really talk about this matter."

Dan appreciated her thoughtfulness. "Great. Shall we say about seven? Is that good for you, Charlie? Oh, and just casual, please."

Bert was waiting when they returned. He loved the house. Terry gave him the full tour before showing him to his room. Dan told him to freshen up, get comfortable and come up to have a drink after.

By half past five, after the lovers returned from taking the dog for a run on the beach, they all gathered in Terry's studio for a drink. Dan opened two beers in the kitchen, picked a bottle of wine out of the refrigerator, took a wine glass and carried them upstairs on a tray to where Terry and Bert were enjoying the telescope.

They sat down on the divans, and the investigator began to tell his boss what conclusions he'd come to.

"Would you two like to be alone?" Terry said pleasantly. "I really need to see how Marge is getting on anyway."

After she left, Dan explained what had happened that morning in the restaurant.

Bert fumed. "What is it with this guy?"

"I think he is mad because Terry agreed to marry me."

The full face expanded into a broad smile. "Hey, Dan, congratulations. Terry is quite a catch." He winked and took a swallow of beer. "I hope you both will be really happy."

"If we live long enough. It seems somebody doesn't want us to have any peace." Dan shook his head, and there was serious concern in his look.

"Are you worried?"

"Yes, frankly, I am. I think whoever murdered the captain is after Terry to frame her. That damn Delaney is trying to make a name for himself at our expense. He has to know she didn't murder anyone, and it's all circumstantial, but people have been indicted for less."

"Didn't you hire Jess Timeron to be her legal advisor? Hell, he's a tiger. I wouldn't want him after my butt."

"Yes. And that reminds me, he's going to call as soon as he gets back from court."

"Look, Dan. Before Terry gets back we got to pow wow."

"Okay. Shoot."

"I want your permission to put the state police on alert. I got this bad feeling about tomorrow. Ted is supposed to be checking on something for me. He'll be calling soon. If it's what I think it is – we got problems."

Dan frowned. "Like what?"

"Like I'm figuring that Czechof is on his way here with Mexican divers and guns. I don't think these guys will give up without a fight. It could get really nasty."

"What the hell is he doing out?"

"He made bail. And, don't get me started on why he was able to get bail set. My cockles get crazy over this stuff."

Terry came back into the room and picked up her glass. "I want to toast us, darling."

Dan lifted his glass. He grinned and saluted her. "To my bride-to-be."

Bert said, "Here, Here. To two of the nicest people I know. I'll dance at your wedding."

They all laughed, and for the moment, things actually seemed normal.

The phone rang; it was for Dan. Terry and Bert went out onto the balcony to view the lighthouse with her telescope.

"Jess, yes, Dan Levine. I've got a problem here, and I need you to take care of it." While Dan explained the situation, Bert asked Terry to point out the probable location of the sunken ship. They took turns scanning the horizon; it was very interesting to the man who listened attentively as she explained the sinking and what was on board. After awhile they scanned the lighthouse. Terry said, "You know, I love that old building – as you can see from my paintings. It now has so many rotten memories, I feel really sad about it."

Bert listened attentively. He understood her pain. He felt anger that there was still an enemy out there who wanted to harm them, and he firmed a reserve to protect them both no matter what.

Dan came out after he'd finished the call. He cupped her shoulder affectionately. "I heard a car drive up below. I think Charlie is here; let's go down and greet him."

Dinner was served shortly. Bert eyed the tasteful dining room thinking how lucky Dan was to have found someone who could help him with his career and be a good partner. His own wife had run off with someone a long time ago. He never got over it. It was, perhaps, the reason he was so cynical. There had been other occasions to love someone, but he could never trust anyone again. He watched Dan and Terry feeling remorse.

Charlie's pleasure at having been invited was apparent. He and Bert exchanged ideas readily and with verve. Terry watched happily knowing they were all trying to protect her. During dinner, Ted called. The big man went downstairs to use his cellular.

*   *   *   *   *

"Listen, I followed the leads and you were right. Czechof was meeting in bars with thugs the likes of which I haven't seen in a long time," Ted said. "Our tap was removed and the judge wouldn't reissue, but I still got a guy on the inside. I honestly believe Jablonski is clean. It looks as if Soto and Jesus were in bed with Czechof, but there has to be someone down there in Crescent City who is feeding them current information. Bert, these people are smart. I always give the devil his due. I think they were receiving calls on Jablonski's telephone in the fish company."

"What makes you say that?"

"Because I found out that Jablonski was never there. His office is in the National Ship Salvage Corporation building. They listed the telephone in his name to throw anybody off who might be listening. Pretty smart, huh?

"Anyway, to answer your big question, they sailed this evening – four boats. I got some suggestions. Do you want them?"

"Sure. Why not?"

"Well, I'd like to call INS because I figure we can't stop them for a crime that hasn't yet been committed. But, I'm damn sure half of those birds are illegal. That way they could pick them up and if the attorney general were to ask the feds, I think they'd do it." He paused to give Bert a chance to respond.

"That sounds good, Ted. I think you are right on."

"There is something else. If they get picked up, they are going to say they are just going fishing. We'd have a tough time getting them off the water unless we can prove some kind of crime."

Bert sounded suddenly reluctant, "Stephen Landry is going to want proof before he is going to call in the INS. Wets are a political issue here. I know he won't stick out his neck until we prove who they are. And you know, Ted, we can't do that."

Ted sounded dejected. "I know you are right dammit."

"Hey, maybe, Dan can do it. If he calls and asks for state police, they will send them. I know they have high-speed chase units fully equipped for apprehensions, and they have harbor patrol boats. But, I want a helicopter standing by close. I just gotta hunch we might need it."

"What for?"

"That's the hell of it, Ted. I don't know, but my gut never fails me – so, I'm gonna go with it. Better safe than sorry."

"Okay. What do you need from me?"

"I want you to get to the telephone company with a sub-poena to get telephone records, business and personal, for the assistant district attorney and the sheriff."

Ted whistled. "Are you sure? They'll raise hell if you're wrong."

Bert grunted, "If I'm wrong I'll say *mea culpa*. Hell, I hope I'm wrong, but I don't think I am."

"I hate to admit it, but your gut is right more than it's wrong. I'll get it tomorrow, first thing."

They were all in the den when Bert returned. Terry had saved dessert for him with coffee. It was waiting on the tray near his chair. He grinned. "Hey, that's more like it. I love chocolate cake."

"Charlie was just describing his theory about the dives and what might happen here," Dan said.

While the investigator began to savor his cake, the young deputy expounded on his thoughts.

"It all makes sense," Dan admitted when he'd finished.

"We agree, Charlie. In fact, I think we should call in the state police now, and have a chopper standing by," Bert said still chewing on the cake.

"Why?"

Bert didn't know why, so he had to do some quick thinking. "Well, we are all going to be out there." He pointed toward the ocean. "The fastest way to get back and forth is by chopper. You don't know what might come up. Even if there were a fight and someone got shot, you could fly them to the hospital. It is just expedient."

Terry said, "He's right, darling. I know I'd feel better if there was a helicopter nearby."

Charlie nodded thoughtfully.

Dan's capitulation followed. He went to the phone in the next room and ordered the equipment they had agreed upon.

Charlie left and Bert excused himself to go to bed.

"Wait!" Terry said. "I have something for you. I'll go and get it."

After she left Bert said, "Dan, do you think Martin Delaney is the killer?"

Dan nodded. "It's beginning to look that way. I hate to think that, but evidence is evidence."

Terry entered and handed her guest a wrapped package.

"Hey, what is this? I'm not used to presents." He looked secretly pleased scrinching his face up in anticipation while his fingers tore at the string surrounding the cardboard. "Wow! What's this for – it's beautiful. I love it."

Terry grinned. "You were so nice to arrange that wonderful place for Dan and me. I wanted to do something for both you and Ted. I have one for him also. I'll give it to you to take back when this awful mess is over."

"Terry, this painting is really good. I'm not much on art, but I'll be so proud to have it. I'm going to put it over the fireplace in my living room. Thank you so much." The big man literally flew to his room. He felt on top of everything for the first time in a long while.

After they went upstairs Dan took her into his arms. "I'm so proud of you. You don't mind sharing what you have with others. And, you never pull rank with anyone. That's a really nice quality."

She blushed. "What he did for us was special. I've never had such a wonderful weekend, darling. I'll never forget it. So, if I have something to give in return – it's pleasant for me."

Dan unbuttoned the blouse and slipped it off. He kissed her neck and shoulders and slipped the bra straps off exposing her breasts. They lay down. His lips caressed her breasts slowly, deliberately while he slid off her slacks. Shortly, she wrapped her legs around him and clutched his shoulders close. He pulled away and got up to undress. Their bodies felt hot as they clung to each other, kissing over and over, rubbing closer until Dan thought he would explode. He entered her quickly and the rhythm of their coupling brought their delirium closer and closer. She moaned. He knew he brought her to that place, and their love was as perfect as he ever could have imagined possible. He gathered her into his arms whispering his joy and the thrill of loving her. He told her of the emptiness of fighting to achieve but having no one with whom to share it. He told her of the love he would give her forever and of the life they would have together. He told her he had never been this happy in his life, and he begged her to be careful.

She sat up. He felt her shiver. "Oh, Dan, maybe it is too perfect, my darling."

"DON'T SAY THAT!" He sounded angry.

"Why not. Look at what keeps happening. I'm terrified that I'll lose you. I need you, Dan. I need you as I've never needed anything before in my life."

He put her into the bed and crawled in next to her pulling her close and feeling her breath on his chest. They clung together in that quiet place. Finally, they slept a deep and troubled sleep.

Chapter 17

Hunting for Treasure

The morning seemed electric. Dan, eager to look for the wreck, jumped up and hurried to the shower at 6:00 A.M.

Terry put on a pale pink robe and went down to the kitchen to prepare them both a decent breakfast. Having made the coffee, she plugged it in and listened for the sound of it perking; then, she brought fresh cantaloupes to the cutting board, sliced and cleaned them. After setting the table, she put out the fruit, jam and butter. Marge had previously been to the bakery; Terry hummed as she put the Danish into the microwave. Sitting down with her first cup of coffee, she gave some thought to Dan's upcoming day just as her guest appeared in the doorway.

"Hey, that food smells great. You sure know how to roust a guy."

"That was the idea," she said grinning. "Sit down and I'll pour you a cup. Can you handle some ham and eggs?"

"You bet. I don't get a breakfast like that very often."

"Okay, how do you want the eggs?"

"Over easy."

While Bert sipped the freshly brewed coffee, Terry busied herself at the stove. A succulent aroma of honey cured ham filled the room by the time Dan arrived. He kissed her on the cheek. "I'll have mine soft scrambled with ham, Mrs. Levine-to-be," Dan announced sniffing the tantalizing scent.

Terry's look became winsome. "All right, sit down and I'll get you some coffee, Mr. Levine, husband-to-be."

Everyone laughed; it was a happy atmosphere.

She didn't want Dan going out to the unknown without smiles and a really good breakfast. That, at least, was her contribution to the search. She'd decided not to worry. It seemed expedient to think that the worst was over. She also thought, looking over at him eating with Bert, that their life was taking on some normality and that was very satisfying.

By 6:40 A.M. the men were on their way to the docks. The state police had agreed to be there for a least a week. Two of the trollers, which had been hired, were already in the channel awaiting orders from the state police harbor patrol. A motor dingy moored near a floating pier was ready to take the pair out to their ship. After climbing down the wooden ramp, Dan followed Bert into the dingy. Immediately, the buzzing sound of the outboard motor rose around them while they moved out toward the waiting ships. The captain of the harbor patrol boat, Ro Birch, waited on board the Chris Craft. As they neared he extended a hand.

Birch told them to get comfortable before he climbed up to the flying bridge. He had already explained that his navigator had been studying Captain Tillman's map and was pretty certain where they needed to be. Shortly, the navigator established radio contact with the other captains and the armada prepared to sail. Finally, they cruised in tandem toward the jetty, through the channel and out into the ocean. Birch had been scanning the horizon from the bridge. He yelled to Dan that they did not see any other ships in the vicinity.

Dan only hoped he was right.

Overhead, scudding clouds emitted a thin mist. The fog, clinging to the cliffs up and down the coast line, seemed to dissipate out on the open sea. Overhead, trailing gulls sang their unique song. The ship, a thirty-five foot Chris Craft, cut through the swells evenly, swaying slightly as it rose over the waves. Dan looked behind watching the others bobbing in their wake. The air felt damp and fresh, inhaling deeply the lawyer absorbed it and the raucous sounds of the cawing birds following as his excitement mounted. He was nearing the place where his goal could be attained.

By then they were cruising in the area they believed was their destination. The ships slowed and stopped. It suddenly sounded unusually quiet as the engines idled. Divers were ordered below. Three, wearing scuba gear, went over the side and disappeared beneath black water that was deep. Their job would not be easy.

Bert spent a good deal of his time sitting on a flotation cushion on a bench in the stern. Every time Dan observed him he was talking on his cellular phone. Dan wondered how much he was getting done. There were still a lot of unanswered questions and, maybe, the investigator would get them solved.

The radio crackled incessantly. Dan went down into the cabin to listen to the information being relayed by the other ships and the divers themselves.

The attorney general's office had selected the divers from a list prepared for them by the United States Navy. It had been a coordinated effort because of a request made by the governor of California. That usually got the job done. California was a powerful state as far as electoral votes were concerned, and Washington didn't want to cause political problems there. Dan thought the entire matter had been handled so efficiently, he was equally proud of the outcome and his staff. The group had been hand selected and there were specialists in every field available. Two archaeologists from U.C.L.A. were on their way to Crescent City, but no one thought there was any rush. Dan could only hope they would locate the site within a reasonable length of time. All of this equipment and manpower was costing a bundle. Although it wasn't being taken from his budget, he was responsible, and he didn't carry that burden lightly.

* * * * *

Charlie Stevens knew about the search. He was nothing if not discreet. It didn't seem reasonable to discuss it with anyone in the office. He imagined that Dan had already told the sheriff and the assistant district attorney. There was no reason to tell anyone else, and Charlie had the distinct impression that Dan Levine trusted him. He smiled remembering the relaxing, interesting evening he'd had with Dan, his girl and Bert Maxmillian. The puzzle they presented caused him to spend a lot of time thinking. In fact, they hadn't said so, but he had the impression that they thought someone of note was the contact in Crescent City. He'd decided to try to figure out the plan coming at it from that angle. It wasn't unheard of to suspect a high official. Very often they could cover up better than anyone else because folks were usually afraid to question them. That meant sneaking around when no one was in the office. It just had to be done if he were to help with the case. Besides being dedicated to sleuthing, Charlie definitely liked these people. He really wanted to help them, especially Terry, who seemed to be in jeopardy from some unknown enemy.

Getting a cup of coffee from the office machine, Charlie pushed his ten-gallon hat back on his head and sat down. He leaned way back in the swivel and put his boots on the desk and crossed them. It was quiet. He guessed his boss wasn't in. *Come to think of it, he was gone pretty regular these days.* Charlie frowned. Picking up the phone, he said to the operator, "Charlotte, where did the boss go to that last meeting? Was that in San Diego County? See, I'm supposed to get some papers for him, and I forgot where he said he was?"

"Charlie, no – it was Marin."

He thanked her and wrote the information in his book. He opened his statewide manual and got the telephone number of the Marin County Sheriff's Office. He dialed and listened to the ring. Once it was answered, he pretended to be a reporter who took some photographs of the sheriff at a recent meeting. He asked politely if that meeting was in Marin County? He further stated that he had done several meetings and had mixed up the prints. "Ahm gonna be in a whole peck of trouble, ma'am, ifn I don't get these right."

The operator assured him they had not had a meeting in that county for over six months.

Charlie was very gracious as he thanked her and hung up.

The information was logged into the notebook. Swinging the boots to the floor, he got up and went into the accounting office. The accountant only came in three days a week. He was just finishing up. Charlie greeted him pleasantly. "Hello, Harold. It's nice to see you."

The accountant grunted, nodding his bald head.

"Say, would you be able to let me see the gas receipts for two weeks ago? I'm not sure I put all of mine in the hopper. I'll get into a bundle of trouble if I screw up."

Harold was not known to be pleasant. He looked annoyed, took a deep breath, lifted his eyes impatiently and then, silently, went to the filing cabinet. Shortly, he handed the deputy the cardboard folder.

Charlie thanked him profusely. It only took a few minutes to find what he was looking for. He slipped it out of the folder and left. Seconds later the deputy made a copy of the gas receipt and returned to the accounting office. "Hey! Harold, I forgot to say thank you." He tipped his hat. As the accountant snarled because he'd been disrupted, Charlie slipped the gas receipt back into the folder still laying on the desk.

Later, in his office he sat down to think. Now he had three pieces of evidence. By itself it didn't mean very much, but it was a start. He spent the rest of the morning figuring out his next move, then eventually, went to the patrol car to make a call to the investigator on the patrol ship. "Hey, Bert, it's Charlie."

The conversation was brief; Charlie just wanted to know who Mr. Henry knew in Crescent City besides Terry Hamilton?

"Damn if I know, Charlie. But, if you ever find out, I'd sure like to know." He looked at the phone and grinned. That young deputy was nobody's fool.

It was getting late in the day. Charlie decided to go to the newspaper office and mince around.

At four o'clock the deputy entered the front office of the *Crescent City Herald.* The building, which had been spared by the tidal wave, was old and badly in need of paint. It sat up high overlooking the harbor. The owner-publisher had already left for the day leaving his assistant, young Tilly Leiphart, in charge. Tilly looked old for eighteen. The girl was single and thought Charlie Stevens was just about the most handsome man in town. Her face brightened when she saw him and as the blush rose, tried to hide it. "Hello, deputy, what can I do for you?" she said sweetly, mopping her face with a handkerchief.

"Oh, it's you, Tilly. Good! I need a favor." Charlie's face had a boyish quality. Looking expectant, he grinned softly awaiting her response.

Tilly, small in stature, was extremely well endowed. Taking a deep breath, her voice seemed to ooze out. "Why sure, Charlie."

"Well, you know all of those society functions the Crescent City Historical Society and the Art Foundation has?"

Tilly swung her long curls over her shoulder and nodded. "Yes."

"Well, I was wondering if you could pull the photographs on those – say in the last year. It would sure help me. I'm looking for a particular photograph, and I won't know it until I see it."

The girl was only too happy to serve. She waved at Charlie to follow her into the file room, swinging her hips effectively as she moved in front of him.

* * * * *

Terry spent the day in her studio tidying up and rearranging the paintings. It seemed a good time to get started on a new project. She couldn't paint the lighthouse anymore; at least, not now. The recent calls from Mr. Waxman had been exceptionally helpful. It was wonderful to have some guidance, especially from a man who had clout in the art world. He was recommending that she do some seascapes. Terry remembered that last art dealer suggesting that same thing on the day she'd met Mr. Henry. The thought drew her out onto the balcony. *Honestly,* she thought, *it is all unbelievable. Imagine, all that has happened. People dead and my meeting Dan, getting engaged and, now, getting back to work.* Terry shook her head in disbelief. Her lawyer was right; it did sound like a dime novel . . . whatever that meant? They were getting some matters settled. She'd decided to put the house up for sale. Dan promised they would go house hunting the next time she came to San Francisco.

It had been difficult explaining her wealth to him without causing a problem. They had been discussing the home they would buy, and Dan tried to be diplomatic explaining what he earned and that he expected to take care of his wife. Terry stopped him delicately. She said, "Darling, I want that also, but look, this house is worth about $400,000; it is paid for and we won't have any problem selling it. I need a studio, you need a study, and we need a bedroom for ourselves and one for each of the children; and, of course, we need at least one guest room maybe two. I would like to ask Marge to come and work for us, if you would agree."

Dan's look raised a smile before he said, "What children?"

"The three we will have – oh, yes, darling, at least three."

Dan laughed really hard. Getting up, he went to her and

kissed her with passion. "It is real, isn't it? I'm actually going to have a wife and, according to you, three children and a live-in maid." Terry smiled but he could see her seriousness.

"Honey, I'm going to be married to you for the rest of my life. I want us to have a wonderful home that we can raise our family in, entertain, where I can work and one you can come home to. I don't want to move around at all. Let's take this money and buy our home. It does make sense, doesn't it?"

Dan agreed that it did, but he was reluctant to accept her money. "I'm not used to accepting money from women, honey."

He looked every inch a little boy, and Terry hugged him. "But, darling, I'm worth five million dollars."

Dan gasped. "What?"

"Look, I didn't tell you before because I didn't want to have this conversation, but it is your money now too. I'm having Adam draw up the papers as we speak, and I needed to tell you about it. Dan, my family worked very hard for it, and they wanted me to enjoy it. Now, I want us to enjoy it. We need a big house with lots of room for our family. I want us both to have what we want. And, oh, Dan, what fun we'll have looking for our home."

He saw how happy she was and decided not to fight it. She was right. They needed lots of space even for his family when they came to visit. He held her close and grinned before whispering, "Okay. Mrs. Levine-to-be." Then looked at the ceiling he said in awe, "Five million dollars – my Lord – that's overwhelming."

A thrill overcame her; getting married was exciting. They still had to call Dan's family to tell them their news, but that could wait until this whole business was settled. And, then there was Adam Linquist, her old friend. Terry hoped he would give her away. She wanted a beautiful gown and train in a church with an organ with Dan's nieces as flower girls and his sisters as her bridesmaids. She hoped they would like her. Thinking that, she sat down and grinned. It was so much fun to think about. Glancing at the clock, Terry decided to go see Marge about dinner. Dan thought they'd be back around 7:00 P.M. Baron yipped. "Okay, boy. First, we'll talk to the housekeeper about the food, and then I'll take you for your run." She stooped to pet her animal who licked her hand as they went on down to the kitchen.

The day was considerably clearer when they arrived on the beach, and the gunmetal ocean seemed at peace. Terry was glad of that, being seasick was pretty terrible. It occurred to her that the two men might not fare so well in the swells when the ship wasn't running. She picked up a stick for the dog and tossed it. He raced away to retrieve it. Terry watched his graceful movements. "Good boy." Collecting it, she threw it again only farther, laughing at the muscular form the dog used to meet the challenge. The wind was rising. It felt good on her skin. After they played awhile, Baron was tired and Terry sat on a big piece of driftwood to think. There was something she had been wanting to do. That young woman who had lost her baby and her home needed help. Deciding it was rewarding. *Tomorrow I'll go to the hospital and make arrangements with her. Jess can take care of the legalities. I'll call him first thing tomorrow.* She grinned; it felt good. *Captain Tillman would be very happy to know his money went to such a worthy cause.*

* * * * *

The search had been on for two days. They hadn't located the wreck but did find a few pieces of a broken mast. They had to be close. Captain Birch called Dan into the cabin for coffee. "Look, Dan, we need sonar and none of our ships have it. I believe the coast guard has a sonar vessel near here. I'll put a call in and see if they would consider coming up the coast to help us."

Dan agreed. It had been expensive and totally unproductive. There had been no sign of the armed intruders, and he was

219

beginning to believe they might be able to locate without problems. Ro Birch had been on the radio for a long time. Finally, he came topside grinning broadly. "Hey, good news. Captain Lucas of the cutter *San Diego* is about a half a day away. They said they thought they could get permission to bring her here tomorrow. She has every piece of equipment known to mankind, and she is fully operational."

Dan yelled. "Great! That will make me sleep good tonight. Okay, let's head for shore and the drinks are on me."

The morning dawned stormy. A steady downpour outside the bedroom didn't look welcoming. After breakfast Dan stood at the windows glancing down at the shore bemoaning that fact.

Terry approached and hugged him. "Maybe, it's a good omen."

Dan snarled. "Right."

"No, hon, it just might be. It was a day just like this one when she went down. Just, maybe, it'll be a day like that when she's found."

"That kind of reasoning could be contagious." He kissed her on the top of the head and hugged her close. "I'll certainly be glad when we locate and you and I can get back to some kind of normality. We have a wedding to plan, Mrs. Levine-to-be."

Terry laughed lightly. "Oh, I love having you here. I don't care if you ever find it."

"I hear Bert, love. We've got to move. Wish me luck today."

Terry blew him a kiss and watched out of the window to see them drive away.

They were all wearing slickers and hats as the ship raced out to sea. The divers had left a buoy anchored to the fallen masts. It gave them a place to start. Everyone was anxious to see what the cutter's sonar equipment would show. The coast guard had promised to radio Dan when they were close to the site and had given an ETA of 0800 hours. Dan watched the ocean impatiently. He honestly believed this was their only chance. Eventually, the *San Diego* came into sight. She was trim, 180 feet, cutting a huge swath through the slate-colored sea. Their radio transmissions increased. The radio man came topside.

"Her skipper wants to know if you'd like to board, Mr. Levine?"

Dan's face reflected his surprise. "Tell them yes. My investigator and I will board with pleasure."

A boat was dispatched from the cutter now circling the area in slow speed. The motor dingy came alongside, and the two men climbed down into it. Shortly, they boarded the *San Diego* and were greeted by Captain Lucas. After they shook hands, the slim, white-haired skipper invited them into his ward room where a map had been spread. "According to your map, which we received by scanner, we are here." He pointed to the place where they had placed the buoy. "If you will follow me to the sonar room, we will get started."

The room looked very futuristic. Bert whistled when he saw it. Two men were operating the equipment that was registered on a large screen in front of them and sounded exacting with its steady ping as its echo bounced back from the target. The captain pointed out the broken masts that had been identified. There were also laser and radar screens operational and sounds emanating from them. Captain Lucas said, "Well, I'll be damned."

"What?" Dan sensed something was afoul.

The captain moved closer to the sonar screen. "We're being invaded."

"What does that mean?"

"It means, gentlemen, that we have company." He pointed to the blip on the sonar screen. "Get your divers up now. Lieutenant, radio the patrol boat to recall their divers on the double, mister."

"Yes, sir, Captain." The officer disappeared into the radio room.

Dan was aghast. "Captain Lucas, do you know what it is?"

"Yeah. It appears to be a small submarine – I would guess a sea searcher. Let me explain how the sonar works, gentlemen. Under our keel we have a sonar dome. We have one or more transducers to send and receive sound, electronic equipment for generation and detection of the electrical impulses to and from the transducer and a display for the observation of the signals." The captain pointed to the computer generated receiver. "There, that is your submarine coming up on the enhancer screen now."

"Is it capable of lifting material or just observing?"

"We are doing some tests now, and we have a laser that will actually outline the ship or anything else down there. I'll have that information as soon as my officer gets back. We will also monitor their radio frequency. We might be able to get you some additional information. For now, I'm going to insist on radio silence among your ships. We will use an old-fashion method to signal. They will get it immediately."

"Morse code?" Dan questioned.

"Yes, let's go topside and watch how fast these captains respond."

It was cold on the deck. The rain was heavier now, a solid drizzle. The ship began to rise and sink deep into huge swells as the storm buffeted them. Dan watched a corpsman closing and opening the shutters sending Morse code messages to the trollers and the harbor patrol boats. Flags went up to signal their receipt of the information. They would maintain radio silence as long as the intruder was beneath them.

Captain Lucas led the way to the board room. He asked them to sit down and offered them coffee. They both declined.

"Would you like some Dramamine instead?" It was said with stoic indifference.

Dan said, "I believe that would be a welcomed addition to our cruise."

Everyone smirked. A corpsman appeared shortly with a tray. Each man helped himself to pills and water. He also gave them plastic wrappers to pocket. "These are patches, sir. After today, wear one before you board. It will dispense the medicine according to your needs. It won't be long, this new medicine works fast."

"Now, let's get to work," the captain ordered. "We are not authorized to bomb the invaders. I know you probably would like to do that."

Bert's answer was caustic. "Damn right."

"Unfortunately, those days of fighting on the high seas are at an end, unless, of course, there is a declaration of war." He laughed. "Or, the admiral issues an order," he said with a wink.

Dan's frustration was mounting. His voice had gone up an octave. "What the hell can we do? I've had it with these bastards."

"So, Mr. Levine, we can do the next best thing."

"Name it."

"If we maintain radio silence, they won't know where we are. I have them in plain sight on sonar screens and on radar if they surface. They aren't going anywhere unless I know it. We will just wait them out."

"What good will that do, Captain?"

Captain Lucas smiled. "You have the California State Police Patrol boats who have authority and apprehensive capabilities. I will find the mother ship, they will follow and apprehend."

"That's fantastic," Bert yelled. "Boy, am I glad I came. I wouldn't miss this for the world."

"I can only assume they do not know we are here. The mother ship is too far away and we cruise these waters all the time. They don't know we have sonar and that we have identified them. It is good for 100 miles and that ought to be enough."

A corpsman approached. "They have used an electronic arm to place an underwater marker, Captain. After that is completed, we believe they will return to the mother ship where their divers are probably waiting."

The captain issued his orders before they all went topside to send the Morse messages to the other ships. He said to the corpsman, "Tell them we should lay off shore until they actually come to the site. Then, we can apprehend them in the act. Ask the state police captain to decide if they want to get behind the jetty out of sight. Once the pirates are on the target, we will send a Morse message, and they can come out to the site, board and apprehend. Either plan will work – tell them to make that decision."

They waited for what seemed an eternity. They talked it over and thought the second plan was the wisest. Dan, of course, was contemplating the legal ramifications considering a trial and the potential arguments used by the defense. He also noted to the captain that the site was inside the 12-mile limit where the California Harbor Patrol still had jurisdiction.

Within a half an hour the answer came. They needed to catch them in the act. The corpsman came back with the decoded Morse messages. "They think you should all go into shore and leave the cutter circling out here. We will circle far enough away until we spot them. Once they are on site and have men in the water, we will close in. We are being asked to give them Morse messages aimed right at the jetty; they will be parked there. They are asking Mr. Levine to concur."

"Tell them we will stay on board this ship, and they should proceed as planned. Oh, and tell them good luck."

It was done. Captain Lucas smiled. He knew they would have these criminals within a few hours – a more than satisfactory day's work.

Chapter 18

The Ghostly Return

A throaty roar raised as the ship prepared to move. Dan and Bert went topside to watch the retreat of the rest of their fleet. It was a miserable day, and the sea seemed choppier than before. Dan chuckled seeing the big man rubbing his stomach unconsciously and burping, ignoring the rain. The sky was darker, swirling low hanging rain-filled clouds all around the ship.

"It's a good thing they gave us the sea-sick medicine," Dan said.

The investigator shook his head. "I think I would have died without it. What a rotten feeling." He slumped, pulling his slicker close around his burgeoning middle. The slicker hat dripped water off its brim, but Bert didn't seem to notice.

"Off the subject, has anyone called you back with the results of the subpoena you mentioned earlier?"

"No. I'm waiting for the call now. Ted's like a dog with a bone, he won't let up until he gets it, but that kind of information takes awhile. I'll give it to you as soon as I get it."

The ship had turned and was going south while the rest of their fleet moved closer to the bay in Crescent City. Shortly, they were all beyond the jetty completely out of sight. The lawyer suggested they return to the sonar room where the captain was marking an electronic chart.

"There he goes. That's our submarine headed due west and very slow. Now, we might as well go up to the galley and get some food. I've been up since five, and I'm hungry."

They ate in a small but compact, immaculate dining room. A corpsman appeared to take their order. They deferred to the captain. He ordered chicken sandwiches, vegetable soup and lemon custard for dessert. It arrived in record time and was very tasty.

"I think we will have success, folks," Captain Lucas said looking smug as he finished the dessert. "I'm always impressed with what the electronic equipment will do. We can actually track this sub until it is met and then track its mother ship." He shook his gray head and winked. "In fact, I'm really pleased that you called us. Too often our jobs are mundane, but this one is a real challenge. The whole crew is enjoying the work immensely."

"I can't thank you enough, Captain Lucas," Dan said sincerely. "California will be exceptionally grateful to the coast guard if we are successful. There is a great deal of gold down there, not to mention the artifacts."

"I'm really interested, Dan; please, tell me all about it. I've never actually heard the whole story."

While Dan relayed the history, Bert excused himself to make some calls. Later, when he returned, Dan could see his frustration.

"Any luck?"

"There's a problem. Ted says not to worry he'll nail it down shortly. He'll call us back. He's had another idea."

* * * * *

When Terry returned from the hospital she found a message from Martin Delaney's office. It said he had arranged to meet her at the lighthouse at 3:00 P.M. to view Captain Tillman's

226

belongings. He included the fact that he would notify Dan and have him join them there. It further stated that the tide would be out around 3:00 P.M. Terry read it over again thinking they must be coming in early today. "Good," she said out loud. "I wouldn't want to go there without Dan. And, it was Dan who originally told Martin to get this set up."

Terry had gone up to her bedroom. She saw the envelope lying on the dresser with the key to the lighthouse taped to it. *Oh, Captain,* she thought, *why did you have to die? Well, you would at least be proud of the joy your money brought to that young mother and her little girl.* Terry smiled remembering the scene at the hospital when she offered the legacy to them. Glancing at her watch, she decided to have some lunch before meeting Dan. It would also be a good idea to place a call to Jess's office in San Francisco to ask him to take care of the legal work connected with the gift.

* * * * *

Charlie Stevens stood in the dark room of the newspaper office with Tilly Leiphart. She was a little too close for comfort. Charlie edged away to hang the newly developed blow-ups on the drying line. The room looked infrared. It enhanced Tilly's coloring, and he resisted the compliment forming on his lips. He wasn't interested in getting involved; he had too much to do right now.

"There, Charlie, that one is pretty clear now. You can even see the people in the background like you wanted." She pointed to the third photograph on the line. The group was toasting a newcomer and Charlie could plainly see Mr. Henry and Sheriff Ripley standing side by side. As the photograph dried, he could also see Martin Delaney nearby and Mr. Jablonski of the National Ship Salvage Corporation and an unidentified woman.

Charlie swore softly under his breath.

"What did you say, Charlie?"

"Oh, nothing, Tilly. I'm just frustrated. You have been really helpful, and I won't forget it. My boss will be sending a letter to your boss for all the cooperation I've found here. Thanks, ma'am." The deputy tipped his hat and backed out of the small enclosure leaving an unhappy Tilly huffing angrily behind the rapidly closing door.

* * * * *

At 1:30 P.M. the *San Diego* turned sixty degrees to the west leaving the *Moravia* a wide gap. Everyone was in the sonar room and their adrenalin was up.

Dan watched in awe as the tanker sailed toward the marker the submarine had left.

Once the ship was actually over the sight a beeper sounded from the sonar computer. It gave off a steady, repeated sound that caused smiles all around.

"Steady our course, Mr. Lonaker," Captain Lucas said into the speaker connected to the bridge.

A voice returned, "Aye, aye, sir . . . steady as she goes."

They could feel the ship surging as the powerful engines propelled them back toward the site.

All eyes were on the screen. It was evident that new activity had been initiated as blips appeared to be moving toward the ocean's bottom.

"There they are, gentlemen. We have divers in the water." The captain picked up the microphone to call the radio room. "Mr. Bernside, have a radio signal sent by Morse code to the jetty."

"Aye, aye, Captain."

"Tell them the enemy is on the target and there are divers in the water."

Dan felt his innards tighten. The entire scenario had the feel of a James Bond movie. He wasn't given to excesses, but he knew he could get very used to this. It seemed the captain of the cutter was getting as much kick out of this as they were.

Bert said softly, "Holy shit. Will you look at that thing?"

There were smirks on everyone's face in the sonar room. It was true the electronics were invincible. The screen began to tell a story as the figures moving below swam to the marker, stopped briefly and then began to fan out. Totally captivating them was the sonar's pulsing ping that echoed in their ears.

"Please use our finder, Mr. Gaston?"

"Aye, aye, Captain."

The sonar man's fingers danced across the computer's keyboard while up on the screen an electronic beam searched the ocean's floor. They could actually see the shapes forming around the divers. There were huge rock formations, debris, kelp beds, fish and eventually the prize itself. They all cheered when the beeper sounded and kept sounding until they wanted to jump up and down.

"There is your wreck, Mr. Levine," the captain said proudly.

"Wow! That machine is a beauty. I don't know what to say." Dan felt his blood surging through his veins, the adrenalin was up, he was as excited as he'd ever been in his life – victory . . . *I'm going to do it* . . . Dan was beside himself with joy. All of the legal battles, the chicanery, the threats, the attempts to destroy and murder were over. It was all unbelievable, and now, in one moment, they were actually within a hair's breadth of winning.

"Please plot the charts, Mr. Gaston. I'm certain these gentlemen would like to be able to relay the information just as soon as the police have made their arrests."

* * * * *

Ro Birch had been a captain on California's State Police Harbor Patrol for ten years. He had gone through the frustration of having ships without equipment, which weren't fast enough to apprehend, and he knew the agony of defeat. These days, with all the new electronics, speed and especially built ships to apprehend drug smugglers, Ro was in heaven. This particular job raised his pulse. He pushed the patrol boat to the limit and wallowed at its thrust, watching the rain sheeting across the wind screen. The hull lifted in the water, fleeing at peak speed toward the small, rusting tanker that was now poised at the site. Having control of the other ships following, he gave them directions on a special radio band that could not be penetrated. They had been given special radios during the long wait. Unless the pirates had a watch out, they didn't know they were about to be apprehended. Of course, it was reasonable to assume there was a lookout, and it would only be a question of time until they were spotted. Ro gave instructions to all of the pursuit team to be armed and ready to use their weapons before and during the boarding. His men's safety was of a grave concern, and these perps were dangerous. Picking up the speaker, Ro said, "Watch your backside. This is a rough bunch. I don't want anybody hurt."

The two men went topside with the captain. Nobody wanted to miss the action, but they were actually reluctant to leave the sonar equipment until the very last minute. The coast guard, having been given permission to join in the actual apprehension, decided to help if needed. Captain Lucas ordered two corpsmen up to the bow gun. They removed the canvas covers and prepared to shoot.

"One across the bow will probably be enough, Mr. Henson."

"Aye, aye, Captain. One across the bow it'll be."

By this time the police patrol boats were almost to the target. There were shots fired into the oncoming patrol boat as the lookout spotted them racing toward the scene.

"Now, Mr. Henson, and don't leave too much room above her gunnels."

The corpsman grinned broadly. They heard the boom; it was loud even in the wind and exploded just beyond the tanker's bow.

"Good job, son. Now, give them another one just to let them know we mean business."

"Aye, aye, Captain."

This time Dan and Bert held their ears. They cheered when the explosion came.

"That ought to do it," Captain Lucas said grinning satisfactorily.

It was as if they were watching a movie. Soon the patrol ships idled in the water while boarding parties went onto the tanker. They now had a clear view of the coast guard cutter and were not resisting.

Ro Birch had boarded and faced Olaf Czechof, the captain of the *Moravia*, who stood glaring at the invading force commandeering his ship. His hands were raised because he knew it was all over. They put cuffs on him and led him below. The action took over an hour. The cutter was in radio contact now, and each bit of information was radioed to them as it occurred. Ro placed a skipper in command of the *Moravia* to take her into port.

Captain Lucas opened the speakers in the radio room so Dan and Bert could actually hear the encounter. Czechof was ordered to bring the divers up. That took a long time. Dan went topside with the binocular offered by the captain. The *Moravia* had drifted into their view blocking his sight of the men coming out of the water. Dan hurried below. The sounds of the ship actually being secured, thrilled him. In fact, he couldn't believe they now had the location on a map and their acquisition could be completed. He pulled off the wet slicker as he went down toward the sonar room. Bert was coming out of the radio room almost running toward him. He was sheet white.

"What's wrong?"

"Dan, I had Ted trying to get a subpoena to pick up the telephone records of the sheriff and the assistant district attorney." His look widened.

"So, what?"

"That call was from Ted. He couldn't get the subpoena

because the judge was unavailable. He figured he'd go to the telephone company and try to get the information from some woman who knew his ex. He figured what we needed was current information and we could subpoena the stuff later."

Dan was getting impatient. "What the hell are you so wrought up over? Spit it out."

"The woman was pretty helpful. It's the sheriff. He called Czechof five minutes after you were in that office to tell him about the proposed raid. They were on their way to this destination that night armed for bear. They just didn't figure you'd have the United States Coast Guard gun ship with you."

Dan frowned. "So . . .?"

"I got that feeling in my gut again."

"About what?"

"Terry."

"What about Terry?"

"That bastard knows that you know. He had to have killed Captain Tillman and tried to frame Terry. Don't you see. If he can get rid of her, no one can prove it."

Dan's brain was racing. Bert was absolutely right. "CALL CHARLIE, NOW."

It took only seconds to punch in the telephone numbers.

Charlie Stevens was in his car. He answered immediately. Bert explained the situation, and Charlie said he'd race to the house and get back to them.

* * * * *

Terry and the dog ran across the spit after parking the Jeep in the A Street parking lot. It was raining steadily. Terry wore a jogging suit covered by a slicker and on her head she had an all-weather hat. The dog's coat darkened as they crossed. Once they hit the island and started up, Terry called to him. "We're almost there, boy. I'll dry you when we get into the kitchen." At the top of the path she noticed the door was open. *That's funny. There were no cars in the lot. Oh, I guess Martin got a deputy to drop him off,* she thought.

She went inside and pulled off the wet clothes, dropping them onto a bench in the hall. "Martin, Martin. It's Terry, are you here?" her voice sounded hollow in the silence.

They moved into the kitchen where Terry grabbed a towel to dry the dog. She avoided looking into the alcove. Her mind was still trying to forget the horror of finding the captain with his head bashed in. "There, boy, that's better huh?" The dog licked her hand and made a soft growling sound.

"Martin must be up in the captain's room, Baron. You wait and I'll go up and see." She started for the room surrounding the spiral staircase. The dog bounded in front of her, barking loud and refusing her entry into the circular hall.

"What's wrong, boy?" Her pulse raced and she felt fear creeping through her body.

Suddenly, the dog leaped away down the entrance hallway barking loudly. In an instant there was silence so deadly she felt sick. *My God, someone was able to get Baron outside and locked him out.* Terry knew the building. Other than going up to the tower room, there were no doors heavy enough to hide behind. She made a split second decision and started up the round, narrow staircase, clutching the rope railing with shaking hands. Her brain wasn't functioning properly and her instincts were in terror. It occurred to her that her feet seemed rooted to the twisting stairs. She tried to look down and up simultaneously, fearful that someone might be waiting above as well. There was no one in sight. Once she reached the lamp room, she ran inside and slammed the door hearing the lock click, she gasped. Leaning against the wood, she tried to swallow, but her mouth was dry all the way down her throat. Her heart felt as if it were going to run away. It pounded loudly. She actually believed she could hear it. Fear had taken control. Could it be true, was she going to die here? Terrorized eyes fled to the counters and shelves beneath them desperately looking for a weapon. *The captain's telescope, it's metal. I'll use that.* Groping for the counter to hold herself up, she moved closer to grasp the scope. As she reached for the object, Terry inhaled heavily just as a hand clasped her mouth. She fainted.

Charlie's car screeched to a halt in Terry's driveway and in seconds he was pounding on the front door. It took the house-keeper a minute to answer, but it seemed hours to Charlie who knew what the consequences of a delay might mean. Marge was quick to see his impatience.

"She left about twenty minutes ago. I wouldn't tell you, but you are the law. She went to the lighthouse to meet Mr. Delaney and Mr. Dan."

Charlie was in the car and moving before she finished. He dialed as he drove. *Five minutes, tops to reach the parking lot,* he thought and drove to the edge where he could plainly see the island.

"Bert, listen," he said into the cellular, "Terry's dog is on the edge of the island, and he's having a fit. Somebody has got her trapped inside, and I don't have a key. You'd better get the chopper over here pronto. Tell them to bring axes. There's no way into that building without a key."

Yelling into the phone, the investigator said, "You come back to the island, immediately. I'll call them right now."

Dan's face drained of color.

"You okay?" Bert yelled while he dialed the state police chopper pilot. After they answered, he explained while watching Dan go cold.

"WHAT IS IT . . . YOU TELL ME, NOW," he shouted.

Bert started trying to be explicit without making it sound as bad as it actually was.

Dan could only imagine what was going on inside that build-ing. He had never experienced such frustration and helpless-ness. He went up on deck with the binocular. It was so close and yet so far. It might as well have been a thousand miles for all the good it would do him.

Terry felt the rush of cold air caressing her face as the rain pelted her skin. She opened her eyelids and squinted into the blustery sky. Beneath her was the iron balcony outside of the lens room. It was metal and not solid. She screamed but no sound came out. It was seventy-five feet down to the rocks that were being pummeled by an angry sea. Alongside her was the low metal railing surrounding the light room. It had three rungs, the highest of which was probably no more than three feet. It was rusting. She clutched it and felt the wet metal raw against her hand. It seemed important to stand up, but she couldn't. It occurred to her that she must have fainted, but that was inside the lens house. *How did I get out here?* Then, she heard him yelling her name and banging heavily on the wood. The sound was muffled by the wind, but she knew she didn't imagine it. The door was quite thick, so he couldn't breach it easily, but she knew he would find a way. Looking down she shivered. "Is that how I will die? Oh, Dan, I need you." Suddenly, she screamed a blood curdling scream. "HELP! HELP ME! GOD – SOMEONE HELP ME."

"I WILL."

Terry's mouth gaped. The captain of the *Brother Jonathan* stood spread legged in front of her. The rain didn't touch him; he looked handsome and full of life.

"I'm delirious. Oh, help me, I'm delirious."

The pounding had increased and now it was being done with a weapon, either an ax or a sharp instrument that she could hear splitting wood.

The captain's strong hands lifted her up. "Stand very still, lass."

She looked down at the waves crashing onto the rocks below and sluicing into the air in great white fans. "I'll fall."

"NO. LISTEN!" he demanded. "I will not allow him to hurt you. Just do as I tell you, and you will be saved."

Terry had no choice. Her limbs shook noticeably and the tormentor was almost through the door. Finally, the crashing stopped. A large hand came through the tear in the door and unlocked it. He was still carrying the ax when he came out onto the balcony.

Terry stared at Sheriff Ripley. He looked crazed. His gray-white mane was getting wet from the rain that ran down the flabby pale skin, his eyes were rage darkened and his mouth turned cruel as he spoke. "You are going to die rich, lady. I wonder if people who have everything die like everyone else. It won't take long. You were so upset because you killed the captain that you came here and ended it all." He laughed sardonically. "Now, you can join that old fool. If he had given me the map as planned, this wouldn't be necessary . . . although, I will enjoy it." He laughed, sounding crude and caustic.

"WHY?" she cried out in a shrill voice.

"I can't get caught now. I went to so much trouble to find that gold. It all blew up on me because of you and that lawyer you brought here. Martin will gladly accept the fact that you killed the old man for his money. I even wrote a note. I'll leave it on the counter by the captain's sexton. Ha! Ha!"

He's insane, Terry thought. Her hands were clammy now, and she was very cold and wet. The wind was howling, and even her bones felt cold. To Terry the moment was surreal. Maybe it was a dream and she wasn't going to die. She would marry Dan and have beautiful children; they would have Christmas every year for them and she would paint their portraits for posterity.

Cameron Ripley waved the ax as he spoke. Terry wondered if he meant to hit her with it. She felt nauseous. "What do you want? I'll give it to you. I have money; I can pay you. Please don't do this." She was crying softly, the tears mingled with the rain running down her face.

Suddenly, the big man growled. It was an animal sort of sound, and he ran toward her with his arms outstretched to hit her and force her body over the railing. She cringed screaming. Just before he reached her, Captain DeWolfe materialized in front of her. Then, when he saw the apparition, Sheriff Ripley's arms flailed. He tried to stop his momentum and failed. Instead, he slipped and went careening over the railing, screaming his guttural fear into the wind. There was a thud. Now there was sudden silence, except for the soft sound of the rain and the wind singing a lonely song.

Terry's dazed eyes perused the broken body spread over the huge rocks below where the ocean was already flooding. Her knees went weak, but Captain DeWolfe clutched her with strong hands. "Go ahead and cry, lass; you've earned it."

Terry leaned into him for security. "Why?"

"Why didn't you die? Because it wasn't your time. That's what happened to me. I wasn't supposed to sail that night. I killed all of those innocent souls, because I was afraid to lose my ship."

"What about the woman and the child?"

"They got on board at the last minute. I didn't know they were there. We drowned together. I tried to save them. We were all caught between two worlds." He smiled. "At least, they keep me company and I've grown quite fond of them. Now, listen lass, I don't have much time. You will have two sons and a daughter. Please, name the first boy Amos, after the captain. He will be very happy about that. What you did today was extremely kind. It will not go unrewarded. The captain hated that he put you in jeopardy. Your wonderful Dan is going to set me free. Those bodies have to be buried and blessed. Then, the lady, the child and I can go home. I saved you because it was destined. I had to wait until you came. Remember this, it is important. After Ripley bashed the captain's head in with an iron crowbar, he threw it into the sea. I retrieved it. I put it under some canvas by the front door. It has the captain's blood on it and Ripley's fingerprints. So, when that fool Delaney sets blame to you, you can give it to them."

They heard the rotor blades; the chopper was nearing. Soon its sound roared overhead deafening them. Terry looked up. She could see the officers clearly. They were armed and poised until they saw his body below on the rocks. The big ship turned, twisting and lowering to the other side of the island where it landed.

Suddenly, she was alone feeling great remorse. Forgetting about the cold, Terry called to him. "Please, Captain DeWolfe, come back. You saved my life. At least, let me thank you." It was silent except for the untiring wind.

Chapter 19

Rescue

Deputy Stevens barely made it to the island before the incoming tide obliterated his path to it. Baron, watching the crossing, slowed his barking. Charlie thought the animal must be exhausted. He stopped to pet him while telling him how wonderful he was to be so loyal to his mistress. *If Terry is alive, Baron probably saved her life*, he thought. They moved up the path to the door that was closed and locked. Charlie knew help was on its way. Fearing what might be taking place inside caused him to cringe and raised mounting frustration. It was only minutes before he actually heard the distinctive sounds of rotor blades moving closer to the island. When the helicopter was actually in sight, Charlie breathed easier. Once they broke into the door, he'd be able to call Dan ship to shore. It seemed a certainty that the lawyer was beside himself with worry over Terry. Charlie could only hope that she was alive and unhurt.

The plane touched down in a downpour. The officers were out onto the ground within seconds and immediately attacked the door with axes. Charlie stood off out of the way, clutching the choke chain on the barking animal whose efforts to reach Terry were his only concern. "Wait, boy. They'll get to her shortly."

Forcing the door, the police raced inside and Charlie could

hear their voices calling. Baron and Charlie entered and went to the kitchen. It was obvious she wasn't in the lower level. The deputy remembered having been there after the captain's grisly murder. He sat down to wait. The dog went to the staircase. Staring up, he barked repeatedly. Moments later they heard the officers coming downstairs talking to her. Charlie felt absolute relief. He got up anxious to see for himself. The girl was soaking wet, pale and unresponsive. Charlie hurried outside to the chopper where he yelled to the pilot. "Hey, Chief Deputy Attorney General Dan Levine is out on the Coast Guard Cutter *San Diego*. That ship is part of your operation going on at the sunken ship site. It would be very much appreciated if you would fly out and pick him up. His fiancée is inside and someone tried to kill her."

The pilot nodded. "Get on the radio and tell them I'm on my way," he yelled closing the door.

Charlie watched the lift off before running back inside to the ship-to-shore radio in the alcove. Sitting down, the deputy's fingers fiddled with the controls until he heard the familiar crackling of static.

"Coast Guard Cutter *San Diego*, this is Sheriff's Deputy Charlie Stevens at the lighthouse in Crescent City . . . do you copy?"

"This is Coast Guard Cutter *San Diego* . . . we copy. Go ahead Crescent City lighthouse."

"Please relay a message to Chief Deputy Attorney General Dan Levine. We are inside the lighthouse and have retrieved Terry Hamilton. She is alive and unhurt but quite shaken. I am sending the chopper to the cutter to pick Dan Levine up by basket. Please, have him standing by. Do you copy?"

"Lighthouse, Crescent City, this is the Coast Guard . . . we copy and that's a go."

Terry was being given brandy to reduce her shaking. The officers were concerned about shock. Suddenly, responding to the sight of Baron who ran to her barking and licking her hands and face, Terry reached for his thick neck and leaned over hugging him. It was familiar and warm. "You are wet, old friend," she whispered softly.

"Where is Ripley?" Charlie asked one of the officers.

"He's dead." It was said with morbid finality. "I think he tried to push her off the catwalk; he may have slipped and gone over. The body is out on the rocks below the tower. He had an ax in his hand; we found it lying close to the corpse. We've got men out there now. You'd probably want to notify the coroner, deputy," the officer said stoically.

Charlie went over to Terry and knelt down beside her. The artist's hands were still petting the dog while her eyes stared ahead absently.

"I've sent the chopper to pick up Dan, Terry. He'll be here soon."

She either didn't hear him or couldn't. The brandy was helping; she had stopped shaking. It was warm in the kitchen, and Charlie put the kettle on to boil. He found the tea bags and prepared a cup. The sound of the kettle was shrill. Charlie grabbed it. Pouring the boiling liquid into a waiting mug, he loaded it with sugar. "It's hot, Terry, come on drink some, please." Kneeling, he forced the liquid into her blue lips. In a few minutes he could see she was starting to respond. The glassy eyes washed over Charlie's face. "He's dead," she whispered.

"Yes! You don't have to fear him anymore, Terry. He can't hurt you now."

The police officers were moving around quickly assessing the scene. One of them approached. "Can you answer some questions, Miss Hamilton?"

The question was met with silence.

Charlie stood and took him aside. Speaking softly he said, "Officer, this woman has been through hell for a long time. I don't know what went on here today, but I can guess. Please, give her time to get warm and for her fiancé to be brought in from the cutter. I think we'll be able to get information as soon as that happens."

"All right. I'll go outside to see to the situation with the body. You stay with her. She seems to be responding to you and the dog. I'll be back shortly."

Charlie watched him leave and brought her more tea fearing hypothermia. "Come on, Terry. You need this, drink it."

He watched her sipping the liquid. It was as if it reached the emptiness of her soul. With each sip she seemed more in control, but her color was still deathly. Charlie rubbed her hands hard trying to bring back some warmth. Then, he put her legs up onto a chair and pulled off the wet shoes and socks. He dried her feet with a towel he found in a kitchen drawer. Lifting each foot and rubbing really hard he tried to increase the circulation.

They heard the chopper coming in. Within a minute Dan burst through the door. He looked ghastly. Running inside, he yelled her name before actually coming close where eager hands clutched the blanket and drew her up tightly. "I'm here now, hon; I'll take care of you."

She mumbled something, but neither of them could make it out.

In a few minutes, Dan set her down. Charlie brought the tea back. "Here, Dan, make her finish this. She needs heat and sugar real bad."

Dan nodded and complied. He could see she was in shock. "Charlie, get to the pilot. Tell him we need to get her over to the hospital on the double. Then, come back and bring the dog, we should take him also."

Charlie waved. The chopper lifted off while the lawman squinted into pelting rain and cringed as the backwash chilled him to the bone. *The sheriff was dead. The puzzle had been solved – almost. There was a big hole in the evidence and Martin would, sure as God made little green apples, want to hang her for Ripley's murder.* The lawman frowned deeply. It was important that he find the solution; some of it had to be hidden in Ripley's office. It seemed to the deputy that even in death Ripley had won. It would be only her word against a dead man's.

The people at the hospital all knew Terry was the woman who had turned over Captain Tillman's legacy to the mother and the child injured by the tidal wave. It was quickly evident that no stone would be left unturned to give her their very best care.

* * * * *

Bert thanked Captain Lucas profusely before he was transferred to the harbor patrol boat to be brought into the dock. As the launch raced away he saluted. They had been magnificent and somehow he felt proud to be an American at precisely that moment. The entire operation was a huge success. Besides capturing the criminals and stopping their intended pirating operation, they had been able to locate and chart the wreck. Now, if only Terry was safe, life would be wonderful. He could see the lighthouse off to the left. He hoped Dan was there and that she wasn't hurt. He thought, *If ever two people deserved to be together, it was them.*

By 8:00 P.M. Dan waited with Bert, Charlie and the dog inside the hospital waiting room.

"It was sure nice of these people to allow Baron to come inside," Charlie said. "He actually saved her life. If I had gone to that parking lot, seen her Jeep and not heard him barking, I would have thought she actually was meeting with Martin Delaney just as the housekeeper said." Charlie shook his head. "Terry was lucky the day she found this dog. He is a genius. He knows just what to do, and he can't even talk."

They all laughed, and it relieved some of the tension.

The doctor entered and approached. "Mr. Levine, I think your lady is going to be fine. It appears she has had a terrible shock. Of course, she was also suffering from exposure and her body temperature had dropped below what is normal. In fact it was in the dangerous range. Whoever was smart enough to give her the brandy and the tea and sugar certainly did her a favor. I've given her a sedative; she needs rest. She is demanding to see Deputy Stevens. I wouldn't ordinarily allow it, but upsetting the patient isn't wise."

Dan instructed Charlie to go to her room for a short visit.

After he left, Bert said, "I figure Delaney will be here soon, boss. I'd like to have two state police officers at her door to bar entrance to unwanted visitors . . . what say?"

Dan nodded. "I've just been thinking the same thing. Why don't you get on that phone and take care of it."

The morgue was in the basement. Martin Delaney had been notified of Sheriff Ripley's death. When he learned Terry Hamilton was with him, he laughed. "Well, well. Now let's hear what excuse they have this time." He moved closer to the body and pulled the sheet away from the face. It looked paunchy, extremely pale and bruised from the fall. Martin said, "I suppose I'll never know what brought you over to the lighthouse, sheriff. This whole affair has been mighty strange." Putting the sheet back, the prosecutor moved toward the elevator.

He exited on the lobby floor and went to the desk to locate Terry's room.

Dan waited until Charlie Stevens and Terry were finished talking before he entered the room. The police protection he'd ordered was now in place in the hallway. Shortly, they bared Martin's entry.

Dan went out into the hallway to face her enemy – eager for the encounter as his rage built.

"Who do you think you are, Dan?" Martin said out of earshot of the officers.

"I'm Terry Hamilton's future husband. I thought you knew that."

"Well, it seems she has been present at another death. Aren't

244

you just a trifle concerned about this? Sheriff Ripley is dead. I think he was murdered . . . what do you think?"

Dan's patience was exhausted. "I think you'd better be on your way, Martin." The terse sounds came out evenly, but there was steel in his delivery.

"If I have to go get a warrant for her arrest, I will."

"You do that, Martin."

"You seem pretty sure of yourself."

"What I'm sure of is this, she'd better not be disturbed until she's feeling better. You obviously realize she has been through a terrible ordeal. I won't allow her to be put through anything else right now." With that statement Dan turned on his heel and went inside Terry's room closing the door in Martin's face.

* * * * *

Charlie Stevens had a hard time convincing Captain Birch that he needed to fly the chopper back to the island. Eventually, after repeating all of the story as he knew it, Birch relented. Charlie and the pilot left immediately. The lights on the police helicopter were powerful illuminating the rain soaked grassy knoll. Sheeting rain pelted the bubble as Charlie advised the pilot to leave her running. "What I've got to do won't take but a few minutes." The California Cypress trees fanned toward the doorway pummeled by the wind and rain. Charlie squinted running under them. Just beyond it, to the left of the entrance, he found the canvas. Once it was opened and he saw the crowbar, Charlie yelled into the wind, "YES!" Rewrapping the metal without touching it only took him a few seconds. He clutched it and ran toward the helicopter and jumped inside. "Okay, Barney, head for home." The deputy grinned, savoring the moment when he could spring his surprise on Martin Delaney. Charlie wasn't vindictive, but this was poetic justice if there ever was any.

Charlie asked Ro Birch to drive over to the hospital with him. He really thought they should have a meeting in the lobby to compare notes. So much had happened that day, it was hard to comprehend. Before they went to the hospital, Charlie stopped at the lab to get forensics to test the crowbar.

Pathologist Tom Barton was an old man. He had been in Crescent City all his life and should have retired ages ago, but there never was anyone to replace him. Charlie's face lit. "Tom, thanks a bunch for coming right over. This is real important. I've got it right here in this canvas. Nobody has touched it but the murderer. I think Captain Tillman's blood is on it. How long will you need to finish?"

"Hmm. Charlie, given it is so late, better call me at 6:00 A.M. I'll just stay here and work the night. I can see you are all stirred up."

"Tom," he said with authority, "Pull Sheriff Ripley's prints to compare. I think it will save you a lot of time." The deputy thanked him and left.

At the hospital, Bert went to Terry's room to collect his boss. They all went to the cafeteria where Charlie bought coffee for everyone.

Ro Birch began to tell them how they processed all the criminals. "I can't tell you how good I feel, Dan. What an operation. We've got twenty-six wets in the slammer. Some were illegals just along for the ride, others were divers who'd been hired. Of course, Olaf Czechof was the leader. There were some crewmen who looked like thugs and fishermen, but I'll bet they all have rap sheets. We are running them through the system now, and someone in your office has contacted INS. It'll get processed one way or the other."

Bert laughed. "Hot dog. That was the slickest operation I've ever been involved in. And, when that corpsman lobbed one across the bow, I thought I'd die laughing. I'll bet Czechof dirtied his shorts."

They all laughed at that remark.

Ro sobered. "Oh, I'm sorry, Dan. How is your girl?"

Dan smiled. "Thank God, she's not hurt. She's sleeping right now. It was exposure and shock. I guess he had her outside on that balcony for a long time, soaking wet and scared. He actually tried to throw her off the cat walk seventy-five feet onto those rocks below." Dan's anger fused into his look. "He must have slipped, lost his balance and went careening onto the rocks. I'm thankful he's dead."

"Did he tell her why he was trying to frame her?" Bert asked.

"I think he obsessed over the fact that her family had money. The guy hated rich people. It hardly makes any sense, but she was at the wrong place at the wrong time."

"You mean when she found Soto's body?" Charlie seemed puzzled.

"Yes. After that she and the captain became friends. Ripley must have come here to force the old man to divulge the wreck site. When he refused, the sheriff murdered him. He figured Terry would be worried when the captain didn't show up for dinner and probably would come here. He had the telephone tapped. That's how he found out the captain had stashed the map at her house."

"Remember, Terry said that she saw a Mercedes in the parking lot the morning she found Soto's body?" Charlie stated. "It had to have been Jesus. He might have been worried about the body floating into the cove and probably came here early to see, but Terry and the dog showed up."

Bert shook his head in agreement.

"I'll root around in his office tonight. I imagine I'll find some connecting evidence there." Charlie stood up. "I think I'll go over there now before anyone else get's the same idea."

Ro Birch followed shortly after agreeing to meet Dan in the morning, and the investigator followed.

Dan tiptoed into her room. He watched her sleep for awhile; then yawning, curled up in an armchair next to the bed.

Terry awoke first. It took awhile to remember where she was and why. When she saw Dan sleeping in the chair she smiled. *God is good.* She was still alive and now, it was finally over.

Dan heard her stirring. Opening a sleepy eye, he grinned. "Hi, Mrs. Levine-to-be." Shortly, he came over to her bed and sat down. "Can I have a hug? I'm sorely in need of one."

Terry grabbed his shoulders and pulled him close. "I'm not going to let you out of my sight from now on." She kissed him and then sat up. "I need to talk to you about something you aren't going to believe."

Dan could see the seriousness. "Sure. What is it?"

Terry watched his face carefully as she explained the events in the lighthouse. At times she could see his anger, there was pathos, fear and, eventually, joy. He didn't react to the information about the captain of the *Brother Jonathan*. In fact, when she concluded he looked strange. "Do you believe me?"

Dan stood up and shook his head. "Maybe you saw all of that out of fear."

"Dan, look at me." Terry's face sobered. "I gave him a promise that only you can fulfill. It isn't a request. Somehow, I must keep my word."

Dan walked around the room baffled. He didn't believe in ghosts. He didn't want to hurt or upset her, especially now. It just wouldn't be fair to argue.

"How would I have known where the murder weapon was if he hadn't told me?"

"I don't know. I do know Charlie went there and is having it analyzed as we speak. It was right where you said it would be. The sheriff would not have left it there, that is certain. Someone had to have put it there so it would be found."

Terry's frustration mounted. If Dan wouldn't bring up those skeletons so they could be given a decent burial and be blessed, Captain DeWolfe would be condemned to walk the earth for all eternity. The man had saved her life. It was a sworn duty to save his. Sinking into the pillow and shutting her eyes, using mental telepathy she said, *Captain, show him, please.*

* * * * *

The *Crescent City Herald* used their largest type to proclaim the tragedy. By 10:00 A.M. the entire coastal area knew that Ripley had fallen from the lighthouse tower and that Terry Hamilton was with him when it happened.

Dan brought Terry home as soon as it was light. He knew the reporters would be all over them and instructed Bert to stand guard. Today was the day they were going down to check the wreck. It wasn't reasonable that he wouldn't be there, but he didn't want to leave her.

"I'm all right, Dan," Terry insisted. "Marge is here to run things, and Bert said he will stand guard. Besides," she laughed and reached for the dog, "I've got my protector here, don't I, boy?" Terry used the back of her hand to shoo him upstairs.

Dan went to change clothes.

Bert went to the door when he heard a knock. It was the deputy, and he was very excited. "Come on in. Terry is in the living room," she heard him say.

"Get Dan. Get him right now . . . have I got news."

Bert ran upstairs while the deputy paced in front of her.

Shortly, they both returned. Charlie asked them to sit down. "I flew to the island last night. I found the crowbar right where Terry said it would be. It was analyzed during the night. The only prints on it were the sheriff's. The blood was Captain Tillman's." Charlie watched their faces for recognition.

Dan yelled, "GOOD GOD, THAT'S WONDERFUL! Now we can get rid of Delaney once and for all."

The lawman looked smug. He knew it was a coup they all needed. "And, that ain't all."

Bert became excited. "What? Tell us quick."

"I found lots of letters from Mr. Henry to Ripley indicating what Terry's grandmother's collection included. It seems that Mrs. Baldwin and Mrs. Ripley's sister were friends of long standing. Mrs. Ripley loved art, and although she couldn't afford to buy it, she studied it religiously. Eventually, she grew jealous of Mrs. Baldwin's collection, which she had never seen but had records of. I guess it took years to accumulate the information via her sister. It looks as if she and the sheriff were in it together. They knew about the Madonna which came from Mexico City, but they really believed that Henry had that situation well in hand. They apparently wanted to leave here and retire to the Caribbean. When they got the gold, they intended to flee the country. I found records of a house they had leased in Saint Thomas."

Terry thanked Charlie. "I can't tell you what you've done for me. This has been a nightmare. Your kindness is really above and beyond anything we might have expected."

The lawman flushed immediately. "Ma'am, I was doin' my job. That's what I'm supposed to do. I do admit that I've grown quite fond of you both, and I'm really happy how it turned out. Dan, would you like to go with me to Mr. Delaney's office? I gotta feelin' you would like to tell him what forensics came up with."

Dan grunted. "Damn right, Charlie. Let's go, but you tell him while I watch."

After he kissed Terry, they left.

* * * * *

Martin had been up half the night contemplating his next move. He knew his anger was coloring all of his efforts. He had to control that somehow. Dan Levine was no small adversary. If he filed on her, he'd better have Terry dead to rights – a cold case. He went to his filing cabinet and withdrew a file with her name on it. Inside he sifted through the clippings from the old man's death and the news stories of the body found in the cove. This was amazing. How could one woman be present at the death of so many people and not be involved? She probably had Dan Levine snowed; after all, he was in her bed. Martin went to the lower drawer in his desk and got out a bottle. He poured himself two fingers of the whiskey and downed it. There were still a bunch of loose ends, and he had to be certain he was right.

He heard footsteps. It was too early for anyone to be in the building. He put the liquor away quickly and sat down at his desk. Listening to the footsteps on the marble floors in the corridor, he realized they were coming straight to his office. The door opened.

Charlie Stevens entered and they exchanged greetings.

"Well, deputy, you are up early. What can I do for you?"

"I just wanted to bring you the forensics report on the weapon I found over on the island last night."

"What weapon?" Martin frowned. He was obviously puzzled.

"The one Sheriff Ripley used to kill Captain Tillman."

Dan entered at that moment eager to see Martin's face.

Martin's mouth opened, he gaped. "Why wasn't I informed that you had a weapon? You don't withhold evidence. Don't you know that?"

Charlie grinned. His slender face looked almost boyish beneath the ten-gallon hat. "You were gone when I finally got permission from the state police to fly back to the island to get it."

"Who told you where it was?"

"Miss Hamilton."

"Well, that proves she is guilty. How else would she know where it was?"

"The sheriff told her when he was about to throw her off the metal balcony around the lens room in the lighthouse."

Martin's face reddened. Anger was fusing through his body and his voice rose powerfully. "I haven't had the opportunity to interrogate Ms. Hamilton yet. How would I know what he told her. In fact, how do you know what he told her?"

"She told me last night at the hospital. It was her intention to have me go over to that island and get the proof she needed to clear herself. I was only too happy to do that, Mr. Delaney. See, I never did believe she killed that old man. They was good friends, and she isn't the kind of woman to do anybody harm."

Dan felt a smirk rising.

"How do you know what kind of woman she is?"

"Well, I've gotten to know her, sir. She's a real nice lady."

Charlie moved closer to Martin's desk. He laid the report on top of the clippings that were spread out there. "It says here that Sheriff Ripley's prints were on the crowbar and the blood stains came from Captain Tillman. Sheriff Ripley was already dead when I found this so he couldn't have put his prints on the crowbar recently, and Captain Tillman's been dead a long time. I figure there ain't a jury in the world who would convict Terry Hamilton. So, how come you called her and left a message yesterday with her housekeeper to meet you at the island at 3:00 P.M. to look at the captain's belongings?"

Martin's eyes widened. "What the hell are you talking about? I had nothing to do with her trip to the island."

"Ms. Hamilton's housekeeper took the message. She'll testify to that, Mr. Delaney. I figure the district attorney will probably want to remove you from this whole matter because of a conflict of interest. Don't you think?"

Dan's soul was being renewed. Charlie's voice had a silken quality flowing over the crestfallen lawyer whose face reflected his utter defeat.

"I just wanted to inform you, Mr. Delaney, because now, I've got to go and tell the district attorney about this recent evidence."

Martin was nonplussed. He couldn't look at Dan who was too much of a gentleman to gloat.

Dan knew this was the end of it. As far as Terry was concerned, there was only the inquest and that would go smoothly. He buttoned his coat and turned, going out into the hall without ever having to say a word. He did have one stop to make before he boarded the state police harbor patrol boat.

Dan went into the lower lobby of the court house to the phone station. He looked up a number in the small telephone book and called the Chairman of the Board of Supervisors for the County, Lewis Latimer.

"Good morning, Mr. Latimer, this is Chief Deputy Attorney General Dan Levine. Sorry to call so early, but I have a matter the attorney general wanted me to convey." Dan talked on for several minutes explaining that they had located the wreck and would be bringing artifacts to the historical society soon. Dan could hear Latimer's mounting excitement as he ranted on and on about the attorney general's wonderful efforts. Finally, when there was an opening, Dan said, "Oh, by the way, sir, the governor is going to give a special commendation to Charlie Stevens, the Crescent City deputy, for his efforts on California's behalf. The attorney general wanted you to know that since you've lost your elected sheriff. He felt you could do no better than to appoint such an efficient lawman to that position. We realize we should not interfere in the town's business, but everyone in our division thinks he is a superior officer. We just wanted you to know that. Oh, and sir, we would all like you and the mayor to attend the ceremony in the capitol. I'll have my secretary contact you and your wife about the dates." Latimer was purring by the time Dan finished. Dan was all smiles all the way to the car.

Chapter 20

The Captain's Sign

The armada reached the site just after dawn. Divers were in the water almost immediately. Prior to sailing, the archaeologists had been given a thorough briefing and everyone in the group was excited now that the ship had been located and the team of specialists were actually working. Dan made it explicit to each of the undersea teams that the top priority of the dives would be the gold coins and bars. It was an educated guess that the leather bags surrounding the coins would have long since disintegrated, but the bars would probably be in a cask of some sort that was being held in a metal safe and could still be intact.

After having met with people from the town council and the historical society, Dan agreed that certain of their members could be present during the search. Three people were selected because of their familiarity with the *Brother Jonathan*. They brought along their drawings, diagrams and research. It was mutually agreed that the information would be of some help. Computers had been hooked up to electronics in the radio room of the patrol boat. All the finds were quickly recorded, described and named by the assistants to the archaeologists. Their preparation had been so thorough that information could be transmitted back to the university where a group of researchers were standing by to accept and compile the current finds. They would also be available to do research in the event that something was found that could not be explained or identified. All in all, electricity flowed through the expedition, and everyone on board was ready and willing to be part of it.

The weather had improved. Although no longer raining, the sky was ominous under heavy, dark clouds lurking over the search area. The sea turned black, floating huge swells that lifted them regularly, sinking them on the down flow. Dan had stuck a seasick patch to his inner elbow, for which he was grateful by early afternoon when the ocean turned choppy and began to whitecap.

The divers were already bringing up artifacts. Precious finds were being examined immediately. Cataloging would be done after they were laid out to dry on huge canvas sheets on the deck of a big troller. Of course, it would be necessary to acid bathe most of the selections that had corroded over time. A big tub had been prepared on one of the boats for soaking crusted items. Some were so encased they were barely recognizable.

Underwater cameras were taken below, and using portable lighting, the wreck was photographed. That film would be used later for the myriad of things that were being proposed.

It went on that way for two days. On the third day, a diver surfaced, pulled off his face mask and yelled, "Gold! I've found gold."

The entire fleet was alerted. Everyone came in as close as possible while the rubber suited figure lifted his net to the ladder and watched it being hauled on board. He dove again. The find was exhibited. The coins from an early minting were rough but solid. They were intrinsically valuable because of age and, depending on the purity of the metal, literally worth their weight. Of course, they weren't contained because of the length of time submerged in the ocean and while the currents moved it about, the coins wound up in strange places in the wreck. The divers had undersea lights, which helped some, torches to cut through metal and one of them had a metal detector. By evening the metal storage containers were beginning to fill. Plans had been made to have an armored car standing by. The collection was to have been housed in the safe of the local bank until enough had been collected to warrant moving it. That would be handled by a SWAT team using the helicopter. The state plane was standing by to meet the helicopter at an undisclosed location for the transfer of the precious metal to a bank in Sacramento.

Dan was becoming agitated. He paced back and forth on the deck. Everything was going smoothly, and that was so unusual he didn't exactly know how to handle it.

When he returned each evening, he kept Terry and Bert captivated with stories and explanations. Eventually, he even brought Polaroid shots of the finds. Dinner every night was as interesting as anything they had previously experienced. It was a thoroughly entertaining experience, which they were all really enjoying.

A determination was made as to how long the entire project would take. Those in authority estimated several years, maybe more, but for now, the most important search was the gold.

Dinner that evening seemed especially festive. Dan proposed a toast to Charlie, Bert and his wife-to-be. Everyone drank and laughed as toast after toast was raised. Charlie told them he had been named interim sheriff of Crescent City. They all cheered and raised another toast. Bert had just received word that he was to be given a commendation from the governor for his extraordinary skills in solving the complicated case. They toasted Bert. Terry stood to personally thank each and every one of them for saving her life and solving the crime. She toasted her husband-to-be in glowing terms.

Becoming very serious, Dan made a speech. He asked the two men to be in his wedding. He said they had saved Terry's life and for that he would be eternally grateful. He looked over at her and saw tears sliding down her cheeks. "Don't cry, darling."

"I can't help it, Dan. I always cry when I'm happy."

Bert left to call Ted, telling them he was expecting some interesting information. He was gone about twenty minutes. When he returned they were all in the living room, drinking coffee and enjoying the newly built fire.

"Well, folks – now I can put this case to bed. I just heard from Ted that he went back to the art gallery for a second search and found a couple of threads that will tie up the loose ends. In the cherry wood desk in the main room he found a letter from an Italian art dealer stating the check for $250,000 was a down payment on the Madonna. The money didn't come to Mr. Henry; it came to his mama. And, of course, it will have to be returned. She was the brains behind this outfit. It looks as if she masterminded the sale of the painting with a European buyer who would not ask any questions. He had already made a deal with the Catholic Church for five million dollars for the stolen painting. Imagine that? Terry could make the same deal but," he looked over and smiled, "I know she is a great lady; she wouldn't do it. I learned that when I spoke to Adam Linquist earlier. He sends his regards and said to tell you that the Pope is sending you a letter with a request for a private audience in the Vatican on your honeymoon to personally thank you and your husband for your gracious gift. He wanted to tell you himself, but he had to leave for Scotland on business tonight. He said he would call you within four days. He said this news was too good to keep."

Dan gasped. "Terry, honey, that is marvelous. You deserve that for being so decent."

"I have everything I want, Dan. I don't need to take money from a church. Letty and grandfather Baldwin would absolutely concur."

On the following day Terry contacted Donald Bataglia, the

president of the Crescent City Historical Society. They spoke briefly before Terry told him what her intentions were.

"I would like to arrange to pay for and organize the funeral for the skeletons that I hope will be brought up from the wreck. I know that funerals are expensive, and I thought, perhaps, your organization wouldn't have the funds to accomplish this matter, Mr. Bataglia," Terry said.

Mr. Bataglia was only too happy to cooperate. By now everyone knew that Terry Hamilton was engaged to Dan Levine who was emerging as the town hero. There were plans being made to build a museum to house the artifacts. Once the entire matter was given national press, everyone assumed that donations would be forthcoming. There was even talk of raising the *Brother Jonathan* and trying to put her back together. Many of the historical society people believed tourists would pay a decent price to climb aboard a famous paddle wheel steamer. All in all, the future looked bright for Crescent City.

That evening they were alone. Marge had gone home for a few days to stay with her sister who was visiting Crescent City. Charlie was busy with his new office, and Bert had flown back to Sacramento to finish up, as he put it, "a few loose ends."

Terry put their dinner out. They sat down and looked at each other. "It seems strange to be alone, Dan," she said eating her salad.

He appeared smug. "I like it. We've got some plans to make."

"I wanted to tell you that I've arranged for the funeral of the skeletons from the *Brother Jonathan*."

Dan's surprise registered. "I didn't think you were serious about that? After all you were quite upset then, Terry, but you are well now."

"I gave my word."

"You don't really expect me to believe that you spoke to a ghost – let alone that you made him a promise?"

"I expect you to believe whatever I say is the truth. I would have thought by now, Dan, you would know who I am." There was suddenly wrath in her glance. "It would never occur to me to question something you told me." Terry clenched her fists and dropped her napkin on the table with force.

The man's face grew solemn. He drank some wine silently, and it was deathly quiet in the dining room. Finally he said, "I can't justify the cost of bringing those bones to the surface."

"I'll pay for it."

"And, what reason would I give my boss for doing something like that? I'd be the laughing stock of my entire agency if this ever got out. I've worked really hard to achieve my position, Terry."

Slowly, the artist stood. Looking directly into his dark eyes she said, "If you don't believe me, then surely, we shouldn't be together." Having said that, Terry took off her ring and laid it beside his plate. "I'm going to take the dog out for a walk. I suggest you plan to sleep in the guest room tonight."

Suddenly, they were gone and shock overcame the man. He reached down and picked up the ring he'd given her. Staring at the stone, he felt sick. "What have I done?" he choked out.

Terry ran hard along the sand. It was cold and the wind was up. She stopped to stare out at the lighthouse looking forlorned and being pummeled by the choppy wind-driven sea. "It is all your fault," she said into the wind bitterly. It was late when she returned to the house. Dan wasn't in sight. Terry went up to her room with Baron and the desolation she felt overwhelmed her. They'd had their first fight, and it might also be their last.

Dan was gone by the time Terry came down to the kitchen the next morning. The ships went out early each day. After she made coffee, she began to plan how she would handle her promise. It took only a few minutes to reach the Scripts School of Oceanography in San Diego. There were a few phone transfers before she reached the proper department. It wasn't difficult to explain the request. They understood the problem and were certain they could accommodate the dive. The instructor was an old navy man. He told her he'd be glad to come up himself, but he needed to check schedules and would be in touch. Terry gave him her number and hung up.

At 6:00 P.M. Dan returned. The artist, who was preparing dinner, saw him standing in the doorway. He looked sheepish. "I was wondering if we could talk," he said softly, sounding very hesitant.

Terry nodded.

"Let's go into the living room. Would you like to have me get you a glass of wine?"

"No."

"I think I'd like a drink. Do you mind?"

"No."

Dan went to the refrigerator and took out a beer, which he uncapped. "Are you sure you wouldn't like a glass of wine?"

Terry just stared at him silently, her huge eyes evidencing her pain.

He followed her to the living room where she sat down on the divan. Her face seemed beautiful but lifeless. Dan was afraid. "I thought about our discussion all day. In fact, I couldn't think about much else."

It was silent in the room.

"I love you. I need you, and that is not a small thing. If I hurt you yesterday, I'm truly sorry. Won't you discuss this with me?" He wasn't used to pleading; it felt very uncomfortable.

"What is there to discuss, Dan? You don't believe me. I don't want to be married to someone who doesn't believe me. Can you really blame me for that?"

"It is just so bizarre, hon. I'm not unusual. Most men would react the same way."

"I just didn't think you were like most men. I suppose I was wrong. Why would I want to be married to someone who thinks I'm a liar? My word is my bond. My grandfather instilled that into me when I was a child. It didn't occur to me that you wouldn't believe me. I loved you so much, I guess, I honestly didn't think you had faults."

"Well, I do. I hate to disillusion you, but I'm human. You are being naive."

The girl took a deep breath. "It doesn't matter, Dan. I've taken care of the problem. You've hurt me very deeply. I don't know if this can be repaired. If you honestly believe there is nothing else in this world besides what you can see and prove – what can I say?"

"You can say you understand." He appeared distraught. "I'm not alone, most people would agree with me."

"Dan, Drew University has a school that studies the paranormal full time. U.C.L.A. also does infrared testing of auras and other paranormal studies. There is proof that energy appearing in a place changes the temperature. There has been evidence of other dimensions for a long time. People – ordinary people – have homes that are haunted by poltergeists; they have been photographed. I don't pretend to understand it, but I know it occurs. I have seen this man three times. I spoke to him twice. The captain and I had two conversations about it. He saw him also. Why would I make this up?"

Dan looked embarrassed. He was a logical thinker. He had to admit she wouldn't gain anything by telling him this story. It also occurred to him that she was going to a lot of trouble and expense to satisfy this request. No one would do that without a good reason. "I'm sorry. I didn't mean to question your integrity. I think you are one of the finest women I've ever met. It is just so . . ." His voice trailed off.

"I understand how difficult it would be to believe something like this. Especially, if you've never thought about it before. But, because it is different doesn't make it untrue. Why don't you ask those people from the historical society? I understand lighthouse keepers have claimed the place has been haunted for a long time." She paused and became terse before saying, "Captain DeWolfe saved my life, Dan. I owe him a debt, and I mean to repay it."

Dan looked sick. His eyes were as sad as she had ever experienced. "Please, Terry, don't throw us away. You mean everything to me. I'm pretty used to having my own way; it comes from being single for a long time. Be patient, hon, but for God's sake put my ring back on your finger."

She couldn't stand to see him in such pain. Moving toward him, she put her arms around him. "I love you. I need you too, but don't question my veracity, Dan. That is very important to me."

They kissed and clung together for a long time before he carried her upstairs. In the morning she was wearing the ring.

* * * * *

Dan stood on the bow of the ship just as they reached the salvage site. In his pocket he carried a copy of a sketch Terry had made for him of the brass belt buckle Captain DeWolfe wore. She said if they found his body he would be wearing it. Also, the captain would be with a woman and a child. Knowing the years, storms and tides could have moved them, Dan agreed to take the sketch. He imagined everything else might have changed, but the belt buckle would remain the same except for discoloration. Terry made it quite clear that there was a symbol of the British Navy in the center and his name engraved upon the brass. Dan shook his head; she was quite emphatic about the matter.

The finds were excellent that day. The divers radioed that they had found the safe and were torching the hinges to break into it. They asked that the hoist basket be lowered into a certain location because of weight. They all waited with baited breath, and it seemed an eternity before the darkened cask swung up over the bow, sea water pouring from its innards. Everyone gathered to see it opened. When that finally happened there were gasps. It was filled with gold bars. Their distinctive dull shine raised a huge cheer as the diver reached inside and took one out.

"There it is, Dan," Ro Birch shouted. He was astounded picking one up and feeling the weight; he handed it to the lawyer.

Dan appeared dazed. "I must admit I was skeptical. Wow! This is quite a find." It felt heady, the excitement flipped the pit of his stomach. In that instant he visualized unveiling the gold at the office for the entire staff to see. What a coup. It was real now – he had actually pulled it off.

They were almost ready to head into shore when one of the divers climbed on board. "Mr. Levine, I found something interesting. Come and look at it." He removed his scuba equipment and walked toward Dan with his hands outstretched.

As Dan approached he could see the metal. "What is it?"

"It looks like a British Admiralty belt buckle. It has a name inscribed on it. Holy Toledo, it is the name of the captain . . . Look! It says DeWolfe right here." He pointed to the inscription. "That is the man who sailed the *Brother Jonathan*."

"Did you find his skeleton?" Dan questioned anxiously.

The diver nodded. "He was with a woman and a child. I know it was a woman because she is wearing a feminine religious medal around her neck. Her hand was entwined with the child's. I imagine she was his mother. They died together."

Dan's expression changed to surprise. The buckle looked exactly as she described it, and the markings were the same. Terry couldn't have drawn it unless she had seen it. The lawyer took the buckle over to the people from the historical society who were just preparing to leave. "Mr. Fergeson, I wonder if I could ask you a few questions, sir." Dan handed the new find to the historian.

"Why certainly. What did you want to know?" Vern Fergeson became excited as he fingered the brass buckle. "This is better than finding the gold." He was grinning broadly and calling to the other members of his team to come and see it. Turning

264

back, he looked expectant asking, "Now, what do you want to know?"

Dan posed the questions as if he was just curious. He always had to watch how he did that. Interrogation came easily to lawyers and people resented it. They talked for quite awhile. Dan thanked him and watched the boat leave and head for shore.

Dan called to the diver. "Can you go and bring them up? It is most important." They all agreed and putting their masks back on the trio jumped back into the sea.

At 7:00 P.M. Dan arrived at the beach house. Terry was in the kitchen taking baked lasagna out of the oven. The aroma was pungent in the room.

"Oh, Dan. Good! You're home. I've made us a really nice dinner, and I'm hungry. I hope you are." She could see his look. It was different almost compassionate. "What's happened? I can see by your expression you have news."

He came into the kitchen and kissed her gently. Then, he said softly, "Will you come and sit down? I have something to tell you."

"Certainly. Just let me dry my hands from washing the lettuce." She clutched the towel and quickly used it, then dropped it onto the counter, anxious to hear what he had to say.

Once they were in the living room, he led them to the divan. "We found the gold today."

Terry's voice raised. "Tell me quick."

"The gold bars were in a wooden cask. It was thrilling. I've never held a gold bar before. No telling what it is worth. I've had the SWAT unit fly it directly to Sacramento. Once the word got out it would be dangerous to have it around." He looked at his watch. "It should be arriving there shortly. I'll be getting a call when it is taken care of."

"Dan, I'm happy for you. It has been a long, hard fight. I wondered at times if it ever would be found and if we'd live to see it." She leaned closer and kissed his cheek.

"That's not all. I found this." He handed her the buckle.

"My God! It's Captain DeWolfe's." Terry's look became ebullient. "You've found them," Terry squealed. "Dan, oh, honey, now – I can keep my promise." She clasped her hands around his neck eagerly as her look brightened into complete satisfaction while she hugged him.

Pride laced the lawyer's smile; he'd made her happy again. It was a good feeling. "I had the divers go down this evening. They were brought up within the hour. In fact, they are being prepared for burial as we speak. It is my wedding present to you. I hope you like it?" He closed his eyelids.

Terry clung to him. "I love you. Thank you." She laughed lightly before getting up and drawing him toward the kitchen. "Let's have some wine. I want to toast the successful completion of the most bizarre project in history."

"Wait!" he said pulling her back to the divan. "I know I didn't believe you. I'm sorry. You couldn't have known what he was wearing or what this buckle looked like unless you had seen it. You also couldn't have known that these people had died together. They found the three of them side by side. The woman's hand clutched the child's. She was wearing a medal. It still hung around the skeleton's neck. Please, accept my humble apology, darling."

Later, after they had eaten and Dan had completed his calls to and from his office, they contacted Donald Bataglia. It was decided by mutual consent that the funeral would take place the following week. At Terry's request the headstones were already being prepared for those who would be named. The others would have headstones which read, "Unknown – died Sunday – July 30, 1865 on the ship *Brother Jonathan*. May their souls rest in peace." Terry elected to have them made of oak stained planked wood. The pertinent information was routed out and painted in off-white. The bottom of the marker would contain a brass plaque which said, "This body was brought to the surface from the sunken ship *Brother Jonathan* on July 30, 1996, and laid to rest August 12, 1996, by the State of California."

Crescent City's newspaper account of the search and location of Captain DeWolfe's remains was the talk of the town. The funeral was turning into the social event of the year; it was not to be missed. A local chamber music group offered to play before the ceremony. The Daughter's of the American Revolution donated tiny American flags which had been placed around the perimeter of the cemetery's fence. Flowers had been delivered to the mortuary all the previous day. In fact, the mortician was forced to hire a van to carry the huge amount of sprays and plant stands that had been sent by local businesses and historical society members. The mayor was scheduled to speak as was the president of the historical society. As a special courtesy, Chief Deputy Attorney General Dan Levine was asked to be the principal speaker.

Terry and Dan ordered nautical sprays of flowers for their three friends. They arrived early to place them at the grave site. The chamber group was tuning up and eventually began to play. It was a glorious day. Down below the ocean sparkled under the reflected sunlight. A slight breeze wafting across the compound cooled them as they stood gazing at the caskets waiting to be interned. Dan held her hand, squeezing it as they waited. Terry glanced over and smiled from under the brim of her black straw picture hat. She looked elegant in her black linen suit. Dan's admiring glance showed how proud he was that she was going to be his wife.

Within fifteen minutes the crowds began to arrive. The mayor approached and offered them a seat near the open graves. There were seven skeletons brought up for burial. Terry had asked that the captain, the lady and the child be buried side by side at the head of the group. She eyed the coffins feeling exhilarated and wondering if the captain was nearby.

Chamber music floated around them as the old cemetery filled with mourners. Mayor Haggerman spoke first, followed by Donald Bataglia, president of the Historical Society, and finally, Dan.

Terry felt proud watching her future husband get up to speak to the crowd. He addressed everyone of note, the townspeople and finally, surprisingly, Terry.

"I honestly believe that my future wife should be speaking to you today. Terry Hamilton spearheaded the funeral for the poor, unfortunate souls who lost their lives on the *Brother Jonathan* over a hundred years ago. She did so because she believed they needed to have a decent burial and resting place. Obviously, ladies and gentlemen, you believed that also. I hope that Captain DeWolfe and those who died with him know how much we all care. I have been told that a fund has been set up to provide flowers for these graves on Easter Sunday each year. I believe that is fitting. Now, please stand while Rev. Jack Ramford blesses the deceased and their grave sites."

The minister stepped up to the small podium and began the prayer. Everyone bowed their heads. Soon it was over. The crowd was polite and orderly, quietly leaving the cemetery. Terry asked Dan to stay. He agreed.

Soon the grave diggers appeared to lower the casket. Captain DeWolfe's was first, then the woman and finally the child. Terry had insisted the child's skeleton be placed in the casket with the mother. The third casket was empty. Only Dan and the mortician knew of the change. Once the dirt was put into the graves Terry asked the grave diggers to stop and return in a few minutes. They obliged. When they were gone she knelt to place the flowers on top of each grave. "Captain, I have fulfilled my promise. Please, go home and be happy. Tell Captain Tillman I will name my first born son Amos in honor of my dear friend."

Terry swiped at her eyes with a handkerchief. Dan encircled her shoulder. "Go ahead and cry, hon. I know they heard you."

They stood up. Dan clutched her to him. He started to speak but stopped his mouth agape. There, at the head of the two graves were the apparitions. The woman was smiling broadly while clutching her child in her arms. Captain DeWolfe blew Terry a kiss and said, "Aye, lass. I knew I could count on you. Be happy the pair of you."

Dan's obsidian eyes glistened, widening as they watched. It only lasted seconds. Suddenly, they saw the ghosts rising above them and disappearing.

Terry smiled. "It was nice of him to show himself to you, my darling. Now, you don't have to wonder for a lifetime whether it actually happened. It was a gift to both of us."

Epilogue

Forever

Living in Dan's apartment had been fun at first, but after weeks of getting up early, driving him to the office and spending frustrating hours viewing house after house, Terry felt drained. There had been some good news. The house in Crescent City, which the realtor priced at $500,000, had been sold for $495,000. In fact, Terry had barely listed it when there was a contract. It hurt momentarily. Dan couldn't believe her reaction until she explained all of the sentiment regarding Letty and her grandfather and the nostalgia connected to it. The new owners wanted to buy it furnished because they, like Letty, were going to use it for a summer house. She agreed. In hindsight she made a request for some personal items, and the request was granted.

Friday, early in the morning during the third week, Terry received a call from the first realtor she'd met in San Francisco. The woman sounded excited, breathless. "It must be important," Terry commented. "Uh, huh . . . uh, huh . . . oh, all right, I'll be there." Putting the phone into the cradle, the artist glanced at Dan busy still putting on his tie.

"Well, what?"

"I can't believe it." She laughed lightly. "It sounds as if this house has everything I want, and I was beginning to think there wasn't such a place."

"Honey, I've got to get going," Dan said impatiently. "Please, let's go, you can tell me on the way."

At 10:00 A.M. Terry drove onto a road marked Hilltop Lane. The secluded tree-lined driveway raised curiosity, but she was unable to see the house until the road turned sharply. Terry slammed the brakes. Up to the right on a wooded bluff sat an extraordinary stone and clapboard, ivy-covered farmhouse. Gaping, she said, "Maybe, just maybe . . . Dan and I have found our home." Beside a parked car in the circular driveway the realtor waited – waving.

"Hello, Mrs. Pierson. Have you been waiting long?"

"No. I've just arrived. The owner isn't here, and I've unlocked the door. Let's go on inside."

The heavy, black front door creaked as it swung ajar alongside a brass plate that read HILLTOP HOUSE. Inside was an inviting entry hall whose polished wooden floors lead to a curving staircase where spindles were white against a pine railing and tread, curving as it gracefully ascended to the floor above. To the right of the hall was a big living room. The center piece, a colonial fireplace large enough to stand in, contained black andirons, a cast iron pot on an iron hinge, iron fireplace equipment and a wide stone hearth upon which sat a brass log holder. The outside fieldstone wall, where six large, white French doors were recessed, faced a clump of mature trees and a garden. On either side of the fireplace double French doors opened onto a stone terrace. The country house overlooked the river far below and the magnificent bay bridge off in the distance. The realtor opened the doors drawing them outside. Fortunately, the day was clear giving the pair an unobstructed view of the distant panorama.

"It is spectacular, isn't it? I knew you'd like it, and I couldn't wait to call you after I'd seen it."

"That's an understatement, Mrs. Pierson."

The library, alongside the entry on the other side of the house, replete with colorful leather volumes, red leather chairs and a couch, a cherry wood claw-footed desk and Duncan Fife tables, seemed cozy and warm. Terry pictured Dan working there. The door to the room closed behind them as they went toward a formal dining room also furnished in cherry wood, which sat upon an exquisite oriental rug in red, gold and navy weave. It too faced the view and opened onto the terrace. Its walls were lined with built-in china cabinets filled with antique plates and cut glass. A huge kitchen off to the left held an unused fireplace, antiquated furnishings and sinks in what seemed to be an ugly, empty room. Terry laughed. Compared to the rest of the house, the kitchen appeared repugnant.

The realtor said, "You can tell the Bartlets didn't do the cooking. If you like the house, that would be a good point to use to reduce the price. I know you like to cook and this kitchen just wouldn't measure up."

"That's true and someone could put in a new kitchen. The room is plenty large enough, and it has a great view." After examining the pantry, cellar and the sun room, which was outside the kitchen all by itself and accessible through a long hallway, Terry's excitement grew. She hoped she was appearing calm and not giving her feelings away. Dan had certainly warned her about that.

Within a short time they climbed up to the second floor. There were four beautiful bedrooms with fireplaces, hardwood floors, and baths; there was also a small sewing room and a laundry on that floor. The master suite, complete with a sitting room that overlooked the view, had its own balcony entranced through French doors. Although very formal with thick luxurious carpets and dark, heavy period furniture and drapes, Terry was already mentally redecorating it. At the end of the hallway, a doorway led to a small staircase that served two additional bedrooms and an adjoining bath on the wing. In that same stairwell was a back staircase leading down to the kitchen.

Terry went down the main staircase and entered the living

room where she sat down. "I'd like to know the particulars please, Mrs. Pierson." She glanced up and noticed the wide, white beams in the ceiling. Early American furniture, placed tastefully all around the big room, added to its warmth.

"The room is charming, isn't it?"

Terry nodded.

The house was 55 years old. It had been built by the owner's grandfather and left to his son who owned it now. "Mr. Bartlet's wife died a year ago," she said. "They had one son who lives in Europe where he is the general manager of a subsidiary of a well-known American brokerage. Since the son will never be living here – and the elder Mr. Bartlet is getting old – they've decided to sell the family home. In fact, Mr. Bartlet has gone abroad for the winter. The transaction will be handled by his lawyer, Gerard MacDougal."

"What are they asking for it?"

"The house, outbuildings, the garage apartment and twenty-five acres of land are being offered for a million, five hundred thousand. If the purchaser would rather not have all the land, Mr. Bartlet would sell the house and five acres for $900,000. I really think they are being quite fair. He said whoever buys it for full price can have the contents except for his personal belongings. He intends to take an apartment in a highrise in San Francisco and doesn't really want the memories connected with this place. Mr. MacDougal has a list of contents that are to be removed to storage when the house is sold. There is a caretaker, who is away at the moment, but who will take care of these matters."

"I can certainly understand his problem of dealing with giving his things away. Look, Mrs. Pierson, my fiancé is in his office right now. I'd like him to meet me here, but I don't know his schedule. I'll call him and see what we can work out."

Mrs. Pierson was amenable. This would be a sizeable commission. She was amazed that someone so young could even consider buying such an expensive property. "I'll leave you the keys, Terry, so you two can view it at your leisure."

At five Dan's pool car turned into the estate. He made the bend and gasped just as Terry had done. "Oh, boy, this place must be worth a bundle," he said out loud. Sweating, he didn't want to get out of the car, but Terry ran out to greet him. Seeing the look on her face, Dan cringed. It was evident she had found her dream home.

The lights of the city began to come on before they went out to the terrace and, just as they did, the bay bridge was illuminated. Terry sighed and hugged Dan.

"How much is it?"

Terry explained as deftly as her grandfather's coaching had allowed. "The land is worth a great deal, Dan. We can buy it for investment and then, control the resale, besides wouldn't it be great to have the whole mountain to ourselves?"

Dan inhaled, beginning in a monotone, "How much, Terry? You have to tell me sooner or later."

"One million, five hundred thousand."

"WHAT! You must be joking." The lawyer paled; he was appalled.

"Dan, I sold Crescent City for $500,000 after the furniture was added. My estate in Boston is worth $2,000,000 and my grandmother's art collection is valued at over $1,000,000. Adam can sell it tomorrow. Why the hell shouldn't I spend my money the way I want to? The house will be paid for, and I expect you to pay the taxes, upkeep and help. And since I'm going to be married to you for sixty or seventy years that ought to make us even." Concluding, Terry looked exasperated.

Dan started to laugh. He laughed harder and harder the more he thought about her argument.

Terry watched soberly, anger rising. "What is so damned funny?"

"You are. My God, woman, you should have been a lawyer." He laughed again. The black eyes tearing, swelled on his red face, as he doubled over to resume the belly laughs.

"I'm glad you think this is so damned . . ."

Dan took her in his arms and kissed her into silence. "I love you Mrs. Levine-to-be. Now, shall we go inside and take a good look at our new home?"

Terry squealed. "Oh, Dan, yes, darling. I want to show you what I'm going to do to the kitchen." She was ecstatic, chatting away, her spirits ebullient; he followed into, what had become, their new kitchen.

Later, they had dinner at an Italian place on the river that Dan thought was cozy and had great food. Terry's eyes sparkled. Dan could feel the satisfaction building as she talked nonstop about their plans.

"Wait! Wait a minute! I can't keep up with you," he said munching contentedly on crusty Italian bread and sipping on a beer.

"Oh, Dan. I've never been this happy. Now, that I've sold my house in Crescent City, we can actually move here. When we buy the house, I can bring Baron, Marge and my Jeep." She paused because Dan was laughing again.

"Terry, you are wonderful. I just agreed to spend more money than I ever thought imaginable; I'm marrying a woman who positively has control, and I'm sitting here eating pasta as though none of it is happening." His eyes flashed and he laughed again.

Terry took his hand. "Dan, you now have a wonderful study; I have that great sun room for my studio; there is a garage apartment for Marge, who has agreed to come and live and work for us; there is room for your whole family to come to the wedding and stay there. We can even have our reception there."

Dan nodded. "That's right. My God, woman, you've thought of everything."

At 11:00 A.M. on the following day Terry drove into San Francisco and parked in the Skyline Building parking lot. Taking the elevator up to the roof garden, she met Dan for lunch. "Hi, hon," the young lawyer called getting up to greet her. "I've ordered already because we have an appointment shortly, and I know you don't want to be late." Dan smirked, winking. He could see she was agitated.

Terry sobered, sitting down she seemed hesitant. "Dan, would you be angry if I told you what I want to offer and how I want to offer it?"

He looked surprised. "No . . . eh, . . . I've never spent this much money before . . . well, not for personal reasons, and I think your grandfather taught you well."

Terry's smile brightened and she caressed him with her eyes. "You are so wonderful. I love you." Reaching out, she touched his hand covering it with hers.

"Honey, this is your money. I might be a chauvinist, but I've got to be fair. I also am not used to dealing in such large sums; that will take some getting used to."

"Okay." A huge sigh escaped. "What I want to offer is one million, three hundred thousand to be paid in increments of five hundred thousand and five hundred thousand, six months apart, and three hundred thousand six months from then. That will take approximately one year and a half. We will then have time to consummate the sale of the estate in Boston. I want a clause in the contract that is subject to approval from plumbing, electrical, heating and structural contractors. If there are serious problems in those areas, I expect the owner to be responsible for repairs. We will select the contractors and be responsible for their quality. I want to close and have occupancy within 30 days. We should offer twenty thousand down today . . . you know to show good faith." Terry removed a prewritten check from her purse handing it to her fiancé. "It would be expedient to also have the contents of the house minus Mr. Bartlet's personal belongings and the list that he left with his lawyer. I want to be able to have access to the house from the signing of our agreement, so I can have contractors in to examine the kitchen for rebuilding. If we do not acquire the contents, my offer drops to one million two hundred thousand."

Dan had written everything as she spoke, becoming sanguine at the conclusion. "Wow . . . lady . . . I'm impressed. That sounds very acceptable." His black eyes leveled on her. She never ceased to amaze him . . . he knew then what a wonderful life they would have.

"I expect they will haggle, and we will pay a little more; but the land, if we sell it, will bring almost a million dollars. I called an appraiser. Of course, there would be expenses preparing it and keeping the neighborhood as nice, but it is something to consider. Dan, darling, I also called Adam and he has prepared all the documents for our legal agreement so we will hold everything in joint tenancy from the day of our marriage. There is well over five million in stock plus three million in the estate, including Letty's art collection, plus the $500,000 from Crescent City. We will have to fly to Boston soon to consummate these agreements. I hope that you concur?"

"Terry, this is overwhelming," he seemed dumbstruck. "I'm feeling strange about this. I always believed I would take care of my wife when I married." The black stare drifted while he digested the facts. Suddenly he said, "Terry, honey, that is almost nine million . . . is there anything else you haven't told me, and, what happens to me, now? I want to take care of you."

"And, so you shall. Dan, you are my life now. I waited for you for a long time. I never discussed my wealth because my grandfather warned me that a lot of men would go out of their way to have it. I didn't dream I would be fortunate enough to find you. I'm certain, darling. Now, we have to do what is necessary when one has this much money. You are a very good lawyer, and you know exactly what I'm talking about." The look she had warmed him: her sincerity, her intelligence, her beauty and personal magnetism. Dan wanted to grab her, just then, and make love to her.

"Adam is very trustworthy," she continued. "He also needs us to sign the agreement releasing the painting back to the Catholic Church." Terry paused watching him, afraid it might be upsetting. It was a lot to swallow at one time, but they didn't have much time. "So, I wondered if you might not think it would be the time to see your family and tell them of our plans? I also want you to tell me if we could plan our wedding for Thanksgiving weekend. Your whole family could come and stay with us." Terry was obviously pleased at the prospect.

"Well, I agree, that would be nice, hon, but I can't do it. We want to have a honeymoon, and I can't get away right now. We could fly to Boston, I would like to see your home and your grandmother's art collection, especially the famous Madonna. Imagine that painting being worth so much? So, why don't we call my parents tonight. You can invite them for however long you want them, and we can tell them about the house. We can fly to Boston next Friday night and meet Adam. How does that sound?"

Terry, too excited to sleep, paced in Dan's apartment living room where he found her after his shower. "Well, are you up for a call?"

"Oh! Dan, it's so late back there," Terry cautioned, frowning.

"They won't care, hon. They will be thrilled at our news. I promise." Picking up the phone, Dan dialed and winked at his fiancée.

The call lasted forty minutes. Barbara Levine became so excited, she cried. Then, Terry cried. Dan and Dan Sr. had to put a stop to the water works, and they were clever about it. Terry made a wonderful gesture to Dan's mother by asking if she would come out early and give Terry guidance about the wedding; then, asked if the rest of the family would consider being in the wedding? Barbara assured her they would. They seemed surprised that there was room in their new home for everyone. Dan made huge fuss about the house. He told them in his whole life he never expected to live in such a grand place. He could tell they were happy for him.

Terry changed the subject and made Dan tell them about his recent coup in Crescent City. They knew she was proud of him. That particular conversation dredged up the pain of nearly being killed. Dan saw her look and changed the subject by asking his father if he could take some time off and come out with Barbara for at least two weeks. They agreed and it was settled.

The following week became tumultuous: the plumbers invaded their new home along with heating experts, carpenters, masonry and, finally, electrical contractors, all selected by the realtors. The group, although efficient, was somewhat troublesome. Terry decided it was necessary, especially if they were going to have a wedding soon. It also seemed expedient to allow the contractors to overlap each other, confirming her ideas and theirs simultaneously. While the turmoil was going on, she met with the old caretaker who was to gather and ship the previous owner's personal possessions. She though it advantageous that they could collect the things together and check them off the list.

On Friday exhaustion had set in. After the last of the objects was loaded into a moving van, the artist sat down in her new living room with a soft drink and sighed. It had been hectic. But, at least, they were working on the project and had, to a man, told her that for its age the house was in good condition. Dan decided they should replace the old furnace with an oil burner. That work was currently being done. Terry frowned listening to the repeated hammering coming from the basement. The noise was giving her a headache. The kitchen was also being remodeled. She had just approved the plan and was anxious to see the finished product.

After she ate the sandwich she'd brought, Terry decided to

climb up to the attic to root around. There looked to be some interesting antiques stored in a dark corner near a small attic window. Clutching a big flashlight, she followed the light past several old chairs and a large pine cupboard. Above one of the chairs was a string attached to a light bulb. Terry grinned. Pulling the chair close, she climbed up and tugged the light on. It was still dim in the big room. There were cobwebs everywhere. "Oh, wow!" Terry gasped while pulling the webs from here hair and brushing them away. "Looks like a trunk in the corner," she said aloud. That really intrigued her. It was locked. Using a screwdriver lying nearby to lift the rusting latch, she worked diligently. Within several minutes it popped. "Hey, that's great."

Opening the lid, she shined the light inside. There were newspapers, letters, old envelopes and photographs. She pulled up a nearby chair and began to examine the contents. The letters were mostly old records that were relative to the building of the house. Some deeds explaining the surveys seemed exciting because they were so old. Other letters were personal correspondence she decided to read later. The newspapers were from the 1880s; Terry became enchanted reading them. It was all so long ago. Shortly, she opened the third paper and saw a photograph of a ship that looked all too familiar. "Heavens!" she exclaimed. "It's the *Brother Jonathan* just before it sailed on that fateful voyage." Terry's innards contracted and she gulped air. The articles were from San Francisco newspapers. The sinking was a prominent topic and was given its rightful place in the news.

Captivated, she gathered the papers to take down to the living room where the light was better. Once on the lower level, she relaxed on the big sofa facing the fireplace and spread out the papers on the coffee table. It did not occur to Terry why the papers had been saved until she saw a photograph of a young woman holding a baby in her arms. The caption read, "Daughter and Grandson of Lumber Baron Drown." An ensuing article explained that Lisel Marie Pointrain was traveling

281

to Portland with her two-year-old son, Jason Ezra, where they were to meet with her father, Ezra Martin Pointrain. The decision to sail had been at the last moment. They were both lost at sea when the famous paddle wheeler hit a reef sinking in a terrible storm just off Battery Point Lighthouse near Crescent City, California.

Terry turned the page in order to read the rest of the article when she realized she knew that young woman. Once the information was absorbed her jaw gaped. Stunned momentarily, Terry said outloud, "My God, that's the woman I saw at the grave with Captain DeWolfe. I buried the pair with the captain." Pulling the article up close, Terry gazed sadly at the beautiful, young face. It suddenly seemed apparent that she and Dan were destined to live in that house. Then she remembered seeing the name of the previous owner's wife. Lisel Marie Pointrain was Mr. Bartlet's wife's great-grandmother whose full name had been written on the original deed. Terry raced up the stairs two at a time to find the photographs that were in the trunk. It hadn't occurred to her yet, but soon those photographs would be beautifully matted and framed to hang in her studio along with the portrait she was painting of Captain DeWolfe.

The trip to Boston came and went much too quickly. Adam was delighted to give Terry away after she broached the subject over dinner at his club. Dan and Adam got along famously. She could see that Adam knew she'd made a good choice; he even proposed a toast to that effect. They spent the following two days at the estate where Terry renewed her acquaintance with the caretakers who were pleased to meet her fiancé. Dan moved through the rooms in awe. The building itself rose four stories, was mostly brick with dark wood trim, had eight bedrooms, a library, sitting rooms, a formal living and dining room, a solarium, a bar-keeping room and a huge kitchen with an attached apartment for the couple. Outside, the lawns were manicured except for the formal garden surrounding a fountain and brick paths. The entire estate was fenced in ornamental cast iron and was accessed through a large electric gate. Terry, cognizant of the couples dismay at the upcoming sale, assured them they would have wonderful references and probably could continue in that position. Adam was sending a letter to that effect to the potential buyers.

They spent an unusual amount of time examining Letty's art collection that was spread throughout the house. "Here, darling," she said pointing up the staircase to the first landing. "The famous Madonna." Their attention caused them to pause in reverence. "I can't believe how beautiful she is." Terry's voice softened suitably, "Imagine, Dan, the painting hung in the private apartment of Pope Pius V. What I can't imagine is that it is worth five million dollars. That is incredible."

Glancing at his bride-to-be, he appeared impressed. "You know, hon, not many people would have given it away. No one would have ever known that you have it."

"God would know – I believe that is called theft." Terry's look reflected indignation. "Grandfather Baldwin wouldn't want it any other way, and I agree." They spent hours selecting pieces they both wanted for their new home. Terry marked each piece with masking tape; then, asked the caretakers to see that they were packaged carefully for shipping.

Dan was still talking about it as they boarded the plane to return to San Francisco. He couldn't understand why she had left her magnificent home. Terry clasped his hand and said, "I was looking for you, darling. I would never have found you in Boston." Sobering, she offered, "Besides, Dan, Captain DeWolfe needed me. It was destined that I go to Crescent City, and Letty definitely wanted me to be there. I couldn't live in that huge house alone. Now, could I?" The blue eyes widened questioning.

Dan had to admit it probably would have been lonely.

MacDougal had seemed extremely happy to consider their offer. Dan was nothing if not business oriented; Terry was satisfied at how he represented their business. It had been difficult for him, she knew. Wanting to spare his feelings, although important, was not the primary factor. There wasn't enough time before the wedding to prepare for the arrival of a houseful of guests. Terry knew they had to get the business dealings out of the way. Many men wouldn't have been able to accept her position suddenly thrust upon them. In fact, Terry wondered if they would survive it, but there was absolutely no use to pretend she wasn't who she was. Now that he had signed the papers, Dan was her partner. From now on the decisions would be based on their money. She chuckled, thinking to herself, *I'm actually going to be living in Hilltop House as Mrs. Dan Levine – oh, that sounds wonderful. I'll have my three children and my Dan, Baron and Marge and the entire Levine clan.*

The plane's engines roared into action and they felt the enormous thrust as it raced down the runway for takeoff. Shortly, they were airborne; Dan reached for her hand and squeezed it. "You look pretty happy, darling," he whispered.

Terry smiled softly and gave him a kiss on the cheek. "You cannot imagine my happiness, Dan." Her sentient gaze washed over the handsome man at her side. In an instant she conjured up the gown hanging in the apartment that had been especially designed for the nuptials. The rings which they selected at Tiffany's were being engraved. The furniture for their new bedroom was being shipped within a week, and they were taking possession of their home as soon as they returned. It seemed extraordinary, a dream, but Terry knew they deserved it after all of the trauma they'd experienced. Dan's mother sounded genuine and his sisters all said they would love to be bridesmaids, even the grandchildren were to be in the ceremony, and Adam would give her away. How proud Letty would have been.

The steward brought the drinks Dan had ordered for them. Terry accepted the champagne and lifted the glass to his.

"To us, hon, forever," he said taking a sip.

"Forever, my darling," she answered before adding softly, "to never being alone again."